DEAD ENDS

STORIES FROM THE GOTHIC SOUTH

EDITED BY

NEW YORK TIMES BESTSELLING AUTHOR

J.T. ELLISON

TWO
TALES
PRESS

TABLE OF CONTENTS

FOREWORD

For years, I've been telling people (new writers, especially) that while everything is derivative—there are only seven plots, after all—what makes their story distinctive is voice. The treatment a writer gives their novel or short story will always be unique unto them: their voice, their experiences, their vocabulary, their writing style, all will converge to make even the most tried-and-true plot trope unique.

Said more simply, if you give thirteen writers a photo and ask them to write a story, you'll get thirteen completely different stories.

I've seen this happen when I teach. I like to use visual aids to help the writers in my classes, to give them a jumping-off point. A kick start. I think it's a fun, stress-free way of starting a story. I show them a man, a woman, a setting. Something, anything, so they don't have to conjure up a tale from total scratch.

I've been using this example for so long, and so often, that when I came across a photo in an article I was reading, I knew I had the perfect opportunity. The photo showed a man in a dusty black suit, his back to the camera, standing in a roiling mist at the ornate gates of a broken-down gothic mansion. There was longing in his stance; though his face wasn't visible, the lines of tension running through his body were clear. I immediately wondered: What was his story? What was this place he stood before? What was the house to him? *

With this evocative photo in hand, I approached my publisher and posited an idea: Let's create an anthology of stories based on the house in the photo. I mean, why not put my money where my mouth is, right? I hand-picked a group of writers whom I thought would do a great job at showcasing (and proving) my theory—that no two writers will approach the page the same way. We had only two requirements for them: that the house appear in the story in some way, and the theme of the story was Southern Gothic.

These talented writers did exactly what I thought they'd do—they created wildly diverse stories about, in, and mentioning the house that are in turns chilling, haunting, and downright scary. From writers going mad to demons inhabiting young girls; ancient caves to ancestral feuds; gardens of stone angels to evils seen and unseen—the stories you're about to read cover the gamut of the best themes of Southern Gothic fiction.

They clearly had so much fun with it that I had to join in.

And so, I give you DEAD ENDS. My brilliant friends and I have cooked up thirteen original, never-before-published spooky tales for you to enjoy this Halloween season. I hope you enjoy reading them as much as we did writing them. But be sure to lock the doors and windows first… you never know what the road ahead might bring.

J.T. Ellison
Nashville
2017

★ For legal reasons we can't include the photo here. But if you'd like to check it out, visit twotalespress.com/the-house.

THE PERFECT BUYER

JEFF ABBOTT

"IT JUST NEEDS THE PERFECT buyer," the real estate agent had told him in a bright and chirpy e-mail, and Paul thought, *There is no perfect buyer for this horror. None at all.*

He'd agreed to go take a look because Catherine had phone calls with film producers the entire morning, desperately trying to get her career back in order, and looking at houses was better than sitting in Starbucks and pretending to write. So he'd driven a couple of miles outside the city limits of Fort Sheldon, North Carolina, to where this Gothic pile stood. The real estate agent was running late, and Paul walked through the sagging, broken iron gates and surveyed the overgrown gardens with a stare of dismay and then amusement.

It was wonderful and awful.

He could almost imagine the e-mail to his agent: *Viv, you won't believe it. I'll only be writing horror novels from now on. I know that's an abrupt change but wait till you see our new house. It's as if* Dark Shadows *and* The Shining *had a threesome with* The Haunting of Hill House. *I'll send you a link to the Zillow listing, be sure and do an exorcism before you open the web page.*

Paul double-checked the address on his phone; how disappointing if this was the wrong house. But it was. There wasn't another house in hailing distance, not even across the road, where a huge field of some sort of produce—he had no idea what, he was a city boy—grew.

He slowly walked up, watching the windows facing him, half-hoping he would see a ghost, a shade, an echo of a lost child, a lost bride, a vengeful father… what an odd thought.

He texted Catherine, although she hated when he tried to contact her when she was talking with film people: just a perfect place, ha ha. She probably hadn't even looked at the original e-mail or link. *You pick the house, darling. It's only fair. I'm the one dragging us back to my hometown, you should get to pick the house.*

He stood there and thought, *There's a book in this house. I could write one about a couple trying to save their marriage and remodel the house.*

And then the better idea came, clear and golden.

Us redoing this could be an HGTV show for a whole season. Maybe that would help with the costs. And Catherine could probably handle being on camera that much; it would be different from the strain of being in a movie. It would be easier. It would show the world a different side of her. Perhaps he'd mention it to her agent before he mentioned it to Catherine.

He reached the door and touched the front door knob, and the door swung open.

Well, the last real estate agent to show it was careless. He stepped into the large foyer. Dusty, but he could see the tile was good. The rising staircase seemed like something out of a film set from a period piece. Sheeted paintings hung on the wall.

He walked toward one of the paintings. He yanked on the sheet and it slid free, like paper from a birthday present, and beneath it was a portrait. A family. A father, a mother, a boy and a girl around twelve, a younger boy of three. It was only after he stared at the painting for a full ten seconds that he realized someone had cut out the eyes of the children in the portrait. He gasped and took a step backward.

"Oh, was it unlocked?" said the bright cheery voice of the real estate agent. Her name was Melody and it suited her—she always sounded like she might be about to break into song. "Hi, Mr. Duvalier, how are you?"

"I'm... I'm okay. This house is a bit overwhelming."

"Is it not just amazing?" Melody said. "I know it looks a little Addams Family from the street, but there is no house in the greater Fort Sheldon area with more potential. And size." She peered around. "Oh, is Ms. Manning here?" People were always disappointed when Paul showed up without Catherine. He thought perhaps he should put her Oscar award in his pocket and produce it for the times when Catherine didn't show. It might allay their disappointment.

"She has some conference calls. New film in the works. Or new TV. I can't keep track." He smiled.

"Oh, how exciting. Maybe something they'll film here? They did a movie here with Sandra Bullock, oh, like, ten years ago. So fun!"

"Not sure. We just want a house where we can spend most of our time... we're tired of Hollywood." *Or Hollywood is tired of us, or Catherine can't decide what she wants to do and she's scared she's losing everything so she wants to run home, where she will always be a big star even if no one is sending her scripts right now.* He almost said all this aloud and instead he looked up at the painting. "This portrait looks like it's been vandalized."

"Oh. Unfortunate. Well, as you might guess, this house has a colorful history. And sometimes kids dare each other to stay here."

"This is the local haunted house."

"Oh, it has a sad history. I'm sure your wife told you, being a Manning and all."

"Maybe you could tell me while we tour it. Catherine's not so good at storytelling."

She looked at him like she didn't believe that Catherine Manning was bad at anything. So they started a slow walk, through a grand parlor and living room, a spacious kitchen, ground-floor library and bedrooms, all in need of repairs and updating, and she talked.

"Since the town was founded, the two big families in Fort Sheldon were the Mannings and the Pallisters. Both wealthy, both established. In 1857 there was bad blood between them, though, as the oldest son from each family quarreled over a girl, and they held a duel. Right out in front of the house."

"Who won the duel?"

"The Manning boy won. The Pallister boy died as soon as they carried him into the house. He wasn't even badly hurt, they said, but he died as soon as he crossed the threshold." Her happy voice turned to a sad one.

"A murder on the doorstep," Paul said. "You really want to sell this house." He laughed.

"You'll hear the stories sooner or later if you buy it," Melody said, and for the first time he saw her as a slightly tougher negotiator than he'd imagined. "I'd just as soon you hear it from me. That way you can't say I held anything back."

"I appreciate the honesty. So it's haunted by the poor young duelist?"

"Oh, it gets better," Melody said. "Think of how gorgeous that kitchen could be with an island range and new cabinets."

"Yes," Paul agreed.

"Of course the Pallisters wanted their vengeance on the Mannings, even though it was a fair duel. So, years later, a drunken Pallister heir kidnapped a Manning daughter. He brought her back to this home, intending to, um, defile her so as to force a marriage out of respectability."

"I didn't think the Mannings would go along with that," Paul said.

"I didn't say the Pallisters were really bright," Melody said. "But as he attempted to ride here into the yard, the

Manning girl grabbed his gun and she shot him through the throat. He staggered into the house and he died on the spot."

"That front door has issues."

"Oh, every local legend needs the common element," she said. "You put off yet? You want to see the upstairs?"

"Yes, please." He wasn't put off. The house was in disrepair but the bones, as they said, were good. He could guess that some rooms had seen more recent use than others; whoever had lived here last had limited themselves to only a few rooms: the kitchen, the dining room, the library, a study, a downstairs bedroom he suspected had once belonged to the housekeeper.

"The house became empty two years ago. The last of the Pallisters—old Hank Pallister—lived here, alone. He could hardly afford the taxes, but he stayed."

"Let me guess, insane old hermit type who would chase off the kids?"

She laughed. "Try much beloved English teacher at the high school."

"So the Pallister money is gone?"

"It's all in the house. And there are no more Pallisters, at least with the surname. Hank never married. His will left the house to three distant cousins of his in Charlotte... they only agreed to sell now."

"Did any more Mannings kill off any more Pallisters other than the two you've told me about?" They were now moving up the stairs.

"Oh yes, but neither of the first two Mannings were prosecuted, obviously. Two more chapters to the story.

In 1919 a Pallister girl got pregnant by a Manning boy and died in childbirth—here in the house, of course. The baby died, too, and according to local lore was horribly misshapen. I know it's not the same as murder, but at that point if a Pallister got the flu and died, you'd say he caught it from a Manning. And then…" She stopped.

"Yes?"

"1946. That was the worst one. The final rift between the families. Hank Pallister's father, Adam, had gone into business with Joseph Manning. Joseph cheated Adam and bankrupted him, and Adam came home and he picked up a knife and he killed his family… except for Hank, who hid from him while Adam searched the house. But he killed his wife and his two other children, and then cut his own throat."

Paul could say nothing. It was horrible. What a story. He could imagine the TV series now. And maybe a novel to follow. Exposure and money, to put them back on top.

"I know. Horrible. But that's all the past. You and your wife could give this house such a bright future."

Paul arched an eyebrow. "Even though she's a Manning?"

"It's just a name. And this is just a house. I can't afford to scare you off… there are not many buyers around who could afford the renovations and then the upkeep. It's had a few looks from a couple of software millionaires out of the Research Triangle who might want to play at country squire. But you and Ms. Manning are the first who might be able to afford it and who could live here nearly full-time. And it would be a wonderful place to write."

Melody smiled. "Obviously I'm a fan of your wife's, but I want you to know I've read your books and I'm a fan of yours, too."

"I appreciate that." People said this and he was never sure how much to believe it.

"Think how great this house would look behind you as an author photo."

He laughed. For all its tragic and bloody history, he didn't feel particularly scared or repulsed. The inside was grand. And there must have been happiness here as well to balance out the darkness. Generations of Pallisters had lived here for decades; tragedy was inevitable, and it was part of life.

"I almost feel sorry for this house," Paul said, touching the wall. "It's just a house. Tile and brick and wood. What did it do wrong?"

"Nothing," Melody said. Her voice was now almost a purr. "Nothing."

They walked around the property. A distance from the house there was a small graveyard. Perhaps twenty graves. *A pall of Pallisters,* he thought, then silently chided himself for insensitivity.

"I suppose we could have those moved," Melody said. "It would be expensive."

"No, I wouldn't want to disturb them," Paul said. For a moment he scanned the graveyard and realized the rows were all filled, except for the last row, where there was room for two more graves. *Don't be morbid,* he told himself, and he increased his pace past the tombstones. He and Melody continued to walk; the cleared land gave way to a thick growth of pine and oak. The air felt fresh and clean. He thought with excitement of what his schedule would be like here: brisk walk in the morning, coffee, working in the study with its window view (if that was not too distracting), then five daily pages written. The library he could stock with the books he loved. Hollywood money would go far here.

Her money. Not so much yours.

He pushed that thought away. Of course, if Catherine didn't like it they wouldn't buy it, that went without saying.

The TV show, with Catherine's family past... it could be great. Just what she needed.

And it was a place full of stories—writerly catnip. No, he wasn't scared. He was intrigued. This could be a fresh start for them both. He was careful to keep the excitement off his face.

They were back in the foyer when Catherine called him. "So what kind of house are you looking at?"

"I've heard all about how awful your ancestors were," he said, smiling at Melody. She excused herself into another room.

"What?"

"It's the old Pallister mansion."

Catherine fell silent. "You are *not* at that house."

"I am. I think you should come see it."

"Have I not told you the legends?"

"I've heard them already. That's overblown history. It's a great house."

"Um, all right."

"How did the script calls go?"

"Not well. Not well. No one is hiring me right now." Her voice wavered.

"I have an idea." And he told her about remodeling the house as a TV show that would star her. She said nothing for several long seconds. Then she said she'd think about it.

His phone rang again a few minutes after he hung up with Catherine, while he was pacing the house's library (it had an actual library room; it made his chest thrum). He glanced at the caller ID—Catherine's aunt Josie, her oldest relative still here in Fort Sheldon. Paul always thought of her as a preview of what Catherine would be like in old age. He realized, from her age, it must have been Josie's father who cheated the last Pallisters.

"Paul," she said, by way of greeting, "you're not at that house, are you? Catherine just told me."

"Yes."

"Get away from it. Get away from it now."

"Aunt Josie, I don't believe in ghosts."

"There are things worse than ghosts."

"It's just a house."

She was silent for several seconds. "It sure ain't a home. I won't visit y'all there. It's not a place for a Manning."

"Catherine and I need this place. It will be fine. Perfectly fine." He got off the phone with pleasantries, and he thought of the stories he could tell inside these walls. He stared up at the ceiling with a surprising smile.

⚜

Catherine and Paul ate at the nicest restaurant in Fort Sheldon, people at nearby tables smiling at the hometown girl made good, the Hollywood queen returned to them. No one was thinking about her drunkenness on a set or that her last three movies had bombed badly.

Paul quietly pitched his fleshed-out vision for a TV show while they renovated the house. "We'd call the show *The Catherine Manning Project*."

"Like the house and I are both projects? I don't want to be a project."

"You have to sell your own redemption story, babe. Just come with me to go see it. And see the possibilities." He was reminded of when he'd first pitched a screenplay to her, the day they'd met. She'd optioned it on the spot. He knew how to make her want something.

So Melody met them at the house, and let them wander the rooms. Catherine looked at the floors and the walls and the ceilings as though it was not her future house but a set.

"It's a thought," she said. "But is it a good one?"

"Yes. And with the backstory of your family..."

"Ugh, we wouldn't have to play up all that Manning versus Pallister stuff, would we? It doesn't make me look great, does it?"

"It's called authenticity, sweetheart. Let your family history be your family history. No one can blame you for your ancestors. People will tune in. I think it'd be genius."

He added, "And if you didn't like the house, we could sell it after the remodel. But I think you'll like it. The house needs some happiness."

He knew which seeds to plant. And if she was a producer on the show, it might cover some of their investment in the remodel. After another hour she agreed, and he called her agent to start the wheels moving.

That night, Melody went home and poured herself the good wine and thought, *Thank God I found someone for that place. The perfect buyer.*

✤

Six months later, and the renovations were done. The HGTV series—*The Catherine Manning Project*—had been the number-one show on the network the entire run. They'd done a crossover episode with SyFy Network's *Ghosts R Us*, where the paranormal investigators claimed to be creeped out by the Pallister House (as they called it) but of course there was no evidence. Nothing appeared on their films, the odd noises a house made as part of its existence were amplified to invoke a mild shiver or two in the audience, and statements about "energy" and "presence" served to fill out the hour.

"There is something here," the clairvoyant blond cohost intoned dramatically, "and it seeks release."

Don't we all, Paul thought, watching a rerun of the ghost-hunting episode on the couch with Catherine. It was strange to see the couch on the screen, inside the very house. "This doesn't scare you, right?"

She had a new script on her lap that a leading director

had sent her, but she hadn't begun reading it in earnest yet. Like it might vanish if she started. "The house feels so homey now. Almost like the show was filmed about someplace else. Not our home."

"I told you it would be fine."

"You always do. You always reassure me." She stared down into her iced tea glass. "How's the book coming?"

He shifted slightly against her. "Fine." He hadn't gotten much writing done during the renovations. Now he should dive back into the novel, but it seemed a flaccid, uninteresting lump. He thought writing about the Pallisters and Mannings might make for a more interesting book than the one he'd been working on. But he wasn't going to tell her that. Not yet. He kept thinking of the stories Melody had told him, the horrible tragedies of the Pallisters, and imagining them as scenes in a book or a film. That was what he should write.

"I think I'll go read this script upstairs," she said. "I'm tired."

Finally, scripts were arriving for her to read. Her agent was in talks with directors. Hollywood wanted her again, her past sins and tanked movies forgiven in the wake of the suddenly hot TV show. He'd put her back on top. "Any good ones yet?"

"Hopefully." She kissed him on the cheek. "You coming up soon?"

"Yes, in a few. You know I'm happy to read anything you want me to." He was, after all, a writer. He knew story. She gave him a half-smile but she didn't say, "Yes, please, honey, I'd love you to do that." She never did.

Like she didn't trust his taste, or know what roles would suit her.

Which was annoying when he'd known that the home renovation TV show was the perfect vessel for her. She didn't appreciate him, he thought, and the idea of it was so alien and odd and unlike him that he nearly choked on his wine.

She went upstairs, and he refilled his glass of Malbec from the nearly empty bottle on the kitchen island. She had told him she had no problem with him drinking in front of her, but he always felt guilty about it, since she'd stopped.

He stood there, with his wine and his resentment, and he heard the soft whispers of men. Outside the window, in the front yard, which had been stripped of its thorns and vines and landscaped with flowers and shrubbery and a cool green lawn. Autograph seekers, maybe; there had been a number of them during the renovation show, and he'd hoped that would abate once the show was over. He went to the largest window facing out on the yard. He didn't want to stand in the doorway and argue with them or ask them to leave. He'd count how many there were then call the police.

In the yard, the moonlight hung like a screen, and a picture played against it. Two men, outlined in smoke, back to back, antique pistols in their hands, the spines meeting like two clouds merging, and then they started to walk away from each other, one of them staring at Paul with a face that could have been a brother of Catherine, turning, firing, the other man dropping, crawling toward the house, wounded, dying, vanishing as he crossed the entry steps.

Then the shooter offering the coldest imaginable smile at Paul, and then vanishing.

Paul blinked. He blinked again. He gave a soft little sigh of shock and moved his feet and heard the crunch of glass and looked down. Broken wineglass and spilled Malbec pooled around his shoes.

The yard was night-empty, the moonlight a pale gleam.

He looked where the first apparition—he didn't know what to call it—had reached the house, but there was nothing there.

Because, he told himself, *there is nothing there. Just the house. It's just a house. It's not full of hate for the Mannings. Or for Catherine.* That last thought drifted in, surprising him.

He busied himself cleaning up the wine off the tiles and carefully gathering up the fragments of glass. Catherine liked to walk barefoot, and it wouldn't do to leave shards where she could step. Halfway through he laughed at his own ridiculousness.

This is the book you want to write, asserting itself. The scenes are simply coming to life in your mind. Your imagination is supercharged and ready to start. That's all that was. Nothing more.

He said nothing to Catherine.

❧

The house took hold of them; it stopped being just a TV project, just a grand mansion. It became home. At least for him. Catherine was spending far more time in New York and Los Angeles than he'd planned. But that was good; they each needed their work.

He slept later than Catherine most days; she was an early riser, and she liked to jog around the property. He went into his study; it had been Hank Pallister's study before, and before that his father, Adam—the family murderer. That thought unsettled him slightly, but it was a warm, homey space, with ample bookshelves and a window that overlooked the back acreage.

On Hank's shelf he'd found a thin book about the Mannings and the Pallisters, written twenty years ago and published by the local college's press.

And the author was Catherine's own Aunt Josie. That was a shock. They'd invited her to the house several times, but she'd always declined. This morning, though, the sun was bright, and he decided to try her again. And to his surprise, Josie agreed to come over in an hour. He found himself tidying the house for her arrival; he remembered her initial opposition to them buying it.

Catherine had gone to Los Angeles for the week. She had picked a script and a director; she hadn't shared the script with him. It seemed such an odd, passive way to make him feel small. It did not occur to him that she might fear his sarcasm, or want to give such a performance that it wasn't ruined for him by already having read the script. He only saw a pettiness.

Aunt Josie arrived at the door. She was dressed in a

denim skirt, a colorful blouse, and slippers. She walked with a cane. A college-age boy waited in the car—Paul recognized him as Josie's great-grandson. When she waved at him, he drove off.

"He's going to meet his friends at Starbucks, and I'll text him when we're done. I love the texting, don't you? So convenient."

"I'm so glad you could come, Aunt Josie."

"Well, I'm here," she said, and she crossed the doorway into the house and took another deep breath. "I guess if Catherine's been here for six months, it's safe for me."

"Would you like some tea or coffee?"

"Life is short. Do you have bourbon?"

"Yes, ma'am, I do."

"You're treating me like the guest of honor. I approve. I watched every episode of *The Catherine Manning Project* on the television, but I want the tour."

He obliged her. Josie nodded and didn't frown at the modernizations they'd brought to the house. At the end, when they'd retired to the sunroom with their bourbons, she smiled at him and he felt an odd tension jar his bones, instead of relief. "You've changed so much in this house," she said. "Yet nothing has changed at all."

"I don't understand."

"This place... you have to wonder how much hate lived here. The Pallisters, all that hate for the Mannings. It would ebb and flow, naturally, that's how you'd find these détentes between the families, where a Manning and a Pallister would make peace long enough have a doomed romance or to go into an ill-fated business together... but mostly this was a bottle full of hate."

"The people who hated the Mannings are gone," he said. "The hate died with them. This is a Manning house now."

"I don't know that I would have brought a wife here," she said. And then he saw her, as if for the first time: the hard edge of her jaw, the deepness of her wrinkles, the fierceness in her gaze. "You know, I was here right after Adam Pallister killed them. It was my daddy, Joseph Manning, who had the sour business deal with him. He wanted to talk to Adam, and he brought me along to play with Hank—Daddy thought he and Adam wouldn't quarrel so much in front of kids. Door unlocked and we came inside. The blood... the blood was everywhere. Daddy made me wait outside. But I could see through the windows. Mrs. Pallister and the twins, lying on the floor... it was my daddy who found Hank hiding in the kitchen pantry."

"I had no idea. I'm so sorry."

She took a long sip of the bourbon. "He cut out their eyes, you know. His family. After he killed them and before he killed himself. Standing at that window, I could see their faces. I always wondered... what didn't he want them to see?"

Paul thought of the painting, with the Pallister eyes neatly clipped out. A vandal, echoing the legend. It was time to stop reminiscing.

"Well, I hope you enjoyed the show and will be a frequent guest here at the house."

"I won't," Aunt Josie said, setting down her bourbon.

"You did this for the TV show and the attention it gar-nered Catherine's cleanup effort and career relaunch. Fine, you've gotten it. Sell the house."

"I like the house."

"You sure you don't have Pallister blood in you?"

"I'm not even from North Carolina."

She stared at him for several long beats. "Have you experienced anything unusual here?"

He thought of the duelists in the yard, the dying ghost crawling toward him, the grinning victor. Just a scene he wanted to write, playing out in his imagination. "You mean ghosts?" he said. "Of course not."

"I mean echoes... hate echoing down through the years."

"I didn't know you could see an echo." He gave her an indulgent smile at her poor choice of words.

"But the house sees you," she said, and for one moment he wondered what it would be like to crush Aunt Josie's fragile throat beneath his fingers. He could reach out and it would be over within a minute. He stuck his hands in his pocket, felt a flash of fever.

"A house can't see me. But I should save that line for my next book."

"I don't mean to frighten you."

"You couldn't," he lied.

⚜

That night he saw another chapter he'd been thinking about for the book, inspired by Melody's stories, perhaps urged on by Josie's comments about echoes that weren't sounds but were images. The girl in the yard. The Manning girl, seized and brought against her will by the Pallister heir, laid across a shadow of a horse. She was made of smoke and light, and she wrenched free from the shadow of the Pallister; there was a flash, the gun firing, the Pallister falling, clutching at his ruined throat. Lifted by unseen hands, carried in the door.

Paul didn't run downstairs to see if the ghosts cavorted in the foyer. He knew they didn't. They weren't there. It was simply the book in his mind, trying to stir to life.

So he sat down with his Clairefontaine notebook and began to write furiously. He wanted this on paper, not on computer, he wasn't sure why. The words of the two scenes he'd imagined poured out of him. After an hour, his hand beginning to cramp, he looked with surprise at the last words he'd written.

You brought a Manning here. You made me hers.

It was almost like a whisper, he'd heard the words. Just his next book trying to work free, the long story of this house. He needed to write the book and stop daydreaming about its violent, tragic scenes. He'd never written a ghost story, but he could. Based here, drawing on her family history. Manning versus Pallister through the centuries. A follow-up that would be a bestseller, and Catherine could stop acting like she was their sole means of support.

He scratched out the last line he'd written and he

wrote, with a steady hand: *A house cannot remember. A house cannot see. This is a ghost story without ghosts. Stop trying to scare yourself.*

❖

"I think we should sell the house," Catherine said, a week later. She had signed a deal on the script, which she still hadn't shown him, was back in North Carolina briefly for Aunt Josie's birthday, then would return to California. He'd spent the past week in the library here in Fort Sheldon, scribbling furiously in his notebook, leafing through local histories, looking deeper into the stories about the Mannings and the Pallisters, starting at the very settlement of Fort Sheldon.

Because the ideas for the book kept playing out before his eyes. The Manning who survived the duel, his triumphant smile the clearest thing on his face. The Manning girl shooting her attacker, with resolve and cold nerve. The Manning boy standing outside the window, unexpected relief on his face as the Pallister girl died in childbirth. Smoky movies that played quickly, briefly, reflections in the windows. But not the final tragedy, the worst one, the massacre of the Pallisters by one of their own. His mind had spared him that, and he knew that it would be the final chapter he would write. He had started drawing the curtains and leaving them shut, turning the house dark. And he wrote, bringing to life the biographical notes he'd made on the earliest

Mannings and Pallisters. He thought it was the best stuff he'd ever written. Except for that one line in his notes: *You brought a Manning here. You made me hers.* Like he was going to give the house itself dialogue in the story. But he would stare at those words before he started to write each day, as if trying to find a scene where he could place them.

Leave? Now? When he was doing his best work? A rage filled him, and he struggled to keep a calm, studied look on his face.

"Are you not comfortable here?" he asked slowly.

"Well, you always wanted this place more than me."

"This was to be our home," he said. "I wanted it for you. This got your career back on track."

"You wanted it for the TV show. You ought to write a ghost story set here, what with all the old stories." She said it like an afterthought, but he hated that she'd suggested the idea before he told her he was well under way writing that very book. He took refuge in a long sip of his wine.

"Well, maybe I will."

"You get that book done by the time I'm done filming with Brice, and then we'll sell it and be done with it." She spoke as though her words weren't small bombs landing on him.

"Brice?"

"Oh. Did I not tell you? Brice got the other lead role." She seemed to study her fingernails, then crossed her arms, as if bored with the conversation.

Brice had been an issue, long ago. He'd dated Catherine when they'd done her first very successful movie together, the one that had made her "*that* Catherine Manning" and won her the Oscar. There had a been a fling. There had been a highly public breakup, magazine covers, news crews from the entertainment shows, endless gossip. Then, on her next project, she'd met Paul when he pitched his script. But Brice always lurked in the back of their marriage, the lover played out on the magazine pages, her one famous boyfriend.

"I thought you'd decided you wouldn't work with him again," Paul said, quietly.

"Well, I did, you're right, I had. But we had a long talk—a long lunch, it'll probably be up on the Internet by now, I mean, pictures, there were press taking pictures outside the restaurant and we were on a patio so they probably got some shots—and we put all the bad behind us. I think we can work together well. There's on-screen chemistry even if I think he's a jerk in real life."

"Do you still think he's a jerk?"

"Of course I do. Oh, Paul, hon, you're not jealous? You can't be."

"Of an impossibly handsome man who has a past with my wife? Of course not. That would be silly."

"Yes, it would be."

A sudden suspicion flared in his mind. "Are you ever going to let me read this script?"

"The writers are working on a big rewrite, but maybe soon."

"What kind of scenes do you have with him? Love scenes?"

"This is beyond ridiculous, Paul. I won't sit in a house you wanted and that I paid for and be grilled by you this way."

"You could just answer my question."

"It's unreasonable."

"I wouldn't care if it was any other actor. I care that it's him."

She got up. "Go write your ghost story, you can piggyback on my TV success. Sell it, write it, I want to be done with this house. I've got two other projects lined up. I want to move back to California, I want you there with me."

"Do you?"

"Of course I do." She sounded like she was losing patience.

"You're a Manning. You use people. It's in the blood. Have I reached the end of my usefulness to you? My idea, that show, got you back on the public's radar, got the scripts coming back to you, and now you don't need me. I know. You could go renovate a house in L.A. with Brice—there's season two." His voice had risen faster than he thought it would, faster than he meant, and he blinked and stepped back from the table.

"You have lost your mind," she said. "I did the TV show because yes, it was a good idea, but it helped us get this house you were in love with. A house I've not liked my whole life, but you loved it and I love you. So I did it. And I've been working my butt off to line up the right kind of projects, so we can keep this house and you can keep writing..."

"You think I don't earn my keep?" he said. "Is that right?"

"Of course not. But it's been three years since the last book, honey. I have to keep us afloat. I'm sorry if that insults your male ego..." She broke off.

He realized he'd stood, hands clenched into fists. Trembling. Slowly he sank into the chair. What... what was he doing? "I'm sorry," he murmured. "I'm sorry. You're right. I think... I think I want to write about the house. Get it out of my system. Sell the book and then join you in California."

She stared at him. "Paul, you know I love you. You know that."

"I know. I love you, too. And I know I have nothing to worry about with Brice." But he said that because he felt he must; a small dark seed of awfulness moved in his chest, like it had found fertile soil.

"You don't." She came around the table. He stood and turned to her and as he embraced her he saw, in the window, the hazy image of Adam, the father who had killed nearly all of the last Pallisters.

⚜

He wrote like a madman for the next few weeks. Four thousand words a day, the story pouring out of him, a retelling of two families sundered by hate and resentment. When he thought of Brice and Catherine, he put the emotion he felt into the story, as if it were a purging.

At night the images came. He would see their smoky figures in the windows, and at last the final chapter played in the glass, Adam Pallister watching him, but not killing his family: Instead it was Adam Pallister walking in on his wife in bed with a man with the thick dark hair of the Mannings. The smoky image faded. He went to his desk and paged through Aunt Josie's history of the families. Josie's own father was the lover in the image; the man who had bedded Mrs. Pallister. The stabbings hadn't been about a business deal gone wrong at all. The house had shown him the truth.

Like Adam Pallister. This room had been his study as well. Had the house shown him what was happening in his wife's life? Shown him again and again, so when he killed his family he cut out their eyes because blindness was preferable?

Paul started to cry and forced his tears away. He couldn't do this. He was losing his mind. Just write the rest of the book and be done. He drank the rest of the wine; he wanted to sleep, to forget this nightmare.

He had nothing to read on his bedside table, so he went to Catherine's side of the bed to look through her stack of books. And there it was, at the bottom. The script for her new film. He read it, his grip tightening on the pages. Then, finished, he tossed it on the floor.

He heard a noise—or so he thought—and turned to the window and saw, like watching through a rain-streaked glass, Catherine and Brice together in bed, writhing. Her face clear in the haze for a moment, contorted in ecstasy. The image faded. He stared at the glass. Only the night stared back.

I'm imagining this, he thought. *I am. It's one thing to see images from the past that are part of my book, it's something else for the house to show me people who are alive. No. This isn't happening.*

He slept, fitfully. The next morning, he roamed the house for hours, thinking, and then called Catherine. And as wonderful an actress as she was, he could tell in her voice something had changed. She was trying too hard for cheer. She was with Brice now, he could feel it in his heart, his chest. The realization was like a lit match dragged across his skin. She talked of the filming and minor problems with the director and mentoring the young costar whom she liked so well, a young actress from Australia. No mention of Brice.

"I found the script," he said. "You left a copy on your bedside table. I read it. It's very good. Except for the part where you cheat on your husband."

"It's just a story," she said. "Please stop doing this."

⚜

Two sleepless days later he finished writing the book and sat back from the keyboard just as he heard the distant click of the door. Catherine, calling up to him, "Sweetheart? Are you here?"

He got up from the chair, remembering to bring something he wanted to show her, putting it behind his back. He stood at the top of the stairs, watching her in the foyer, setting down her suitcase. "I... I rented a car. I thought you were going to pick me up." She didn't sound angry, just puzzled. "I left you messages. Texts."

"I had to finish the book," he said, quietly. "I'm sorry. I turned off all the distractions."

"All right," she said. "I understand that's important to you. Congratulations. Shall we collect Aunt Josie, take her to lunch to celebrate?"

"You slept with Brice," he said. "The house showed me. In the window. I saw it. The two of you in bed."

She seemed to struggle to understand his words. "The house... showed me doing something I haven't done?"

He started down the stairs. "In the windows. It shows me every bad thing the Pallisters suffered at the hands of the Mannings."

"You're not well, Paul." She kept her voice steady.

"It's like an echo of a movie, stuck in the house itself." He told her about seeing the duel, the kidnapping, the childbirth gone wrong, the adultery.

"I am not with Brice. I haven't been. Paul, this house has affected you..."

"Show, don't tell," he said. "Isn't that the writer's rule? Show the scene, don't tell the reader about it."

"Paul. We're leaving this place right now. Come with me, come back to L.A. with me right now..."

As he reached the bottom of the stairs, he pulled the kitchen knife from behind his back and plunged it into her chest. Her face distorted in shock, but he'd struck her heart and she fell to the floor, dying, saying, "No, no, no, not true..."

True. The last word from a liar. From a Manning.

He watched Catherine die and then he walked to his phone, resting on the table. "Aunt Josie?" His voice sounded normal. "Catherine's here, she'd love to visit with you. Can you have your great-grandson drive you over? Sure. I'll have the bourbon ready for you."

He disconnected the call and waited, the knife in his hand, for the old woman to arrive.

He was the house, and the house was him.

WOMEN AND ZOMBIES

HELEN ELLIS

THE FIRST THING YOU HAVE to accept is we're all going gray. Just look at my roots: I've got a skunk stripe. In three months, if I live that long, I'll look like somebody whacked a blackboard eraser over my head. So leave your beauty ideals at the gate, and make friends with us women who wear our roots like crowns. We've survived the longest. Vanity is for the weak. There's no time for hair dye in the zombie apocalypse.

As you know, by what you brought to get in, this here's a women's compound. We call it The Frizz. It used to be a high school, Hillary High, home of America's number-one text team. Their captain, a kid with a face paler than a forty-watt light bulb, could text two hundred characters a minute, including punctuation and caps. The team's motto was "We're all thumbs." But those boys were snots. Never looking up from their iPhones. Privileged. Always cutting in line and expecting extra tater tots.

Rumor has it: It was the tots that got them. Poisoned tots. Their captain was patient zero. He popped a tot, and two hours later his face turned green. Then he was dead. And then he was undead. And then the text team was undead, too. Their coach locked them in the walk-in freezer to protect the other students. Then the principal let them out to avoid a lawsuit from their parents.

The tots came as a bulk order from Iraq. A buck for a twenty-pound bag of tots is irresistible to school budgets. The principal didn't ask questions. He just high-fived the Amazon Prime delivery guy. It was chemical warfare, if you ask me. I always told him mashed potatoes were worth the extra trouble and money, but he never listened.

You should listen to me.

I used to be a lunch lady, now I make the rules.

You'll be rooming with Purell. Her real name's Ann or Jennifer or something a lot of other girls were named at this high school, so that when we talked about them, we were forced to call them by their last initial. Like Ann P was valedictorian, and Ann G was the cheerleader who bit her tongue off in a car accident. Ann G thought *that* was the worst thing that would ever happened to her, but surprise, Ann G: Your fate was to find a boy who loved you for you, only to have him turn zombie on spring break and eat you, along with the housekeeper who folded your towel into a swan. The point is: Girls didn't like being called by their last initials before the zombie apocalypse, and they don't like it now. So call your roommate—Ann A, B, or C, or whoever she was in high school—Purell.

Everybody in The Frizz goes by what she steals from the outside to stay in. And you will, too. The reason I'm giving you a chance to join us is: You knew just what to steal and just where to bring it. Purell steals Purell. Banana Boat steals sunscreen. Pony, the nurse, steals ponytail holders. Cigs and Dildos are dead so, I'm sorry to say, we've had to forget about those extracurricular activities. I'm Cats. We eat cats. There's no such thing as pets anymore. And just so you know, cats don't taste like chicken.

Purell keeps travel-size hand sanitizers clipped to her belt like ears. She also keeps ears clipped to her belt. Men's ears, not zombie ears. Zombies are easy to kill, men even easier. Unlike zombies, men have to sleep. The ears are gross, and she's gross, but count the ears. Compliment the ears. Purell is a girl you want on your side. Otherwise, you'll never see her coming. She knows how to hide. Case in point: Purell is the only student survivor of Hillary High.

Five days after lockdown, all the kids were zombies. One bit another, who bit another, and then they all had it like herpes. They *wished* they had herpes. The school nurse laughed at the thought.

Pony is a laugher. She laughs when she's happy, and she laughs when she's scared. She laughs when she's angry, and that's the laugh you have to watch out for. One minute she's laughing, the next she's screaming, "What's so funny?" and threatening to quit. You have to put up with her laughing because if there's one thing you need in a zombie apocalypse, it's a nurse.

What we don't need anymore is a librarian, and the librarian is pissed.

The staff killed the zombie students in what used to be her library. Her library was the crown jewel of this school, freestanding on the quad like a pot on a stove. Books burn quickly, and burning a bunch of zombie brains in a contained spot is efficient, so I gave the order to herd the zombie students into the library like they were eggs for hard-boiling. I barred the door, lit a match, and burnt it all to the ground.

No more library, no more zombies inside The Frizz.

Now, I'll admit it: Burning all the books along with the zombies was not my best idea. But who knew we'd have so much downtime in the zombie apocalypse? You can only stand guard and mourn the dead for so long. You've heard of ghost limbs? We get ghost books. My hands itch for Jodi Picoult.

Do me a favor, don't tell the librarian I told you that. And when you do meet her, tell her she's pretty. She's not pretty—she has bug eyes and an underbite—but the librarian is the kind of woman who eats compliments like zombies eat flesh. You're new here, so compliments mean more coming from you. So you tell her you like her hair bun and eyeglasses chain. And you say it like you mean it. Once she's happy, you remind her that she's hearing what she's hearing from you because I let you in.

If she says anything against me, you say: "Shhh."

It's kind of creepy, but she'll do it. It's a reflexive response. Like how I roll my eyes when someone says *sneeze guard*.

The librarian steals super glue, which fixes everything, and I mean everything, except bonfires and a broken heart. She blames me for both. Super Glue was not-so-secretly in love with the principal, but when the proverbial brains hit the fan, she found out what kind of man he really is. Was.

He was a know-it-all. He went against the text team coach and let those zombies out of the fridge, and before that he went against me and ordered tots from a country our own president says wants to kill us. But, before any of that, when our greatest threat was cyberbullying, he took the tampon machine out of the girls' room.

It was the first of many budget cuts under the heading: Not His Problem. Menstruation was not his problem. Menstruation blood on skinny jeans was not his problem. Midol in the nurse's office was not his problem. He said bloat was just fat. He said there was no such thing as PMS.

He said this last bit for the umpteenth time to a cafeteria full of women whose periods had synced up without sanitary protection in the zombie apocalypse.

When I said, "Kill him," no woman hesitated.

We beat him with lunch trays, Purell cut off his ear, and then he was dead. And then he was undead. And the rest of the men ran away cupping their hands over their ears like Beats by Dre. Except for two: a nice man—the text team coach—and a bad man, who taught U.S. history and sexually assaulted Banana Boat.

It was a tit grab, but in The Frizz, there are no shades of rape.

Banana Boat used to be the school secretary. She has a pencil cup of Magic Markers that will make you see colors. She smells like a fruit bowl. The tip of her nose is always orange for the reason it was always orange before the zombie apocalypse: Some people sniff markers. Don't mention the orange on Banana Boat's nose. She's not proud of it, like Purell and her ears.

When Banana Boat's not foraging for sunscreen, she sits guard over her old office, which I've converted into a prison. The zombie principal is chained to a radiator and acts as a kind of watchdog between the nice man and the bad man. The nice man lives in the principal's office and is not chained to anything because he is not a threat. He tried to save us by locking his text team in the freezer, and then he physically restrained Super Glue when we lit her library on fire and later murdered her crush. The bad man is chained to Banana Boat's desk. He's still here because he's married to Pony. When we talked about kicking him out, she laughed and we compromised.

Pony visits the bad man, and we all visit the text team coach. There's no sex in The Frizz because there's nobody nicknamed Sheepskin or Rubbers. Getting pregnant in the zombie apocalypse is worse than going gray. If you don't die in childbirth, your baby cries, and crying draws zombies like a lunch bell on pizza day.

That's why no more men are allowed in The Frizz.

Until now.

Normally men sneak their way in. And they always sneak. No man has ever read our "No Men Allowed" sign and knocked.

Until you.

In the past, men have sometimes gotten in, but we get them. And sometimes they get one of us, but we eventually get them. And, for reasons that are entirely her own, Purell gets their ears.

Don't give her a reason to add your ear to her belt.

My advice: Keep stealing what you've stolen. What'd you do, rob a bunch of dead ladies' powder rooms on your way here? *OB, Tampax, Playtex.* No generic. Nice. Congratulations, you're a feminist in the zombie apocalypse. For your foreseeable future, you'll be known as White Bullets.

NO TRUTH TO TELL

PATTI CALLAHAN HENRY

THERE ARE BEDTIME STORIES TO soothe and bedtime stories to forget. Alice's mother had told her the forgetting kind, but there was no *real* forgetting.

⚜

The woman driving the minivan, Alice Lister, was as annoyed by this trip as any she'd ever made. Why she had to drive four hours on a sweltering summer day to look at an old house was beyond her comprehension. At forty years old, she had bigger and better things to do with her life. With two preteen kids at home, and a husband who wanted to know what was for dinner and her own house that needed more from her than she could ever give, what was she doing driving south from Atlanta?

Actually it seemed that everything in her life wanted more from her than she could ever give, but that was an entirely other issue. No one was forcing her to drive to Linton, South Carolina, unless you counted the fact that Rufus, her best friend, was prodding her to do so. Though this was the problem with the situation at hand—Rufus was imaginary. She didn't hear him talk out loud, nothing that crazy; his voice was more like a memory. Usually he comforted her, but ever since she'd seen that limestone house on the Internet, he wouldn't go away.

The highway changed from its simple, unfurling black ribbon to thin country roads lined with moss-draped trees and boiled peanut stands. Alice's hands were sweating, slick on the steering wheel even as the air conditioner pumped cold air. A warm Coca-Cola sat in the cup holder, and open bags of Fritos and gummy bears slumped in the passenger seat just within reach.

She was angry at Rufus, and at herself because she didn't want to waste her day driving four hours only to gaze at a house that had been lurking in the crevices of her mind for all her remembered life. A house she could see in her mind's eye as right as anything in her life. As clear as the blue eyes of her husband, as clear as the oak tree in their backyard with the tire swing hanging from it, as clear as the newly-etched lines on her face and the half-spiderweb creases at the sides of her eyes.

A week ago she'd seen the house as she was scrolling through her Realtor company's website. AUCTION! it stated. The photo on her screen shimmered and moved as if it were alive, almost reaching out for her. It was an old house, from 1910, the brochure said, built as a plantation home for the Worthington family when they grew indigo and rice in the rich Lowcountry of South Carolina. It had changed hands many times, been reincarnated as hunting grounds and then a bed-and-breakfast. Now it was being sold at auction "as is," a great opportunity on ten acres.

Alice hadn't been in the real estate business for long, just a little over a year, but everyone knew that "as is" was never a good thing. Something was always hidden in that phrase, a glitch the buyer wouldn't find until they'd signed on the dotted line.

Alice had stared at that image on her screen for so very long that when the children ran in the door from school, tossing backpacks and asking for snacks and an hour on their video games, she realized that hours had passed. It was the house of her dreams, not the kind of dreams of what one might want in the future, but the real kind of dreams, where she awoke at 2:00 a.m. with her heart pounding against her ribs like a bird trying to escape. She clicked on the picture, opened it to see the slide show of rooms and hallways, of ancient bathrooms, and it was *her* house. It was the house of her memories. Not exactly, there were some things that were off. But still, she knew the minute she opened the photo that she had to go see it; she must walk its hallways.

For days she walked through life untethered and half aware, so obsessed with the stone house with the iron gates and double-gabled roof. She'd called the listing agent to ask more questions, find out who owned it and why it was being sold. The owner had died alone and the money would go to a family estate, that's all she was told.

It was impossible that Alice had ever seen this house before. Mother had told Alice that they moved to Atlanta from Louisiana when Alice was four years old. Every time Alice asked her mother about their childhood house, and the days when they'd lived there, her mother would shake her head with the gray perm curls wiry and tangled, wave her French-manicured hand through the air, and make a noise that sounded very much like *pooh-pooh*. "It doesn't matter now, Alice, dear. It's in the past and you don't want to look at the past, trust me on this."

Alice didn't trust her mother on anything, so why she would trust her about this was beyond reason. There was nothing Alice had ever been able to do to get her mother to discuss Alice's childhood home. Not once. Not even after her mother's fifth vodka tonic, which didn't have any tonic in it and was the exact right count for when Mother's lips were loosed.

Mother wanted Alice to forget that her years from ages one to four happened. There weren't photos. There weren't videos. There weren't memories that made much sense. But Alice damn well knew that memories would not be denied—problem was that Alice was never sure which were imaginings and which were true memories. How could she know without someone to ask?

"Was it as big as I remember?" Alice would ask casually as she basted the Thanksgiving turkey.

"I don't know how big you think it was, dear."

"Did the yard really have a graveyard in the back, or did I make that up?"

"Oh, my Alice, you are so very good at making things up."

That answer wasn't a yes or a no. Actually, not much her mother ever said about those years was a yes or a no. *That* answer was also a dig at Rufus—Alice's childhood imaginary best friend. For God's sake, Mother had even told Alice's husband, the lanky sensitive soul Leon, about Rufus. Leon had, of course, thought it adorable that Alice once had an imaginary friend. He'd said it made Alice even more wonderful than he'd believed.

"But you see," Alice's mother had said, slurring her words around a cigarette with an ash an inch long about to drop onto Alice's new sea-grass carpet. "You see, Alice wasn't *just* friends with him when we lived in that back-water swamp—Alice took Rufus with her to Atlanta."

"How long did Rufus live with you?" Leon had kissed Alice when he asked this question. It was his way of making sure she knew that he was on *her* side.

"A long time," Alice said, not wanting to tell her husband that sometimes she still saw Rufus. Well, she didn't *see* him as a ghost, nothing that wackadoodle. She saw him as he once was—as real and solid and wide-eyed as he'd been. She could bring him to mind even now as she drove to the house in Linton.

Yes, back to the house, she thought. Enough of her mother.

Of course, there was no way this was *her* childhood house. And why she was annoyed was beyond her scope of understanding, because no one was forcing her to go to South Carolina. No one but Rufus, that is. He wanted to see if this was *the one!* He wasn't asking her to go, and he wasn't asking her to not go—he just stood there with his wide brown eyes and stared at her, insisting that it must be, at the minimum, checked upon.

So there she was in her Volvo, wearing her hair in a bun with a tortoiseshell clip, and smoking cigarettes, one after the other like she was a smoker, which she wasn't, or hadn't been since 1998. She was listening to radio stations go in and out along Highway 17 as she crossed marshes green and blue with unorganized creeks and estuaries winding among each other. She'd lied to Leon, telling him that she had a conference in Savannah. He'd believed her, and why wouldn't he? She'd never lied to him about anything, except how much a new pair of boots might have cost, or that she had a headache as he moved closer in the bed wanting some of what she wasn't in the mood to give. But on the whole, she counted herself as an honest and devoted wife and mother, at least better than her mother. Not that this was a good yardstick to measure with, but it was all she had.

When they'd lived in that house, it had been just the three of them—Mother, Rufus, and Alice. There'd been laughter and running through empty rooms (in her memories, most of the rooms were always empty). If there was ever a Father, Alice didn't know or remember. Another off-limits subject with her mother that was always met with, "I met him. I was seduced. I never saw him again. Sweetie, that's all you need to know because it is all I know. But thank God he was so handsome, because Lordy, look at you, so beautiful you could stop the moon in its path."

Alice drove, thinking of these things, and the closer she came to the plantation house for sale at auction, the more foolish she began to feel. But now she was almost there, and she might as well go look at it.

For the last thirty minutes of her trip, Alice tried to empty her mind of the thoughts that pushed at her. There were many techniques for this, and she'd been taught all of them in the never-ending quest to rid herself of Rufus. Like an alcoholic who hides their vodka bottles in strange places around the house, or the insides of their boots—she knew this one because she'd tried on her mother's cowboy boots one time and almost broke her toe shoving her foot in the bright red leather—Alice hid Rufus in the invisible realms of her mind.

She talked to him less and less, but talk to him she did.

And she succumbed now, just like her mother swigging straight from the bottle when she thought no one was looking.

"Do you believe it, Rufus? I lied to my family and I'm driving four hours to look at a house that reminds me of the one you and I used to live in. Remember those days?"

He never answered, but the silence never stopped her from continuing to talk.

"Remember when we'd run through those hallways as fast and as far as we could? How we'd play hide-and-seek? How Mother would sing us songs while she cooked in the big kitchen? You were always laughing. You never got mad or upset, even when Mother cried or the thunderstorms shook the house. There was the oak tree outside, the one with the gnarled branches and the hole in its side big enough for us to hide in, but only one at a time."

Alice realized, dammit, that she'd been babbling to Rufus for a while now and she shut her mouth and turned up the radio, a country music song about a pickup truck and a case of beer. She was almost there; no turning back. If she parked, stared at the house and turned around, found a motel to sleep for the night, and then returned home the next morning, no one would know better.

At the last turn onto Beachhead Road, Alice slammed on her brakes. There were cars parked end to end down the length of the road. Signs on sticks poking out of the grass shoulder every few feet stated in large red letters: AUCTION. An arrow pointed up the street, which was shrouded by oak trees and hanging Spanish moss clinging to the afternoon sunlight.

Maybe she would just drive by. Yes, that was a good plan.

Alice swooped the car around the parked ones and drove slowly until the house came into view.

Her heart stopped; she knew it did because when it started back up again, it banged against her chest and startled her with the pain of a hammer into her breastbone. She slammed her hand over her breast. Was that what a heart attack felt like? No. Nothing else hurt at all.

Slowly she found a parking space and walked toward the house, step by step, slowly as if sneaking up on it. She was dizzy.

It looked just like the photo—a limestone house inside a wild menagerie of waist-high weeds and oak trees crowding each other to the point of being tangled. The seven-foot-tall iron gate swung open, the scrollwork's gold paint peeling. The walkway to the wooden double front door was made of broken stones, wiry yellow grass and dandelions forcing their way through the cracks. Alice stood so still that other buyers bumped into her, but she didn't notice; she just stared.

Her mother was a liar. Why this came as such a surprise was hard to say. This was the house.

"This is it, isn't it, Rufus?" she asked out loud, and a man in a blue suit and yellow tie walking by stopped to make sure Alice wasn't talking to him.

Alice knew her way around and she found herself winding around nameless, faceless people, feeling as if her body floated more than walked across the wide-plank hardwood floors, through the hallways to the back room where Mother had once slept.

The smell of sex was pungent and sour, and as a child Alice knew the aroma meant trouble without understanding what it was, and always mixed with the smell of the liquor in the glass decanter at the bedside. The bedroom, it was in *this* bedroom.

⚜

Alice held Rufus's hand, warm and dry, as they burst through the bedroom door to spy on them—her mother and the dark man. Mother was underneath the bulk of the man, and she was hollering all hell for him to get off, to stop. It was Rufus who had lurched for them, who had pulled at the man's hairy arm, who had hit the man over the head with the bedside lamp.

But the man, large enough that a lamp was as silly as a rubber ball tossed at his head, merely laughed. Rufus began to cough; Rufus always coughed. His little body bent over, and the man picked Rufus up, not in a kindly way, and Alice charged after them. The man carried Rufus down the hallway and plopped him onto a rumpled single bed and walked away. Alice crawled into bed with Rufus, his body as hot as the sidewalk in the middle of the summer when they used a magnifying glass to fry the ants.

"Mommy!" Alice called her name over and over and over, but she never came. She was with the man with the hairy arms and the slick hair, flopping around underneath him and ignoring Alice and Rufus.

Alice continued to call until her voice went dry and nothing came out. They believed that eventually she would come because that's what mommies did. Alice cried and she held Rufus and placed wet washcloths on his forehead because that was all she knew to do. They fell asleep together and when Alice awoke, in the dawn of a thunderstorm morning, Rufus was as limp and pale as her china doll. She started to scream.

Maybe she'd never stopped.

✤

The real estate agent Alice had seen on the advertisement ran into the bedroom in a gray suit and a white silk shirt, her hair with so much hair spray it looked like it had been painted on. She whirled Alice around by her shoulders. "My God, stop! What is it?"

Alice opened her eyes, the aromas of sex and whiskey fading. Her hands rose to her neck, and she slapped her hand over her mouth that was still screaming. There was no bed or sex or dark man, no Mother or Rufus or fever. The room was empty and dusty, a skeleton of what her memory revealed. The bones of the room disintegrated like cancer had eaten them away. The wood-trimmed walls were pockmarked with wormholes, chunks of it missing. The chandelier hung sideways, a spider clinging to it from the remnants of a web. The windows, three of them, were broken with various-size holes: one the size of a bullet, the others a baseball, maybe.

"What is wrong with you?" the real estate agent asked again. "Do I need to call 9-1-1?"

Alice turned around to face the woman with the bleach-blond hair and black eyeliner so thick and dark, it looked like a tattoo. "I'm fine."

"I don't think so." The woman spoke in a quiet voice as if trying to calm a toddler. "Let me help you out. You're scaring the other prospective buyers."

Her mother was right. That boyfriend from college was right. She was crazy. Literally.

Alice would not be deterred, though. Even as her mind

told her that she wasn't crazy, she understood that she was acting as though she were. And that's when she ran.

✤

The graveyard behind the house was overgrown to the point of hiding the gravestones, although there were only a few of them. Maybe twenty, or was it less? Alice wasn't sure because she was lying flat on the ground, the wet earth soaking through her favorite Real Estate Agent navy-blue fitted dress. Her hair was spread around, undone from the low bun. Twilight spread across the earth, soaking into the grasses and weeds, casting long shadows of the gravestones as thin rectangles, one on which Alice rested.

Her head was cranked to the left, and her hand rested at the base edge of a stone. She took in small sips of breath. How had she landed here? Hadn't she just been standing in an empty bedroom screaming? What was happening to her? Where the hell was she? Far off she heard sirens and the overlapping voices of a crowd.

The cold earth slapped her in the face and she came to herself, as if she'd left for a long, long while. She sat up with a bolt and understood something awful—those sirens were for her. She ran her fingers along the gravestone's lettering—*Rufus Worthington*. Then the dates for a child aged eight years old. She spoke to him again, as she always had. "You are real."

There were other gravestones with the same last name, but Alice didn't take the time to read them because she understood that if she didn't leave, those sirens would descend and men would take her and they would inject her with meds to calm her down and there would be a hospital.

She stood barefoot. She'd lost her shoes and her nude-colored stockings had been ripped so her toes poked out like tiny sausages. That didn't matter. Not much mattered except escaping the sirens coming for her. She slunk into the woods, toward the marsh, into the tall spartina grasses of the estuary.

First the ground was soft, and she sank ankle-deep and then to her knees and then her waist. Soon there was the water—she was chest-deep as the memories, so long locked inside, chased her into the depths. She swam for as long as she could, but soon she knew she wouldn't be able to stay afloat, and that was okay, too, because now she understood everything there was to know.

She wasn't crazy. Rufus was her brother. The man was her father. The woman her mother. The house her childhood home. She'd slept next to her brother while he died, and her mother slept with a monster of a man in the next room, never answering their calls.

It was the last memory that swam with her, slowly swam with her until she couldn't swim anymore.

✤

The limestone house didn't sell that day, what with the ruckus from the woman who had started screaming in the back left bedroom. They'd found her late that night, poor thing, naked and stranded on a sandbar in the middle of the marsh. Her husband had come to retrieve her from the local hospital. It was whispered that she must have believed the ghost stories told in jest to buyers who roamed the hallways, attempting to decide whether to buy or renovate or destroy and start again.

There was once a family who lived here, it was told, and the little boy died, the mother ran away to leave the father there alone with his ghost son, who still roamed the grounds. The pitiful woman had believed it and come undone. The woman's husband couldn't explain why she was four hours away from home wandering through a house that she had no intention of buying. It was all a great mystery, and the story added to the lure of the house, which sold a week later in a new auction that drew even more buyers, upping the price.

✣

Alice awoke as she had every morning for a week now, in a small room with a single cot and a nurse reminding her to take her medicines. But that morning Alice's mother sat at the bed's edge, her hands folded in her lap, the smell of whiskey sour around her as a haze.

"What are you doing here?" Alice asked. Today she was going home. Her sweet husband was coming to get her. Her children were waiting. She had told them—the doctors, the nurses, and her family—not to allow her mother into this room.

"I am here to see you, darling. To make sure you are well."

"I am well, Mother. I am completely well. You know that." Alice brushed her trembling hand through her hair.

"No, I don't know that. You seem to have suffered a break from reality. Probably the stress of the job and kids and trying to be so perfect all the time. Why would you have gone to a house you've never seen or heard of?"

"Mother, stop." Alice bolted from the bed, grabbed her mother's bony shoulders. "I saw his gravestone. I saw it. I remembered."

"You must rest," Mother said and shook off Alice's hands, and then wiped her fingers across her mouth, smearing lipstick as red as blood across her face.

"I know now, Mother. I know. Everyone does. It's time to tell the truth."

Mother's face went serene, calm, the lines smoothing themselves out. "There is no truth to tell." She kissed Alice's cheek and wandered slowly to the door. "No truth to tell at all."

THE DEATH DOULA

AMANDA STEVENS

HABELLA PEACE WAS A WOMAN of indeterminate age and origin, although every now and then I could detect a bit of the Sea Islands in her lilting speech. She called herself a "death doula," someone who eases the passage from this life to the next. I didn't know her well, but I saw her often. The people she cared for almost always ended up at the Charleston mortuary, where I worked the nightshift.

My job at the DeLande Home for Fine Funerals was simple. I made myself available after hours to receive deliveries. For that minimal effort, I was paid a small monthly stipend and given the use of a rundown carriage house at the back of the property. The arrangement suited my needs perfectly. My family had been in the death care business for generations, so I wasn't squeamish about bodies and the schedule allowed plenty of time for my studies.

The garden that separated the carriage house and mortuary was used by the bereaved for meditation and reflection. I tried never to intrude upon their privacy, but on the day of Agnes Brant's funeral, the death doula lingered for so long among the allspice that I finally went outside to ask if I could be of assistance.

She greeted me with a numinous smile. "I'm Habella."

"Yes, I know you by reputation."

The eyes twinkled behind the netting of her veil. "As I you, Alice."

"Really? I have a reputation?"

"Indeed you do, child. I've come to make you an offer."

Her lovely cadence blended so well with the sultry sea breezes that I found myself strangely enchanted. She was tall and reed-thin with skin the color of melted chocolate. Despite the heat, her silk suit and white gloves were immaculate, and when she moved, I could smell raindrops and lemon verbena.

She carried an oversized pocketbook in the crook of her left elbow, and in her right hand, she clutched one of the flyers I'd put up in local businesses announcing my availability to do odd jobs around the neighborhood. Nothing was too small or tedious, so long as the task didn't interfere with my graduate studies at Emerson University or the hours required of me at the funeral home.

"What's the job?" I asked.

"You are aware of Mr. Simon Straiker? He has recently

moved into the area. His house is just down the way."

"I've heard of him, but we've never met." The whole street had been abuzz with his purchase of Culleton House, a rundown Gothic Revival that stuck out like the proverbial sore thumb amidst its pastel neighbors. For several weeks, workers had swarmed the property from sunup to sundown, and then suddenly all activity had ceased, followed by the hushed rumors of a serious illness.

Habella confirmed the gossip. "He is a very sick young man. Blessed with the face of an angel and the wealth of a king, for all the good either has done him. He is alone and dying, poor thing. He'll not live to see his thirtieth birthday."

"I'm very sorry to hear that."

"My job—my calling—is to prepare him for his journey and when the time comes, to facilitate his transition."

The back of my neck tingled a warning. My mother had once talked of transitions. *Death doesn't come easy for some,* she would say as she mixed the embalming fluids and inserted the cannula.

Funny how the thought of death and dying didn't particularly trouble me, but memories of my mother could send me into a funk that would sometimes last for days. I tried to shake off the encroaching gloom as I returned my attention to Habella Peace.

"Simon is at that point in his journey where he requires constant attention, but I have other duties that need minding," she explained. "He has a nurse and there's Cook and the housekeeper. He doesn't want for care or company, but he is surrounded by old women. He needs a youthful presence. Someone who smells of springtime."

I gave her a dubious glance. "What exactly do you have in mind?"

"You will come once a day to Culleton House and read to him."

"That's it? Just read to him?"

"He likes the old stories. Classics, you might say." She paused to take my measure. "I should warn you about his tastes, child. He has become fascinated with tales of ghosts and vampires and immortality. I suppose it only natural for someone in his condition to be consumed by the afterlife."

Another warning chill eased up my spine, but I merely nodded. "I understand."

"Money is no object," she said and named a figure that stunned me. An adage leapt to mind: *If something is too good to be true…*

I fought off common sense with another old saying: *Beggars can't be choosers.* My cupboards were empty and tuition loomed. "All that just for reading to him?"

"For two hours a day. When can you start?"

"I haven't accepted."

"Do you require more money?"

"No, I just…" I drew a breath and released it. Who was I kidding? Of course I would take the job. I had no other prospects and I couldn't go back to my aunt. Not after everything she'd done for me already. It was high time I stood on my own two feet. My chin came up and I said briskly, "I can start today. The sooner, the better, in fact."

Habella gave a satisfied nod. "Come at four, child, when the air is starting to cool. Simon likes to read with the windows open to the garden."

"I'll see you then."

I went back inside and settled down to study for the rest of the morning. Normally, my psychology text-books kept me engrossed for hours. A passionate student, I would often lose all track of time, oblivious to nightfall and hunger until the ringing of my phone or the bell at the back of the mortuary would summon me out of my dream world.

But that morning my thoughts kept drifting from my studies to Simon Straiker. A simple Google search revealed a plethora of fascinating details. The Straiker family could trace their roots all the way back to the founding of Charleston, but the line would end with his passing. He had no siblings, no extended family, no wife or children to carry on the Straiker legacy.

His whole life had been one tragedy after another, it seemed. He'd been kidnapped at a very young age and held for ransom. Upon his return, his parents had been so terrified something else would happen to him, they'd kept him isolated and he'd grown into a reclusive young man who lived for his work.

I felt a strange amity with Simon Straiker. I had also been isolated as a child, not by fear or wealth, but by my family's profession. No one had wanted to play with the little girl who lived in a funeral home.

Not that I'd minded so terribly much. My mother and aunt had been young and playful and offered all the companionship I needed. Once my grandparents had passed on, the sisters raised me together as they ran the family business. We had been happy and reasonably prosperous until my mother's illness had eaten up most our savings and my aunt had been forced to sell the mortuary to the DeLande family. She had been offered the position of director at one of their new facilities, and it was only through her persuasion—or coercion—that I had ended up in the carriage house, still a student at twenty-two, scraping by on that paltry stipend and whatever odd jobs I could pick up along the way.

Speaking of which...

At quarter after three, I rose from my desk to shower and change clothes, forgoing my usual shorts and tee for a cotton skirt, tank, and sandals. I packed a few books in my backpack and set off down the street for Culleton House.

I'd walked past the sprawling mansion on any number of occasions and had often stopped on the street to admire the ornate trim that looked faintly arabesque. Despite those weeks of frenzied renovation, the grounds and exterior remained untouched. The wrought iron gates hung askew, and weeds overran the front garden. I lifted my head, scanning the weathered stone facade until my gaze lit on an upstairs window where Habella Peace stood watching me.

Unease prickled, but I kept my nerves in check and even managed to lift a hand in greeting as I entered through the sagging gates. Darkness was hours away, but a perpetual gloom settled over the besieged garden.

The housekeeper opened the door with a silent glower. In response, I gave her my brightest smile. "I'm Alice Morningstar. Habella asked me to come."

She moved aside to allow me to enter. "Wait here."

I stepped across the threshold into a large foyer with checkerboard flooring, dark-paneled walls, and an oak staircase that rose to a wide landing. At the top of the stairs, someone stood silhouetted against the light streaming in through a long window. The shoulders were slumped, the head bowed, and I thought for a moment it might be Simon Straiker himself. Then I realized it was nothing more than a statue.

When I turned back to the foyer, Habella stood before me. She looked very different from the woman I'd spoken with that morning. Her silk suit and white gloves had been replaced with a loose cotton blouse and a full skirt that hung to her ankles. Her long hair had been braided and coiled around her head, and she wore not a speck of makeup. She was older than I had originally thought, but not so much wizened as timeless.

"Alice." She took my arm and I found myself pulling away from her touch, though I couldn't say why. "Simon is in the library. The room has always been his favorite, and it's easier on all of us not to have to deal with the stairs."

I followed her down a long hallway lined with ancestral portraits. At the end of the corridor, Habella slid open heavy pocket doors revealing a sun-washed room with floor-to-ceiling windows and a wall of crowded bookshelves. Most of the furniture had been removed to accommodate a hospital bed that had been placed in front of the open French doors.

Simon Straiker's head was turned toward the garden, but I could see enough of his profile to take in the paper-like quality of his skin and the brittleness of his cheekbones. A lock of blond hair fell across his forehead, giving him a tragic, youthful air that tugged at my heart. He lay so still I thought he might be asleep—or worse—but when Habella called his name, he turned his head, trapping me in the bluest gaze I'd ever encountered.

"This is Alice. She's come to read to you this afternoon. Would you like that, dear?"

He didn't answer but instead continued to regard me with unblinking concentration. He was so pale as to almost disappear against the sheets, but those eyes glinted yet with life and with something I didn't want to name.

"Simon," Habella said with gentle firmness. "Do you wish for Alice to stay?"

Into that awkward silence came the tinkle of a bell, followed closely by a second ring.

"Will you be all right if I leave the house for a bit?" Habella asked him.

The bell tinkled twice.

The realization hit me then with the force of a physical punch. He could no longer speak. He communicated by way of a small bell that had been tied to the index finger of his left hand.

I glanced at Habella, who was smiling. "He likes you," she said.

"I—well, good. I'm glad." The blue gaze remained

fixed on me, and I said with as much cheer as I could muster, "I'm sure we'll get along just fine."

He tapped the bell against the bed twice. *Yes.*

Habella beamed her approval.

The bell tinkled twice, paused, and then tinkled twice more.

I looked from Simon to Habella in confusion.

"He's given you a name," she explained. "He has rings for all of us, don't you, dear?"

Two tinkles. *Yes.*

Then, two tinkles, a pause and two more tinkles. *Alice.*

The tone of the bell altered slightly with the force of his taps. He gentled the pressure until it became almost a whisper. *Alice.*

I nodded in understanding.

"I shouldn't be gone long," Habella said, as she bent to kiss Simon's brow. She seemed very pleased with the way our introduction had gone. I waited until she left the room, and then approached the bed tentatively. "May I sit?"

The bell tinkled twice. *Yes.*

I sat down on the chair next to the bed and opened my backpack. "I've brought some books, but you may prefer something from your own collection."

A single tap of the bell. *No.*

"Very well then. Habella tells me you like the classics." I pulled out my battered copy of *In a Glass Darkly* and held it up for his inspection. "I thought we would start with 'Carmilla.' It's always been a favorite of mine."

He tapped the bell twice and I settled in more comfortably. I read straight through, pausing occasionally for a drink of water and to check on him. He lay with his face toward the garden and I could barely discern the rise and fall of his chest, so shallow was his breathing.

By the time I reached the end of the story, he had fallen asleep. I closed the book and returned it to my backpack. Then I got up and browsed his bookshelves, finding such esoteric treasures as *The Golden Bough* and *The White Goddess* before wandering out to the garden.

A breeze blew through the trees, rippling the leaves and arousing an inexplicable disquiet. I ran a hand up and down my bare arm as goose bumps rose in the warm air. I had the strongest urge to exit quickly and quietly through the garden gate, to hurry away from that withering place and not look back. Instead, I backed my shoulders and returned to Simon's bedside to wait out my time.

Habella returned a little before six smelling of herbs. "How did it go?" she asked as she saw me to the front door.

"Fine, I think. He fell asleep before I reached the end of the story. At least, I think he's sleeping."

"He gets weaker by the day. His journey will soon take a new turn. We must all be ready when the time comes."

"May I ask...?"

"Cancer," was all she said, and I nodded.

⚜

I'd planned to study late into the night for an exam the following day, but I was too preoccupied with Simon Straiker and his illness. Habella hadn't elaborated on his condition and I felt I shouldn't pry. Cancer had claimed both my grandparents, so I was no stranger to the disease. Whatever form ravaged Simon had not only stolen his youth and vigor, but also his voice. I searched online for a bit, but in the end, decided that perhaps I'd rather not know the details. There was something mysterious and appealing about his silence.

I went to bed early and dreamed about Culleton House. I was lost in a maze of rooms with only the faint tinkle of a bell to guide me through the darkness. The sound seemed so real that when I awakened, I fancied I could still hear the distant peal. I even got up and went out into the garden where moonlight dappled the statues. A breeze whispered through the crepe myrtles, raining scarlet petals down upon my shoulders as I turned my ear to the street. Surely I was too far away to hear Simon's bell and yet the sound came to me as clearly as if I stood at his bedside. Two tinkles, a pause, and then two more tinkles. The sound repeated as if he were calling out to me. *Alice. Alice.*

Nothing more than my imagination, I told myself. Or perhaps the breeze had stirred a neighbor's wind chime.

I was not one given to wild fantasies. If my mother's battle with demons had taught me anything, it was to keep a tight rein on illusions. But as I stood there in the garden, bathed in moonlight and dark memories, a certainty came over me that I was no longer alone.

"Simon?" The very whisper of his name drew a shiver. He wasn't there, of course. He couldn't be there. And yet....

I hurried back inside and locked the door, then leaned against the panel and drew a calming breath. "You'd better get a grip," I said into the darkened room.

If you don't want to end up like Mama.

❧

The next morning, I awoke in good spirits despite my midnight fantasies. I ran some errands after my first class and then returned home in plenty of time to shower and change before my four o'clock appointment. I arrived at Culleton House a few minutes early, but instead of lingering on the sidewalk, I walked boldly through the sagging gates and knocked on the front door. The grim housekeeper let me in and showed me down the hallway to the library. Simon lay staring out at the garden, but he turned his head when he heard the pocket doors slide open.

"Miss Morningstar is here to see you," the housekeeper announced formally. She lingered on the threshold as she twisted her hands in her apron. "May I get you anything before I go, sir?"

He tapped the bell sharply. *No.*

Oh, he doesn't care for her, I thought, and was amazed at how easily I could decipher his animosity by the force with which he struck the bell against his bed.

I smiled shyly as I took my seat at his bedside and removed *In the Glass Darkly* from my backpack.

He watched me avidly.

"Today I would like to read 'The Familiar.' Is that okay with you?"

Two taps. Two taps, a pause, and two more taps. *Yes, Alice.*

The time flew by and when I reached the end of the story, I glanced up to find that he had once again fallen asleep. Putting away the book, I rose, stretched, and then pulled the covers up around him. When I turned, I found Habella watching me from the doorway. She smiled her approval and then motioned me into the hallway. I followed her to the front of the house, but instead of seeing me out, she invited me into a small sitting room that looked out on the street.

I wavered in the doorway just as the housekeeper had done earlier. "I should probably go..."

"Come in and sit a spell," Habella coaxed. "I've made tea."

She took a seat on the sofa and gestured to the armchair facing her. I hesitated for only another moment before joining her. She smiled in that mystical way she had as she poured the tea and offered me a cup.

"This is good," I said, after taking a tentative sip. "I can't quite place the blend. It tastes flowery."

"My own concoction," she said, still with that smile. "Sprinkled with a bit of life-everlastin'."

"The scent is intoxicating."

"Drink up, child. This brew is good for whatever

ails you."

We sipped and chatted until I felt enough time had passed that I could politely take my leave. I set the cup aside and started to stand. "I really should be—"

"Are you not curious about Simon, child?"

"Oh, I don't..." The protest faded as I sat down abruptly. "How did you come to know him?"

"I was once his nanny. But that was a long time ago, when he was little more than a babe."

Before the kidnapping, I thought. "And more recently?"

"He needed me and so I came. It has always been that way with us."

She told me a little about his schooling and the business empire he had inherited from his father. Simon had never been comfortable giving orders, she said, and had conducted most of his affairs through intermediaries and online. "He is uncommonly smart. Wise far beyond his years. A clever and curious young man, our Simon." Her eyes twinkled. "You'll see."

⚜

By the end of the week, Simon and I had gone through all the stories in my book, and I asked him to choose a new title from his collection.

He tapped his bell a single time and then tapped out my name. *No, Alice.*

"You want me to pick a book?"

A single tinkle, a long pause. Two tinkles, a short

pause, and then two more tinkles.

I wrinkled my brow as I tried to decrypt. "No, Alice. No…Alice. No. Alice."

Two taps, a pause, two more taps.

"Alice." I took a shot in the dark. "You want me to tell you *my* story?"

The bell tinkled twice in rapid succession.

I didn't like talking about myself even on social media, but I didn't want to disappoint him, and it seemed only right that he should know something about the stranger that Habella had invited into his home.

Settling back in the chair, I folded my hands in my lap. "I grew up in a funeral home. The Morningstars have been in the death care business for generations, beginning with my German ancestors. My grandparents died when I was a baby and my mother and aunt took over the family mortuary. I never knew my father. I don't even know his name. My mother was just seventeen when I was born. Fragile and fanciful, she remains to this day the most beautiful woman I've ever known. But I'm not going to tell you about my mother. Not today."

He watched me with unblinking fascination.

"Today, I'll tell you about my Aunt Fiona, the second most beautiful woman I've ever known. She was nineteen when I came along, her whole life ahead of her. But she gave up her hopes and dreams to help care for an infant niece and her aging, ailing parents. Once my grandparents were gone, she threw her heart and soul into the business. Aunt Fi has a talent for dealing with people. She knows just what to say, how to soothe and comfort the bereaved. When my mother got sick, we were forced to sell the mortuary. That broke Fi's heart, but she has always done what needed to be done. My aunt is nothing if not pragmatic. In some ways I'm like her and in some ways, I'm not."

Simon tapped my name faintly and I smiled.

I talked on about my childhood and about my pursuit of a PhD in psychology. When our time was up, I rose quietly, tucked in his covers and tiptoed from the room. Habella waited for me in the sitting room with an encouraging smile and a cup of fragrant tea.

"He's becoming very attached to you," she said. "I've never seen him so taken."

I didn't know how to respond so I ducked my head and sipped the tea.

"It won't be long now," she said. "It's good that he has you for this part of his journey."

I left as soon as I could, breathing a sigh of relief as I exited the garden and turned down the street. My time with Simon had drained me and yet I felt strangely euphoric. I didn't bother with dinner or my studies, but instead went straight to bed, where I slept the sleep of the dead.

⚜

It was raining the next day when I returned to Culleton House. The gloomy weather matched the housekeeper's expression, but her dourness no longer intimidated me. The windows were open in the library and dampness permeated the room. Beneath the scent of drowned flowers and wet earth I detected the medicinal aroma of camphor.

Simon didn't turn when he heard my footsteps the way he normally did. He seemed mesmerized by the rain. I went over to the window and stood watching with him for a moment. His eyes looked glazed, his skin blanched and translucent.

"Are you all right?" I asked as I moved back to his bedside. "Simon? Can you hear me?"

He didn't stir, not so much as the blink of an eye. I tried to quell a rising panic as I touched my fingers to his wrist. I could barely feel a pulse, but when I would have hurried away to fetch the nurse or Habella, his fingers closed around my hand and he held me with the force of a vise.

I froze, for a moment too stupefied by the action to break free. When I finally did struggle, his grip tightened until I cried out. He released me immediately and I backed away from the bed, cradling my hand to my chest as I stared at him in fear and bewilderment. Then I whirled and hurried from the room, calling to Habella as I all but sprinted down the corridor.

She appeared at the top of the stairs, her expression unfathomable. "What is it, Alice? What has happened?"

"Simon—" My heart was still beating so fast I couldn't get the words out.

She came down the stairs quickly, her long skirt swirling around her ankles. "What about Simon, child?"

"He's not himself. He's…" My voice trailed off as a light flared in her eyes.

She nodded and ushered me into the sitting room. "Wait for me here." She returned a little while later with a tea tray.

"Is he okay?" I asked anxiously.

"A little weaker, I'm afraid."

"Weaker? He grabbed my wrist. See?" I held out my arm to her. "There's already a bruise."

"That's impossible, child."

"I'm telling you he did!"

"Then it was a reflex," she insisted. "A muscle memory, like the twitching of a corpse."

"Has this happened before?"

She hesitated. "He had a bad night. We had to increase his medication and sometimes a stronger dose produces unintended consequences." She sat down on the edge of the sofa and poured the tea. "Drink up," she urged.

"Shouldn't I get back to Simon?"

"He'll sleep for the rest of the day. Tomorrow he'll be back to normal. Normal for him," she added.

I took a sip from the delicate floral cup she handed me. "This tastes different."

She smiled. "A different blend today. *Passiflora incarnata*. Passionflower. It will help calm you. Finish your tea and then go home, child. Get a good night's sleep and come back tomorrow."

For the second time in as many days I went straight to bed when I got home, falling asleep almost at once. But dreams plagued my rest. Strange, psychotropic visions of the afterlife. Simon was there with Habella. I could see them just beyond an ornate gate. He held out his arms to me, but I couldn't make myself go to him. When I would have turned to flee, a hand clamped around my wrist. Habella was suddenly at my side, but she no longer looked like the gentle death doula I'd come to know. Her gaze was brazen and feral, and she said against my ear, "Do not fight this, Alice. He has chosen."

I woke up in a cold sweat, my heart thudding in dread. I lay very still as I oriented myself to the darkness. I was in my bedroom in the carriage house. The doors and windows were locked tight for the night. I was safe and sound, yet I couldn't shake a feeling of impending doom that hung heavy on the sultry night air.

Rising, I went into the bathroom for a drink of water, guzzling straight from the faucet as though I had been trapped in the desert for days. Then I went to the front window and stared out into the garden. The rain had stopped and the stars were out. Moonlight glimmered from a thousand water droplets clinging to the treetops. The garden seemed ethereal and enchanted, but even as I took in the gossamer beauty, the shadows seemed to creep in from all the dark corners.

Someone was out there watching me. Some *thing* hid in the shadows. It was all I could do not to grab my phone and call my Aunt Fiona to come to my rescue. Even the sound of her voice would be a lifeline, but I wouldn't do that to her. I didn't want to worry her. After the hell she'd been through with my mother, the last thing she needed was a delusional niece on her hands.

I went back to bed but I didn't sleep. I rose at dawn and hit the books until my first class at nine. Afterward, I lingered on campus, reluctant to return to the carriage house, though I couldn't say why. Maybe it was the dreams I'd had the night before or the proximity to Culleton House, a place that no longer fascinated but repelled me.

I wouldn't go back, I told myself. I didn't need the money that badly, but of course, I did. My situation was just short of desperate, exacerbated by the astronomical student debt I'd amassed. It would be stupid and irresponsible to turn down easy money because I'd had a few bad dreams. Nor would it be fair to Simon. He had grown used to me, perhaps even fond of me, and it seemed cruel to needlessly upset him when he had so little time left to him.

With fresh resolve, I returned to Culleton House that afternoon and was relieved when Simon turned at the sound of my footsteps. His eyes were clear and very blue and though his expression never shifted, I sensed he was happy to see me.

I greeted him with a jaunty hello and he responded with a light tap of his bell.

"Shall we continue where we left off?" I asked.

Yes.

"Today I'll tell you about my mother. Her name is Katherine Morningstar. Kitty for short. Sometimes my aunt calls her 'Kitty-cat' the way she did when they were little. That always makes my mother smile. For the past ten years, ever since my twelfth birthday, she has resided at the Milton H. Farrante Psychiatric Hospital here in Charleston."

Chin in hand, I stared out the window as I continued.

"As I mentioned before, the sisters took over the family business after my grandparents died. My aunt was the face of the mortuary and my mother worked behind the scenes. When I was little, she would bring me into the prep room to keep her company. She was a true artist, my mother. She had her own special way of blending the fluids so that the skin looked dewy and supple, and she was an expert at facial reconstruction and cosmetics. A magician, some called her. She created such natural presentations that she came to believe her touch really could bring the dead back to life. I came to believe it, too. At first, it was just the flutter of an eyelash or the tremor of a finger. Then I heard their voices. I would catch them staring at me, sometimes angrily, sometimes imploringly. There is a term for such a disorder. *Folie à deux*. The madness of two."

I glanced at Simon to see if he had fallen asleep. He had turned his head to the window, but I could tell that he was still alert. Still clever and curious.

"My aunt found a psychiatrist who took a keen interest in our affliction. He convinced Fiona to have my mother committed for a short time. The separation, he said, would weaken her hold on me. But weeks became months and then years, and my mother didn't get any better. It soon became painfully obvious that the woman we knew and loved would never come home to us.

"I still visit her at least once a week. Sometimes she'll

see me and sometimes she won't. Sometimes she remembers me and sometimes she doesn't. But I still go. Every Sunday afternoon without fail."

I drew a heavy breath and released it. Simon's eyes were closed now. I got up, fiddled with his covers, and then left the room. As had become our habit, I met Habella in the sitting room and she handed me a cup of tea, something flavorful and aromatic.

"Passionflower?" I asked as I sipped appreciatively.

"With a dash of life-everlastin'. Not just good for the body, but for the soul."

I wondered if she had listened in on my story. No matter. I felt as if a weight had been lifted from my shoulders.

⚜

I studied in the garden until twilight. When I could no longer see the text before me, I put the books aside and let my mind wander, back to my childhood, back to my mother, back to that dark place where she and I had once dwelled together. I had an image of her in the prep room, explaining to me about that moment after death when the body still clings to life. *There are those who fight transition even after the heart stops beating. Even after every drop of blood has been drained from the arteries. Their resistance can sometimes turn violent. That's why you must never, ever turn your back on a corpse, Alice.*

The mosquitoes came out and I gathered up my books to go inside. I tried to study in bed, but my eyelids soon drooped and I pulled the covers to my chin, succumbing to exhaustion.

Something awakened me after midnight. Not a bell this time. Not a sound of any kind, but a scent. The aroma of camphor flooded my room.

I rose from bed to check all the doors and windows and to peer out into the garden. Nothing stirred. Nothing seemed amiss, but I had the terrifying notion that someone had found a secret way into my home. And that someone had stood at my bedside gazing down at me as I slept.

✤

The next day I insisted that Simon and I choose another work of fiction to read. I was done with the story of Alice. I could feel his gaze on me as I wandered around the room, searching and searching until a familiar title struck my fancy. I plucked a copy of *The Mysteries of Udolpho* from the shelf and returned to his beside.

I read until he fell asleep, had tea with Habella, and then went home. The pattern continued for days, but on the Friday of my second week at Culleton House, I sensed something was different. Simon looked the same, the house felt the same, and yet something had changed.

Halfway through our session, I paused in mid-sentence and shivered. Without looking up, I knew that he had slipped away. I set the book aside and got up to check his pulse, lingering at his bedside to adjust the covers and smooth back the lock of hair that fell across his forehead. Then I went down the hallway to the sitting room. Habella glanced up as I hovered in the doorway.

"What it is, child?"

"He's gone."

She rose and came to the doorway. "I'll fetch the nurse and call the proper authorities. Arrangements will need to be made..." She took my hand and squeezed my fingers before she went down the hallway muttering to the portraits.

I didn't know what to do so I stood at the front window and watched the street. Habella returned some time later with a tea tray. I didn't want refreshment. I wanted nothing so much as to escape from that house, but Habella seemed to take comfort in my presence, and so I stayed until two of my colleagues from the funeral home came to collect the body.

That night, I sat in the garden and thought about Simon. How strange it was to have him so near. In the old days, someone would have sat with him all night, but that was a pointless exercise. The essence of Simon Straiker was already gone. His body was nothing more than a shell, an empty vessel. No matter my mother's belief to the contrary, the dead did not awaken.

⚜

Habella summoned me back to Culleton House the next day, presumably to settle our account. She had tea waiting for me, and as I sipped the fragrant brew, she explained that Simon had left a gift for me.

"It belonged to his great-great-grandmother," she said as she handed me a velvet jewelry box. The antique diamond ring nestled inside took my breath away.

"I can't accept," I said on a gasp. "This is too much. He barely knew me."

"He knew you well enough. You became like family to him. Please don't deny him this last request."

"I don't know what to say."

"Say nothing at all. Take the ring and wear it in good health, child. Everything else—his houses, his art collection, all the business holdings…" She shrugged. "The staff will be taken care, of course, but the rest will be dealt with by lawyers. I'm glad the ring will be safe from all those ravenous vultures."

I tucked the velvet box in my pocket and stood. "I should be going. I know you must have a million things to do."

"Stay, Alice. Finish your tea, child. Your presence brings us such comfort."

Without Simon, the house seemed more oppressive than ever and I suddenly had need of fresh air. But under the circumstances, I could hardly refuse her request. I picked up my teacup and sipped. She chatted on about the arrangements and I tried to murmur the appropriate response but my mind wandered. It wasn't until she said my name sharply that I snapped back.

"I'm sorry. What?"

"Are you still with me, child?"

"I drifted for a moment, but I'm here."

She smiled that smile of hers. "Have I ever told you exactly what it is I do?"

"You mentioned something about transitions."

"Put simply, I see to the needs and last wishes of the living in order to make their transition into the afterlife more desirable. Simon was the loneliest little boy I ever tended. He never really grew beyond that frightened child who got taken away by monsters. He never had a chance for a normal life. Never met the woman of his dreams, never fell in love, never had a family of his own. His greatest fear wasn't dying, but in spending eternity alone. He summoned me here to Culleton House to find him a companion. His soul mate, you might say. And I did. I found you, Alice."

The teacup slipped from my deadened fingers and crashed to the floor.

Habella seemed transfixed by the spreading stain. "That was another of my special blends. Did you like it, Alice? Do you feel different now, child? A little lightheaded, perhaps? A numbing in your limbs and a thickening of your tongue? Do not worry. It is but another transition. Since that day in the garden when we first talked, I've been preparing you for this journey."

I opened my mouth but couldn't utter a sound and when I tried to stand, my legs were as useless as rubber. I collapsed against the chair, sliding to the floor, where I lay silent and twitching and more frightened than I had ever been in my life.

✦

When I came to, late afternoon sunlight streamed into the room. I was in the library at Culleton House, tucked beneath the covers on Simon's bed. I couldn't move or speak. I couldn't do anything but stare out the window. I lay silently screaming until the sun went down and twilight settled over the garden.

✦

Night fell. The stars came out and I watched the moon rise over the treetops. After a while, I became aware of a weight on my finger. I thought at first it must be Simon's bell, but then I realized it was the diamond ring he'd left me. I had a vague memory of Habella whispering against my ear as she slipped it on me, "Don't fight it, Alice. For your sake and his, just close your eyes and let it happen. One way or another, he'll come for you, child."

✦

I lost all sense of time. Where was Habella? No doubt she'd fled the house once the deed had been done, but what of Cook and the others? If I could make enough noise, someone in the house or on the street might hear me. But I remained mute and paralyzed and growing weaker by the hour. My heartbeat had slowed. Soon my organs would shut down and I wouldn't be able to breathe on my own. Death was coming but not quickly.

Still, I resisted. I fought off the seductive darkness until my fingertips began to tingle. My lungs grew stronger and my heartbeat, bolder. If I could just hang on a little longer…

The garden gate creaked as someone entered from the street. I tried to call out for help, but the plea remained frozen on my lips.

A shadow appeared outside the open French doors. His shoulders were slumped and his head bowed like the statue at the top of the stairs.

Help me. Please, help me, I silently implored.

Into the quivering stillness came the faint tinkle of a bell. Two rings. A pause. Two more rings. And then the sequence repeated.

Alice. Alice.

THE GENTLEMAN'S MAGICIANS

PAIGE CRUTCHER

Because I could not stop for Death –
He kindly stopped for me –
The Carriage held but just Ourselves –
And Immortality.

—Emily Dickinson

ONE

Florence

DRUNK PEOPLE TELL TALL TALES. They tell long tales, stuttered and bizarre tales, fascinating, sad, funny, and inspiring tales. Florence knows this because she hears them all.

If story were currency, Florence would be a wealthy woman.

Thirty is too old for bartending. She knows *this* because Hairless Gus Hoffman tells her so every time he stumbles into The Main Portal. It doesn't matter that he's a forty-year-old bachelor who has hobbies instead of jobs. Hairless Gus, who inevitably will lose his toupee between the hours of six p.m. and midnight, is a man of firm opinions.

His opinions do not bother Florence. Each day is like tasting a hint of the same flavor of sparkling water that is the small town of City, Anywhere. She knows what to expect when Gus comes in, or when the thieving Price triplets, or local librarian/bookseller Susannah Rodgers, or even town recluse Merle Showcaster plop down at their favored stations in her bar. The Main Portal is a revolving door of people, circumstances, and situations. It has been for as long as she can remember.

Until today.

Today is different.

Cecil Fitzwilliam Sterling arrives at The Main Portal every evening at precisely 7:45 for his nightcap of warm milk and bourbon. He's the last of the Sterlings left in City, Anywhere. He walks from his loft apartment four doors down with a cane he does not need. A man of habit, Cecil occasionally stops at The Full Bloom to pick up a daisy or sunflower to pin to his lapel, and he always pops by Turn The Page to inquire after a rare or first-edition book that he's asked Susannah to look into. Lately, he's taken to bringing Florence strange and wonderful tokens from his collection.

A collector by trade, Cecil is an acquaintance to everyone, and a friend to none. He's a Sterling, after all.

There is only one thing that makes City, Anywhere stand out, and that is Hollowland. Built with hands financed by the Sterling family, Hollowland is the biggest home in the state, and the largest mystery in the region. Cecil's parents closed the house up when Cecil was a boy. It sits empty and majestic, overlooking City, Anywhere from its perch on Crater Hill.

Cecil doesn't speak about Hollowland. He doesn't talk about his two sons or their two sons, all of whom live Elsewhere and haven't set foot in City, Anywhere in almost fifteen years—when Dylan and Major Sterling accidentally set the town hall on fire and their father and uncle spirited them away.

No, Cecil doesn't speak about the uncomfortable things. He comes in, takes his stool, orders his drink, and asks Florence about her day. He offers advice when the deliveryman puts her last on his route and her liquor supply runs dangerously low. He brings her roses when her ex-boyfriend starts dating the owner of The Portico, her bar's direct competitor. He hands over a new token and tells her a tall tale about the token's origin of birth. Cecil talks a good game, but never about himself, and he's never late.

Until today.

Today is different.

Gus takes his perch at six o'clock, and two shots of the cheapest bourbon with it. His toupee is lopsided, his smirk a smear across his otherwise nearly-pleasing face. He observes Florence watching the door, presumably for Cecil. Five, ten, fifteen minutes tick by. Cecil's delay is unusual in a town that doesn't thrive on unusual. Florence places a call to Susannah at the library and Marigold at the flower shop. Neither has seen Cecil, both are worried.

As Florence hangs up, Gus belches. Loudly.

"I think that cane finally got the best of him," Gus says.

"What?"

"Old Man Sterling. There were an ambulance and a rescue truck at his place. Saw 'em when I was heading in."

Florence's hand pauses over her dishrag. "You didn't think to mention it?"

He takes his third shot. "Hell, no. You didn't believe

me when I told you his number was up the first, second, or third time. Why would you believe me now?"

Gus has spent the better part of the last year telling her Cecil's demise is imminent. That "doom is on his way."

He's also told Florence she does not belong here, she will find a key to take her to the place only she knows, and that thirty is way, way too old to be a bartender.

Florence tries hard not to listen to what Gus has to say.

When she sees the flashing lights pass by, Florence puts down the rag and walks to the front door. Outside, Susannah and Marigold stand in front of their stores, Florence's expression of concern mirrored on their faces.

The usually quiet streets on Second and Main are full of people and fanfare. It's a strange sight to see. Unnerved, Florence turns and goes inside, shutting the door, wondering why her legs feel as though they are liquefying.

Gus sets a stool under her and goes to the bar phone. He holds his hand over it a second before it rings.

As he goes to pick it up, he winces, turns to face Florence before he's answered the ringing, and says, "Ayep. The old man is dead."

⚜

Cecil Sterling tripped over his cane and fell down a flight of twenty-two stairs. He did not survive the fall.

Florence closes up shop and goes to sit on the stoop, frozen like a human statue as people come and go. She watches three firemen, two EMTs, the young doctor who is doing his case study in town at the local hospital, and two misplaced pugs go in and out of Cecil's door. After half an hour, the young doctor approaches her.

"Florence?"

She stands, noting the tan lines peeking out from under the doctor's collar, a smudge of chocolate on his sleeve. It's a human thing to see, and somehow helps her remember to breathe.

"Dr. Keating," she says, her hands pressed into one another as though she's been praying. "Is Cecil—"

"He's gone."

Florence starts to ask where he went, before her brain wakes up and pays proper attention.

"Florence," Dr. Keating repeats, reaching out to pat her arm, but stopping just before his hand finds its mark. The doctor draws back, likely unaware he never made contact. Florence doesn't blink at the missed comfort. It isn't the doctor's fault people—well, *most* people—can't touch her.

"How can I help?" Florence asks, a quiet plea in her voice.

"Biscuits and Gravy," the doctor says, looking back at the entrance to Cecil's home.

Florence follows her gaze to the two well-fed dogs, French bulldogs. Realization is a fog clearing. "They're homeless."

"Yes," he says, tugging on his sleeve, checking his watch.

"I have room, I can watch over them."

"Good, I was hoping you'd say that." The doctor

absently brushes at the chocolate stain. "I've called Dylan and Major, left messages for them both. There weren't numbers for John or Richard."

Florence's stomach rolls over. Outwardly she shrugs, because what else can you do but shrug when dealing with death. "At least he kept in touch with his grandchildren."

"I've got to get back," the doctor says. "We can figure out a more permanent arrangement for the dogs, once we sort out the rest."

Dr. Keating reaches for her again, brushing air. Florence smiles, but it doesn't reach her eyes. It barely graces her lips. Then the doctor is walking away and Florence is whistling for her newest roommates.

She sets them up in her living room with bowls and beds and blankets. It's odd for her to have Sterlings, even furry ones, back in her home.

The night has encased the world outside. The stars, which normally alight the quiet town, have tucked themselves away. It's a fitting tribute for Cecil.

The pit in Florence's stomach has grown into a canyon. She tells herself it's because she is sad. Cecil was a good man, or as good as a Sterling man can be, and he was kind to her.

She makes a pot of tea, gives Biscuits and Gravy fresh water, and tries to ignore the tremble in her hands.

Normally Florence is as steady as a rock. She can withstand drunken brawls and shouting matches with ease. She ducks thrown cups, dodges insulting jabs, and forces out customers who won't leave, barely blinking an eye.

She handles it all without so much as a single shake.

Until today.

Today is different.

There's a knock on the door, and her knees buckle.

Setting the saucer aside, she goes to the peephole, but decides against looking through it. Taking a deep breath she knows won't help anything, Florence opens the door.

Dylan Sterling stands taller than she remembers, the same curious look in his eyes and concerned downward tug of his lips.

"Hey, Freckles," he says, his voice deeper than it was fifteen years ago. He reaches out and squeezes Florence's upper arm. "It's good to be home."

TWO

The Gentleman

IT DIDN'T START THERE. OH, I know they say it did now, but *they* are rarely right about anything.

If I had to pinpoint when it started, I might be tempted to go as far back as when Adam met Eve. With how way leads to way, when two people are put in an improbable situation, the impossible *always* seems to happen. But since I've never met Adam, and Eve seems like a nice girl whose sweet tooth branded her a harlot, I wouldn't say it started *there*, either.

It could have started back in 1903 when the town let in just about anyone, and Main Street became a stretch of saloons and fisticuffs. When Lady Franklin opened up her first brothel on the second floor and the mayor became her first paying customer.

But *that's* not right, either.

It might have been when Sam Allen fell in love with Esme Tarlington and stepped out on her with Mitchel Breyers. To say Esme's heart attempted to implode from the pain and injustice of it all—she broke up with Mitchel to step out with Sam, after all—is a severe understatement.

No, I would say the elements have been there since the first fool Sterling came to town 206 years ago. Trouble follows a Sterling like light follows the dark.

But the dusting off of the lock, readying it for a key, well, *that* started when Dylan Sterling showed up on Florence Holden's front step the first time, fifteen years ago. When spring was just kissing summer hello and day had slowly beaten back the night. When City, Anywhere was still a town called Hope and death didn't lurk in the shadows with the other hobgoblins and monsters born from Hollowland.

But what do I know?

No one ever listens to me.

THREE

Florence

FLORENCE STARES AT DYLAN. HE is seated on her couch holding her favorite daisy-embroidered pillow her grandmother made for her the year she turned sixteen. It had been too girly for her then, when the last thing Florence wanted was to appear like a child.

Now she keeps the pillow in whatever room she's in, and sleeps with it at night. There is something immeasurably comforting about holding a belonging her grandmother once cared for. It makes her think she was cared for as well.

In the fifteen years since Dylan has been gone, Florence has done well to forget him. Others might assume she's been planning this moment, working out what she would say when she saw him. She has not. Florence has a gift for moving forward, and when Dylan went, she left him behind.

As he sits to her right, filling up the air with his calm demeanor, she wishes she had more in her arsenal than pretty pillows and oversized mugs of tea. The room's silence is not golden, but charged, and Florence cannot stop staring at the way Dylan's skin creases pleasantly around his eyes, or how he wears patches at his elbow. The boy in the heavy metal T-shirts is gone, and in his wake is a person who stares at Florence like he has been planning very much for this moment.

"You seem surprised to see me."

She looks at the pillow, then back up to his face. "Well, yes."

"My grandfather—" he says, but stops. She's gone back to looking at the pillow. He sets it down. Florence resists the urge to snatch it to her chest. Like a barrier, or a shield.

"I'm sorry," she says, with feeling. "I really liked Cecil."

Dylan's brows wing up, and Florence wishes she hadn't said that. She'd forgotten how expressive his face was, unlike his brother.

At the thought of Major's face, Florence swallows hard.

"When I left, you hated him."

"Major?"

Dylan's lips twitched, and Florence briefly closes her eyes. Shit.

"Him too, sure."

Florence opens her eyes. "I never hated your grandfather." The same could not be said for Major Meriwether Sterling.

"Freckles," Dylan says, throwing an arm across the couch so his fingers are mere threads from brushing her shoulder. "You tried to set his hat on fire."

"It was an ugly hat."

Dylan chuckles. "While it was on his head."

"It was an ugly head," she says, unable to prevent the smile from creeping into her own voice.

It had been during the Autumn Awakening, a yearly festival when the town sets out candles and candy corn, filling the air with the scents of burning leaves and pumpkin-spiced everything. A festival meant to awaken the slumbering gods of autumn and bring good tidings for the season.

Cecil Sterling did not like children. He thought they were dangerous, and so he refused them when they came to his booth. His odd but wonderful booth that sold tree carvings in the shape of smaller trees with faces and gnarled hands. Little Ents, Florence's grandmother called them. Cecil called them Protectors.

Florence had wanted a Protector. She *needed* a Protector. She'd been dreaming of trees that grew out of the ground and turned into hands with long thin fingers, trying to catch and drag her under. The nightmares had been so vivid; she refused to sleep unless it was light out.

When she'd confessed to Dylan why she kept forgetting her homework and couldn't memorize her lines for the festival's production of *The Bewitching of a City*, he'd told her she needed a Protector.

The idea stuck.

When Cecil refused to sell Florence one, she waited until he was in line in front of her for Sissy Neighbors' "Unbeatable Kettle Corn" and tried to light his hat on fire. Dylan confiscated her Zippo before the flame reached the brim.

Major stole the Protector for her instead.

Florence clears her throat, well aware Dylan is thinking of the same memory. She wishes she could tug it back and keep it secret. He smiles, a crooked upturn at the corner of his mouth, almost like he can feel her retreat.

"Do you still have it?"

"My Zippo?"

"No, the Protector."

Florence starts to hesitate, and Dylan's hand brushes her shoulder. She sighs, stands, and goes to the small curio cabinet in the corner of the room. The Protector is as ugly and severe as she remembers. She holds it up for him to see.

"It's still warm," Florence says, with a small smile.

Cecil did something to the wood so the little sculptures felt like they had been under a heater. Sissy always claimed it was in the glaze, that he had a special one ordered from foothills of the Great Mountains, and there was an ember of magic to it.

Major said Cecil gave the Protectors pieces of his soul, which explained why he had none left.

Dylan told her to be careful.

Her grandmother found it, said a prayer, and locked it up in the cabinet.

Florence thought Major was wrong and right. There was something soulful about the piece, but she didn't credit Cecil's soul. She credited the town. It was as though the Protector carried a piece of the autumn equinox all year round.

It was just so ugly she couldn't bear to look at it for very long.

"He must have really hated kids," Dylan says, staring at it. "I mean, I'm thirty years old and part of me still thinks when the lights go out that one of those things is going to come and try and carve out my heart."

Florence bites back another smile and tucks it away. "That would be the opposite of a Protector."

"Yeah, well." Dylan stands. "Cecil never did as much protecting as prohibiting."

He moves to the window and draws back the curtain. In the distance Hollowland stands proud, like a light-house, calling all wayward travelers home. It doesn't matter that the night is as black as an oil spill, or the stars never seem to reach the ground Hollowland claimed. The house appears lit from within without ever using a single light.

"Is that why you're home? Because he's gone and you wanted to make sure the monsters were, too?"

Dylan turns around. He studies her face. "You don't know?"

"Know?"

"Hollowland, Freckles. Upon Cecil's death, the house that has been locked up for so many years is finally open."

FOUR

The Gentleman

EVERYONE TURNED UP AT THE Center of Town Square on the morning after Cecil Sterling took his untimely fall down twenty-two rather wide and even stairs. Stairs so well placed, the last way you would think to describe them would be *menacing* or *dastardly*. Which is exactly how Hairless Gus referred to them while donning his toupee and talking to his white tabby, Professor Snatch. The Professor could care less about the tale; he was waiting for his master to go to sleep so he could try once again to attack the large rodent hiding on his head.

This was the first death in City, Anywhere in years. And, if pressed, *no one* could tell you the last person whose demise had occurred in the town. People did not really come and go from City, Anywhere. They came, on *occasion*, but they found reason to stay. Whether it was the seasonable weather with its fall-like temperatures year-round, the affordable housing prices, or how everything in town was within walking distance, there always seemed to be *something* that lured travelers to relocate. It was a fascinating thing to watch, but it was also rare. Because while those who came, came to stay, not very many were *able* to set foot *inside* the city boundaries each year.

There were any number of *oddities* going on inside the town, but this one would be the most intriguing, if anyone in town would pay attention.

People are like sheep. Self-involved and impeccably groomed sheep, but sheep nonetheless. So of course no one *ever* noticed the lack of visitors.

I notice *everything*, so I watched the townspersons gather with their dark raincoats under a gloomy and despondent sky. There was the butcher, the florist, the baker, the librarian, the dog groomer, the tailor, the painter, and, of course, the bartender.

She looked saddest of all.

Well, next to the dog groomer. No one paid more for nail trimmings than the owner of Biscuits and Gravy, and no one loved those craggly-faced creatures more than the lady who did their weekly manicures.

No, people do not *frequent* City, Anywhere and expect to leave again. No one, that is, excepting for the Sterlings.

The clouds, drunk on rain, swelled and expanded. The two brothers stepped into the crowd and moved through it.

If the crowd were a snake, and *believe me* it was *some* kind of reptile with its typically cold-blooded nature, then the head was the mayor, the tail the sad bartender, the body the remaining citizens, and the rats refusing to digest inside the belly of the beast were the two interloping Sterlings.

I suppose it *was* a *sad* occasion, if you believed such occasions to be sad. What with the way Cecil had gone headfirst over that cane so that when he landed his legs were akimbo and all his devious lights were out. *They* say loss is sad.

Me? I am never quite so sure.

What I am sure of is that if secrets were currency, City, Anywhere should be the richest place in the universe, with the residents riding around on waves of the highest coin.

But that's the funny thing about secrets. When they're kept *so well*, even the secret holders forget what they have.

FIVE

Florence

A CHILL TAPS ITS WAY DOWN Florence's spine like water dripping from a faucet. She doesn't have to turn to know who is moving across from her—she can feel Major Sterling's presence the way farmers sense an oncoming storm. It makes her ache behind the knees, and, if she isn't careful, in other, weaker, places.

When Florence finally looks over, Major is not looking at her, but sizing up the mayor. Mayor Fisher also serves as the town lawyer, and is as sharp and decisive as the angles of his face.

In studying Major, Florence can look for the boy she once shied away from. She doesn't think Major has ever *really* been a child, he was likely born with a scowl and disdain for the masses. But whoever he once was, she can't get a read for how he'll be now.

She wishes she didn't care.

Memories try to push their way up from where Florence has secured them in her mind's basement lockbox. Dylan and Major, the faces of her youth, the names she thought would always be synonymous with her own. It is startling how the people you thought would always bring you comfort can end up being the ones you wish to run from most.

Major turns his face then, so she sees his full profile. The prominent nose, dark hair that is as unruly as his attitude. She sees the boy in the man, and that bothers her for reasons she cannot name.

It won't do to dwell on it. Dwelling prevents living, her grandmother used to say.

Florence feels exposed, like a nerve. She tries to see it, the nerve ending raw, battered, and bruised. She hates the image and instead visualizes an electric wire cut off at the tip, so it sparks and charges.

She would rather be electric than beaten.

Slipping to the back of the crowd, Florence listens to the mayor praise Cecil Sterling, a man she has witnessed him hide from a number of times. Fisher ducked into her bar only last Tuesday, watching through the window as Cecil ambled down the road, cane over foot over foot over cane, until he went into the bank. Only then would Mayor Fisher leave the safety of her doorframe and venture back into town.

The mayor is not the only one who feared Cecil Sterling. He also isn't the only one who revered him. Fear and respect are funny little friends. The crowd is full of people who knew and, well, if not loved, admired Cecil. His wealth, his presence… his house.

A house that looms over the town, as if on guard. Which is funny, considering the rumors. If rumors are born from even a speck of truth, then perhaps there really is something evil about Hollowland.

But what *is* evil?

It is a question Florence spends a lot of time on. One she can never answer, no matter how hard she tries. She only knows she hopes evil does not feel, or smell, or taste like her.

Hollowland was not evil, her grandmother told her. "A thing can neither be good nor evil, for it is not the thing that makes the mark, but the person using the thing."

So what does that make Florence? As a person—evil or not?

She shoos the thought away like an interfering mosquito and focuses on the house in the distance. Will they open it today? Will they discuss this as a town?

Major turns his head, just a sliver of a movement, but it draws her gaze again. Is he really home for the house, for Cecil?

Or could it be something else?

Florence's hand flies to her belly as she tries to settle the off-kilter flipping and flopping of her stomach.

The mayor steps up to the podium.

"We're all here about the loss of Cecil Sterling. I won't insult those of you here to mourn by pretending this is something it isn't. While Cecil's loss is a reckoning that will send shock waves through the toughest pillars of this community, I'm here to pay my respects and put an end to the rumors swirling in regards to Hollowland." Mayor Fisher clears his throat and surveys the audience like a runner taking his mark. "The house is—"

"Closed for repairs," Major calls, his voice cutting through the air like a lightning strike. All heads turn to face him, and he cocks a brow. "Or is it open for business?"

Mayor Fisher fails to hold back a grimace. "Perhaps you'd like to speak on the matter, Major Sterling? Now that you've returned home."

"Home?" Major drawls the word. "Is that what this is?"

His gaze finds Florence. Where his brother is dark and light and something sweeter, Major is shadows and shade. He is darkness and danger, and Florence forces herself to hold his gaze even as everything inside her quivers.

The good mayor doesn't answer the question Major poses. Instead he waves him up like it's a challenge, and Major shakes his head. "I'm afraid that's between my brother and me, and the solicitor."

The mayor sighs in obvious relief as Major cuts through the crowd, heading straight for Florence. She holds her head up, even as whispers from the past send her knees knocking.

"And you," Major says, stopping in front of her. "Dylan, you, me, and the solicitor. It appears the reading of the will cannot commence until the whole band is back together."

SIX

The Gentleman

I ADMIT, THIS MOMENT, *THIS* IS the one I've been waiting for.

They should know better, those three. Nothing ever comes in life without a price. I tried to whisper it to Florence when she was three and accepted the first daisy from Dylan, and again when she was eight and took Major's offered hand when she tumbled from her bike.

But no ever listens to me.

After all, I'm only a memory.

SEVEN

Florence

SOLICITOR WARREN CAPAX REQUESTS THAT Florence and Major and Dylan Sterling meet with him at Hollowland precisely at 7:00 a.m. the following morning.

"He's fucking scared of being in front of that door in the dark," Major tells Florence, his eyes lingering on her earlobe, causing the tip to feel like it is on fire.

She doesn't speak, just nods and tries not to rub her ear as she stares at Major's forehead. She is tempted to get lost in gazing at his mouth, and the way his eyes crinkle at the edges tells her he knows.

Major leaves Florence like a ripple in his wake. She returns home to pace her apartment, the two round dogs watching as their new mistress carries a small throw pillow in her arms crossing, repeatedly, from room to room.

Florence does not sleep.

When the sky turns amber again, she finds herself in front of the cabinet housing the Protector. On instinct she reaches for it, sticks it in her bag. Then she stuffs the pillow in the bag, feeds the dogs, and leaves a note for Marty, the morning manager, to check on Biscuits and Gravy if Florence isn't home by lunchtime.

The drive to Hollowland is a quiet one. Florence's nerves are so taut, she can barely tolerate the classical music pouring from the radio. The layered melody of violin reminds her of Dylan, while the heavy bass reverberates through her skeleton, making her think of Major.

She eventually turns the music off and focuses on her breath. In and out. In and out.

"In or out?" Major had asked her the last time she'd come to his door. She meant to say out, to take three steps back and walk the way she'd come, straight home. Instead she said nothing, and he took her hand, pulling her inside.

The next day, he was gone.

She pulls up to the gate, surprised to see it open. She knows they are meeting at the house and they need a way inside the closed grounds, but seeing the gate unlocked sends something skittering down her spine. It takes Florence a moment to recognize the emotion for what it is: exhilaration.

Florence floors the accelerator, cutting over the hills and pathways in mere seconds, cresting the largest hill on a breath. Hollowland rises up like a phoenix fresh from the ash, and she lets out a loud *whoop* of a greeting.

The sight of the impressive manor, the brisk air, and lush landscape fill Florence with life. She does not know why the solicitor has summoned her, what final game Cecil may be playing. In this moment, she does not care.

Florence whips into the spot next to a sleek black Lexus, her hands loose on the wheel. When she exits the car she feels kilos lighter. Major and Dylan Sterling stand on either side of the large wooden door, watching her approach. Florence does not smile, though she is grinning on the inside. She nods to the thin man with the receding hairline. Solicitor Capax nods back.

She cannot imagine what Cecil has left her. Perhaps he has left her nothing at all, but rather knows having her here will cause his grandsons to squirm. If he has bequeathed Florence some token, she considers how to politely refuse. It feels wrong to take anything from a Sterling. Besides, she has Biscuits and Gravy now; surely inheriting two dogs, if she is allowed to keep them, is more than enough.

Dylan gives her a winning smile while Major scowls in the direction of her high heels. The three-inch spikes make her eye level with the eldest Sterling, and Florence feels bolstered by this.

"Good morning," she says.

"Is it?" Major asks.

"Shove it, Maj," Dylan says. "Morning, Freckles."

Major's scowl deepens, and the solicitor clears his throat.

"Yes," Major says, cutting his eyes to the nervous man. "You can get on with it. Don't want the house to accidentally swallow you whole before you can tell us what nonsense my grandfather is holding on to from beneath the grave."

Capax rubs the bridge of his nose, then pats Major on

the shoulder. The gesture shocks Florence. Major shrugs but gives the man a slight smile.

"This is rather unusual, rather unusual indeed, but so was your grandfather. I am to read his bequest once, and then make my departure. From there, it's up to you three what you do with it."

Dylan looks like he wants to interject, but the solicitor holds up a hand. He opens the sealed envelope in his other hand with a flourish and reads the contents.

"Darling Florence, dearest Dylan, and hello to you, too, Major. They say a house is not a home without the heart of a family. While my heart is not buried under the floorboards, the secrets of this town are. If you want them, you can have them. But first you three must agree to live at Hollowland, from this moment forward, with nothing more than what you've come with, until I say otherwise. Capax will tell you when your time is up. If one of you does not agree, the house is boarded for another 100 years. If you accept, I must give warning. What lays dormant here is more than a story. It is more than a promise or a lie or a dream. It is, my dear boys and girl, everything."

Solicitor Capax looks down at the note then back at them. He looks like he wants to say something, but instead turns and walks to his car.

"Capax," Major calls, and the man looks back. "Has this bequest been offered before?"

The solicitor's smile is grim. "To your grandfather and his grandfather before him." He looks to Florence. "Today is different."

Capax gets in his car and drives off. Dylan, Major, and Florence stare at one another.

Dylan takes a breath and tests the door. It swings open. He looks to his brother, winks at Florence, and walks inside. Major follows, pausing to look back at Florence. She meets his gaze, and this time he smiles a real smile.

It is as beautiful as every sunrise and sunset Florence has ever seen.

"So," he says, one hand on the door, the other held out to her like a promise or a threat. "In or out?"

Florence looks up at the morning sky. She can feel her heartbeat tapping out an SOS inside her chest. She looks back to her car, worries about Biscuits and Gravy, knows Marty the manager has a soft spot for all canines. She looks back at Major and wonders if he still tastes like rain. She glances down at his hand, places her own in it, and breathes the word.

"In."

EIGHT

The Gentleman

THE DOOR CLOSES BEHIND HER.

No one sees the shadow in the window of the third floor.

No one sees the *other* shadows—shadows of shadows, really—as they slink from the corners and the cracks in the floorboard and walls, and make their way out into the house.

I see it all.

And down I go to greet my newest guests.

Because no matter what *they* say, or *where* they say it started, they have always been wrong.

It is now, right now, when time in City, Anywhere unfreezes, and the real story begins.

FORTUNATE SONS

DANA CHAMBLEE CARPENTER

"I KNOW I'M LUCKY," SPENCE SAID. His voice sang with the swagger of a fifth-generation eldest son. "That's just how it is for us, you know?"

He shrugged as he looked over at the young woman whose arm was draped gracefully along his. The moon had already set, but the dim light from the scattered streetlamps filtered down onto the smooth, white kid-leather glove that lay against the black of Spencer Hutchinson's tuxedo and stretched up to the girl's elbow where it blended into the whiteness of her arm.

She smiled and gave him a small nod.

He looked away, contented. Delta Blackstone was just what she ought to be, he thought—a good Southern girl who knew how to please a man.

"Just look at tonight," he said, stretching his neck until it popped. "I come into town to escort my cousin to the cotillion—no fun there—and then I meet you, and your escort's gone home sick." Spence pulled a silver flask out of his coat pocket and took a swig of brandy. "Now you tell me, Miss Delta, is that not a stroke of good luck for both of us?"

"Very good luck," she answered as she turned her head to look behind them. The lights from the court-house-turned-ballroom fell in squares on the sidewalk a few feet back. The music from the dance had followed them out into the vacant town square. The sharp, brassy rhythms of the fox-trot gave way to a slow, haunting melody on a single trumpet, and then a soulful voice broke through, "O Danny boy, the pipes, the pipes are calling."

Spence noticed Delta's backward glance and stopped. "You ever heard Rufus and the Red Tops do 'Danny Boy'?"

Delta shook her head.

Spence took another drink, pursing his lips at the sweetness as he brought Delta's gloved hand to his mouth. "You are a debutante in every sense of the word, Miss Delta. Rufus McKay crooning out that old tune is not something a girl wants to miss. All the dancing stops and the girls just sink to the floor, those white dresses spilling out from under them like they've melted." He hesitated for just a moment. "We can head back if you want. 'Course they sing that at all the dances. You'll get plenty more chances to hear it this season, I'm sure. You just tell me what you want, and I'll do it."

"I want to do what you want, Spence."

He smiled, having expected the answer. Any of the girls at the cotillion would've said the same thing. He was considered a fine catch—the son of one of Mississippi's First Families, wealthy, and good-looking to boot. He turned his blue eyes down on her, fully aware of the sway he held over her.

Spence settled her hand back along his arm. "I want to be out here with you where it's quiet, and we can walk and talk—not all jumbled up in there with the rest of them. That sound fine to you?"

Delta nodded and let Spence guide them on down the sidewalk.

"And don't you worry, sweetheart. I'll get you back before your daddy misses you," he said.

"I know I'm safe with you, Spence."

His shoulders relaxed just a little as his body softened into a more natural posture, less formal, less controlled. He wasn't sure if it was the liquor that was loosening him up or the confidence that he'd picked his girl well.

"Last time I was at Willow Falls I was about ten, I reckon. I spent the summer with my granddaddy. Can't say it was much fun. Ain't much to do around here, is there?" He chuckled. "You been here all your life?"

"Yes."

"Don't you find it dull?"

"Sometimes exciting things happen."

"Like fireworks on the Fourth of July?" He laughed, shaking his head.

Delta ran her free hand down the curve of her waist to clench a fistful of tulle and satin, lifting her skirt as they neared the curb where the sidewalk crumbled into the street.

"I can't believe my daddy wants me to move back to this place," Spence said. "It ain't nothing but a bunch of old ghosts and backwards ideas. Except for present company, of course, Miss Delta."

She smiled sweetly at him. He drank down that smile like another swallow of brandy. He figured he could say anything to her and she'd keep smiling with her pretty mouth set in that fine little face with those big doe-like eyes.

"Why's your daddy want you to move back to Willow Falls, Spence?" Her voice was all honey and light.

"I'm supposed to take over the bank from my grandfather." He stopped and nodded at the three-story building looming on the other side of the street. The stonework was patterned in darks and lights with gold bricks set against red in beautiful fanned shapes, but it all washed out in the moonless night and turned a murky gray. The smooth swirls at the tops of the columns looked like they were writhing under the faded lamplight.

"Oh, is old Mr. Hutchinson ill?" Delta asked.

"Nah. He's just old, and the only bank he wants to spend time around is at the fishing hole. But it ain't fair to stick me here." The liquor and the girl were loosening Spence's tongue as well as his body, and he couldn't hide the bitterness in his tone. He found himself suddenly angry. "Daddy jumped at his first chance to get out of here. He went on down to Vicksburg and started up his own bank. This one ain't nothing compared to Daddy's bank. It's twelve stories tall and decked out in marble and polished oak and brass. Now I wouldn't mind being given that bank, but ain't no way Daddy's quitting anytime soon." He sighed with frustration.

"He's just jealous. I ain't tied down by nothing. I'm young. I can go anywhere I want and do anything I want." He spun around, walking backwards as he looked at the tiny town square behind them. "I doubt any of the folks here in Willow Falls know it, but the world's changing. It's 1968, for God's sake! I ain't got to limit myself to what I can get in Mississippi!" He turned back around, his hands balled into fists. "I'm meant for something more," he said fervently as he craned his head back, looking up into the night sky. "Spencer Hutchinson *deserves* more, don't you think?"

Delta nodded.

Spence didn't notice. "I got a roommate up at Ole Miss who comes from New York. You should hear him talk about the money to be had up there... and the parties and the women—"

The clock on the courthouse chimed, telling them it was a quarter to midnight and reminding Spence where he was and who he was with. "I don't expect you to understand, little Miss Delta," he said, his voice silvery smooth once more, his anger tethered.

"Would it be so bad in Willow Falls?" Delta asked.

He looked down at her, shaking his head. "Oh, I'm just talking, honey. I'm sure I'll do what my daddy says. Always do. Stay in Mississippi and be a good Southern son."

Delta let a little sigh slip through her soft lips. Spence's eyes were alight with all he wanted and meant to get for himself in the future—and now.

He stepped closer to her. She half-turned back the way they'd come. The last of the lamplight fell on the ground where the sidewalk ended. They could no longer hear the music from the dance.

"'Course, if I do decide to run off, maybe I should just take you with me." Spence leaned over her shoulder, speaking quietly at her ear.

"Really?" Delta let him put his arms around her waist and pull her close.

"Why not? You're such a pretty thing with them big dark eyes and high cheeks. And that mouth—" Spence whistled. "Like a little bow waiting for me to open my present." He bent low and stepped toward her again, forcing her back against the trunk of an elm tree that marked the beginning edge of the town's cemetery.

His heart pulsing in anticipation, Spence kissed her long and deep, a first test to see how far she was ready to go. He was confident he'd get what he wanted, the easy way or hard, but he worried that maybe he'd picked this fruit a little too soon. He liked them innocent enough that they'd have no idea what he meant to do, but a gentleman had to be careful the girl wasn't so green she'd panic and bolt too soon. It was all part of the game. Spence prided himself on having learned to play it well.

Sure enough, she let him linger at her mouth a few seconds more and then pushed gently against his chest. He moved his mouth down to her neck, and she arched to look up into the skeleton arms of the tree above. December had stripped the leaves from all but the magnolias and pines, though the air was still as tepid and dry as it had been in September. What made it a winter's night was the silence. No bug-song or night birds singing, not even a wind to knock the branches together. Just lonesome quiet.

Delta shivered a little.

Spence worked his mouth down to her collarbone as he slid his hand up to cup her breast.

"Maybe we should..." She pushed his hand away. "If my daddy..."

"I'm sorry, Delta. I'm not acting like a gentleman, am I?" Spence pulled back and ran his hands across his face before leaning over her again. He'd gotten farther than he'd expected; maybe Miss Delta was ripe for the picking after all. "You're just so beautiful it's hard to keep my hands off you." He unfastened the three pearl buttons on her glove and slipped his finger through the opening to caress the soft skin at her wrist. He thrilled at the delicate moan that slid up her throat.

She looked away, blushing. "Spence? Maybe we could just keep walking? If we turn here at the lane that runs alongside the cemetery, it'll double back and come out just north of the courthouse—a nice, long stroll like you wanted, and then we can go back to the party." She smiled up at him and then shyly lowered her eyes. "But maybe that sounds silly to you?"

Spence turned to look at the lane behind him. Acres of silhouetted headstones and mausoleums stretched out to the left of a wrought-iron fence lifted and bent by thick twisted roots bulging from the ground. The darkness ate the lane a few feet past the corner of the last building on the street—a vacated storefront with Miss Verdia's Hair Salon painted and peeling on the front glass. Everything was dark and quiet and isolated.

"That sounds like a fine plan, Miss Delta." Spence threaded her arm through his again and turned them down the lane.

Bits of bracken snagged in Delta's skirt as they walked. The dark shapes against the brilliant white looked like bugs crawling up her dress, but she didn't seem to mind.

"Did you know that tonight is the winter solstice?" she asked as she rested her head against his arm. Spence smirked. He'd eased her along just right, letting his charm soften her up so she felt relaxed. He knew he was almost home with a girl when she started chatting. "They've always held the cotillion on the winter solstice," Delta said.

Spence was about to ask if she'd had to learn the history as part of her debutante training, but they had entered the deep darkness at the far end of the lane, and he was so focused on keeping his footing that all he could manage was, "Hmmm."

"Did you know—"

"Shit!" He tripped and went down hard on his knees. "It's too damn dark back here," he grumbled as he pushed himself up and shoved his hand in his pocket to grab his flask. He took another long swig.

"I'm sorry, Spence. I should have been paying more attention. I know the way. Let me show you." Delta waited until he slipped the flask back inside his coat and then took his hand and guided him into the deeper darkness. The lane here was thickly lined with cedar trees packed so close together that the dense canopy shut out even the starlight. The lane was filled with the sweet smell of something wild and clean.

Spence was panting from the hard walk, but Delta took in a deep breath. "Did you know these trees are more than a hundred years old?" she said against the silence.

"Are they?" He was trying to maintain his charm, but he was growing impatient.

"Folks used to think that cedar would stop the yellow fever from getting them, so they planted them all along the lanes up to their houses to guard the ones they loved." Delta waited a moment for him to respond. "But you probably already knew that, didn't you, Spence?"

"Sure," he mumbled. "Look, it seems a bit brighter over that way. Let's go over yonder so I can see your pretty little face better." As he pulled them forward, they broke through the cedars into a clearing where the lane ended at two large iron gates with a high stone wall stretching out on either side.

"Wait! I know this place—this here's the old Winona plantation," Spence said as he tugged at the heavy gates, half hanging off their hinges and tangled in kudzu. "My daddy used to come out here when he was a kid. He told me this place was haunted."

"Is it?" Delta took Spence's arm again and pulled as if to move them back onto the lane.

"Don't you worry none, sweetheart. I'll keep you safe

from spooks." This was the opportunity he'd been waiting for—out here it wouldn't matter if she put up a fuss or not. She could scream all she liked; there'd be nobody to hear. He wasn't about to let a ghost story keep him from what he wanted. He bent and kissed the top of Delta's head. "I've always wanted to see this place. Bet a girl like you ain't never been out here neither, huh?" Spence tugged at the gates some more until there was an opening wide enough for him to slide through.

"What about the party, Spence?"

"This won't take long." He grabbed Delta's hand through the iron bars.

"But my daddy—"

"Come on, don't you want a little adventure in your life before we settle down like we're supposed to and wither up and get old? Wouldn't it be nice to have a story to tell our kids?"

Delta's dark eyes were wide as she peered in through the gates at the lawn, more wild than not, and then she looked over at Spence's beautiful, First Families face. She nodded and let him pull her through the gates, her wide tulle skirt crackling as she squeezed through the bars and across the threshold.

Something in the air changed on the other side of the wall. It was cold like December ought to be. Breath slipped between their lips in thin, ghostly wisps, and the stars seemed brighter, closer. Overgrown hedges made broken boundaries between the lawn and the lane, and huge trees, with cracked limbs dangling, erupted farther out in the yard.

Not far past the gates, Delta had to stop to gather up her skirts. They kept snagging in the kudzu and ivy that stretched across the ground like a swarm of snakes. Spence smiled, his eyes hungry as he stared at Delta's exposed calves and the soft, white skin of her lower thigh where the stockings ended. He took her arm and led her, more urgently, through the tangle toward the looming silhouette of the manor house.

"I wonder what's inside," Spence said.

But as they neared the house, the hedges fanned out from the lane, opening up the view of what would've been the front lawn. Something in the shadows caught Spence's eye.

"What the hell is that?"

He leaned forward, squinting into the hazy dark. The thing was low to the ground and stocky, but the edges of it blurred into the night, making it difficult to see its shape, to tell if it was a fallen tree or a mound of earth or a beast. Half crouching, Spence took a few cautious steps toward it, working to make it out in the dim light. Then suddenly he took off running at it, leaping over knots of kudzu in his haste.

Delta let out a little squeal.

"Hot damn! That there's a 1941 Ford Super Deluxe convertible coupe!" Spence ran his hand along the grille of the car half hidden under the remains of a giant weeping willow. Its long, thin leafless branches raked across the hood like bony fingers. "I can't believe ain't nobody come out here and gotten this baby and fixed her up."

"Maybe they're afraid to," Delta offered as she picked

her way through the twisted lawn toward him.

"Guess that's right. I reckon this old car means those stories my daddy told me might be a bit true." Spence took a step back from the car.

"What did he tell you?" Delta asked.

"That the folks who lived out here—"

Delta parted the curtain of bare willow branches and laid her hand on Spence's back. He shivered at her touch, half drunk and full of want. He looked down at the starlight on her lips and the curve of her breasts just peeking out over the sweetheart neckline of her dress.

Spence wasn't interested in telling stories at the moment, especially not that one. "Bad stuff happened is all. Same as any other ghost story, I reckon. Somebody died. Folks go and think the place where it happened is haunted."

"Who died?"

"Nobody important."

"Won't you tell me the story? I'm not scared." She leaned her head against him.

But Spence turned and shoved at the mangled and rotten convertible top that still stretched halfway across the car's body. Shriveled slivers of willow leaves flew off in every direction, some floating down to join a scattering of others in the car. Then he spun and swept Delta up and into the backseat of the car, white tulle billowing over the side and spilling into the floorboard.

"Let's go for a ride," he said as he jogged to the other side of the car and hopped in beside her.

She was giggling. "This old car can't go anywhere,

silly, and surely not if we're in the backseat."

"Well, let's just pretend we took a drive out to Grenada Lake. You ever been there?" He slid across the seat closer to her, wove his arms around her waist.

"I've never been out of Willow Falls."

"Well, I'll just have to fix that, won't I?" He kissed her gently on the forehead. "For now, just imagine we're parked at the edge of the lake, looking out over the water, a big old moon hanging low in the sky." As he talked, he inched his hand up to her breast, caressing it through the thin fabric.

"Spence," Delta said, and he stilled his hand a moment, waiting to see if she was going to protest. "Tell the story about what happened here."

He sighed with anticipation. "Okay, I'll tell you." He twisted toward her, let his hand slide even higher to run his fingers along the soft skin at her neckline, easing his fingers in under the cloth while his other hand stretched around to her back, where he played with the dozen tiny, silk-covered buttons. "It's about a boy and girl in love."

"Did the boy or girl live here?"

"The girl. She was an only child, doted on. Her daddy bought her this car. Gave her everything she wanted." Spence kissed her softly as he worked at the buttons. "But the boy was heading off to war and might not come back," he said between kisses.

"Oh no."

"He asked—" Spence was having a hard time kissing, working at the buttons, and telling the story at the same time. He dropped his hands down to Delta's waist and slid her hips along the seat toward him until she was lying flat, and he eased himself into the gap along the back of the seat, his knee settling into the dip between her legs, lost in the sea of tulle. "He asked her to marry him, but there wasn't time for a ceremony before he had to go fight. They wanted to show their love so—"

"Her daddy didn't like him," Delta said.

Spence pulled back a little, surprised at how sure she sounded.

"Daddies don't ever like boys," she explained.

"No." Smiling, Spence stretched his arm down to the floorboard, searching for the bottom of her dress. "But the girl didn't care. She was willing to give up everything for him." His fingers played with the sheer hose at her ankle and along the backside of her calf. "She wanted to show the boy how much she loved him."

"And then the boy died. That's sad."

Something didn't sound right in her voice, but Spence's body was raging with desire. He eased a hand up to unfasten his pants while he kissed the tender skin along the curve of her breasts.

"Spence, wait." Delta pulled at his face until he was looking at her.

"I don't want to wait, Delta."

"Do you love me?"

"Let me show you how much I love you."

Delta stared into his eyes as if she were trying to find the truth.

"I asked you to come with me, didn't I? Show me how

much you love me, and I'll take you away from here," he said.

Something in her face changed, like watching a little girl turn into a woman all at once.

"What do you want, Delta?" He was surprised to hear his voice shake.

"I want you, Spence." And she let him bury his face against her breasts as he shoved at her skirts and pulled her under him.

Delta sighed. "He wasn't a soldier, you know."

But Spence was too busy to hear.

"He was just the wrong sort of boy," Delta said, her voice cold like the December air, indifferent. "But the girl loved him anyway. So she gave herself to him. In this car. Her daddy had bought it for her, but not because she was doted on. He bought it to control her. His money, his car, his gas meant he could tell her what to do, where to go, and who she could love, or not." There was a bite of bitterness in her tone now.

But Spence didn't hear it as he pulled her tightly against him. She arched her neck back to keep the pile of tulle from smothering her. She stared up at the stars through the spindly arms of the willow tree.

"But her daddy caught them," Delta said as she slid her hands out from her waist where they'd been trapped against Spence's body. "And he shot the boy. Just here, in the backseat of this car. The daddy shot the boy in the head while his daughter was underneath him. Shot the boy she loved. She had bits of his brain on her face. Blood everywhere. It ruined her dress."

"What?" Spence asked. He'd reached his climax and collapsed on her chest.

"The boy died."

"I didn't think you knew the story," Spence said, his voice loose and languid.

"Do you know what happened after?" Delta asked. "Her daddy snatched her up out of the car and locked her away in this house. Painted her up like a whore and sat her in a rocking chair in front of the parlor window. Turned the lights on at night so folks could come jeer at her."

"Made her out to be a lesson to other girls who'd give away their virtue to the wrong sorts of boys," Spence said. "That's what my daddy told me."

The sharp, shrill cry of a mockingbird rang out through the cold air.

"Do you know what Winona means?" Delta asked, her own voice soft and pliant again. "It's an Indian word that means 'first daughter.' It's why this place is called Winona Plantation—because the Indians brought their firstborn girls here to honor them. Their mamas would come, and they'd have initiation ceremonies when the girls were ready to become women. They anointed the girls and said blessings over them. Kinda funny, huh?"

"Funny, how?" Spence sounded like he was almost asleep.

"Funny that this was a place to honor daughters, and it's the place where a daddy defiled one."

"She had it coming."

Delta looked over at the dark outline of the manor

house. "You never asked me about my family, Spence."

"Why would I?"

"You asked me to come away with you, but you don't know if I'm the right sort of girl because you don't know anything about my family."

"You were at the First Families Cotillion, so that tells me a lot about your family, and what we just did tells me all I need to know about what sort of girl you are."

The mockingbird raced through one bird call after another, frantic, as if trying to find its own song.

"My mama came from the Lusks over at King's Hill near Alva. Some folks tell stories about them. They've got a touch of oddness. Do you know them?" She waited a beat. "They aren't a First Family, but my mama—she was determined to marry into one. So she said yes to James Blackstone, and he brought her to his family's estate here in Willow Falls, and they had me."

"See, it's what I was telling you earlier this evening. Some people are just lucky." He gave a muffled laugh.

"My daddy, he—"

"I ain't afraid of your daddy, sweetheart, if that's what you're getting at."

"No, Spence, you don't have to worry about Daddy. He's been dead a good little while now. See?"

The lights at the front of the manor house sparked to life, and Spence spun around to look. The neglected gray stone walls were mottled with black and green mildew, stone shingles hung precariously along the eaves, but his eyes were drawn to the room at the right. A full bank of windows exposed the interior. Through the wavy glass,

Spence could see gas lamps lit up along the walls. Empty shelves ran along one wall, cobwebs hanging in the gaping crevices. The room was painted a stark white. There was nothing in the room but a simple cot and an old rocking chair. There was someone in the chair—a man, it seemed, based on the size. Chunks of flesh hung flaccid against the skull, the jaw dropped and mouth gaping, loose and impotent. The rest of the body was shrouded in a black tuxedo, tails draping down from the seat and swaying as the chair moved gently back and forth.

"I sat in that room for twenty years," Delta whispered. "Twenty years' worth of rocking. Twenty years Daddy would come in and paint my cheeks with Mama's special rouge and turn the lights on. Twenty years of Mississippi's most fortunate sons and finest daughters sneaking out here to jeer at me and call me a whore." Her voice was icy with bitterness. "Now it's his turn."

The front doors of the house opened, throwing light out onto the steps and up to the lintel over the entrance where there were words carved into the stone—BLACK-STONE MANOR.

"I don't understand," Spence muttered.

"See up there? The name? Blackstone? That's the name of the people who lived here." She spoke to him like she was explaining something simple to a child. "That's my daddy's family. That's my name, too. Delta Blackstone."

"But that can't be," he said. "You can't be her. That was nearly thirty years ago, and you're... you're just a girl."

He spun back around to Delta. "Oh God!"

There was blood everywhere, streaked all down her white tulle.

She propped herself up on her elbows. "Don't worry, Spence. It's not mine."

He held her gaze, shaking his head as if he didn't want to look, but his hands were already moving to his abdomen. He felt the sticky wetness there before he finally looked down to see the sliced flesh. He looked back at Delta.

She was sliding a delicate little knife back through the opening of the glove at her wrist. The silver hilt glinted in the light. "The blade's so fine you don't even feel it."

Spence pushed himself back against the car. Blood poured down his gut into his pants, and slick, pink intestines pushed at the edges of the wound. He clamped his hand over them to keep them from spilling out.

"It's not my daddy you have to be afraid of, Spence. It's me." She pushed herself up to her knees. "And my mama."

Spence turned to look where she was looking. Just past his shoulder stood a woman in a wedding gown with a veil drawn over her face. Even in the pale light, it was easy to see that the dress was yellowed with age. She held out a small porcelain box with a fine, filigree peacock embedded in the top.

"Thank you, Mama," Delta said as she took the box. She wriggled the top loose and pressed it against the blood flowing from Spence's gut until the box overflowed with red. "He's going to make real pretty rouge, Mama."

Spence tried again to push himself up and out of the car, but he was so weak he couldn't move more than a few inches, and his breathing was fast and shallow.

Delta smiled down at where Spence had slumped into the floorboard. "You're lucky, Spence—you're my first." She giggled at the look on his face. "My first time to do it all on my own. Mama's always done the cutting before."

The sky was starting to turn pink at the far eastern edge.

Delta leaned down and kissed Spence tenderly on the lips. "It's almost time, lover," she whispered. He moaned.

"Did you know the winter solstice is a powerful time, Spence? Especially for people like my mama and me—all us Lusk girls, in fact. Mama said some folks used to call her and her sisters witches under their breath at church on Sundays. Nobody believes that anymore, though." Delta dipped her finger in the box of blood and lifted it to her cheek. "Anyway, the earth gives us what we want if we ask in just the right way. Blood shed in the heat of passion, worn like a shield against time." She smeared the blood in perfectly round circles at the apples of her cheeks, then she curled up against Spence on the floorboard, his head sagging on her shoulder.

She started humming softly the tune to "Danny Boy," but stopped, looking down on Spence's chalky face.

"I want you to know that I learned my lesson all those years ago about the wrong sorts of boys. Only fortunate sons for me now." She kissed him on the top of the head and turned to look at her mama.

"Aren't I a lucky girl?"

STONE ANGELS

LAURA BENEDICT

*T*REWLOVE HALL IS THE LAST *house I will ever see.*
The thought assaulted me with violent certainty
as the chauffeured car made its slow way up the curv-
ing drive leading to Trewlove Hall, and I clutched the
collar of my new spring coat closed to fight the sudden
chill. The drive hugged the house's elaborate gardens,
winding through trees and around massive banks of riot-
ous yellow forsythia and pink-tipped azalea buds. My
panic felt strange and out of place among so much natural beauty. At the other end of the wide leather seat, my
daughter, Theresa, gawped at both the garden and the
charming statues of waist-high rabbits, foxes, geese, and
raccoons scattered here and there. It was like a child's
wonderland. Traveling here was an adventure for her.
Though Theresa was almost nine years old, it was only
the second time she'd ridden in a car. The first time was

three years earlier, when we'd ridden in the car following her father's hearse to the soldiers' cemetery, after he
was killed in the Great War.

Trewlove Hall, home to Mary Trewlove, my new
employer, and her granddaughter, Lilith, sat nestled in
the gently rolling land outside Carystown, Kentucky,
only a six-hour train ride from our former home in Cincinnati. But I felt like we'd been transported a million
miles and a lifetime away.

"Mama, look. Horses! Did you know there would
be horses? They're like giants." Theresa tapped on the
window, indicating two huge gray Percherons grazing
behind a distant fence.

Before I could reply, Jerome, the grizzled, brusque man
chauffeuring us from the train station, answered without
turning around. "Those ain't for riding, and they ain't
for playing with, either. They pull the mowers, and drag
out stumps and the like. So don't you go bothering them.
They'd as soon step on a little thing like you and crush
your head."

Insolence. There was a time in my life when such behavior would have thrown me into a pique, but I held my
tongue. Theresa turned to me, her large, dark eyes as
solemn as her father's on our wedding day, waiting to see
how I would respond. I shook my head, and she turned
back to the window, silent. The shame of the job I was
taking—working as a hired tutor for a child who was
surely as spoiled as... well, as spoiled as the girl I'd been
early in life—kept me silent as well. My pride chafed.
I was the hired help now, and socially little better than

the ill-bred Jerome, with his coarse hands and bullying words.

Trewlove Hall was framed by tall, leafy trees, and a riot of brilliant garden blooms, but the house itself was a grim and dingy Tudor monstrosity out of a dime novel from the last century. The stone walls, where they weren't covered with creeper vine, were streaked with weather and age, and the hall's broad central building, which joined two steeply pitched wings, was crowned with an intricate pattern I couldn't quite make out. Flowers, perhaps, and were those cherub faces in the stone foliage?

Even now, I'm not certain. I spend little time outside of the house.

Perhaps it was the late position of the sun, but the scarce mullioned windows reflected back the blue of the sky, making them opaque, and I gently squeezed Theresa's shoulder, wanting to pull her closer as the house loomed, but she resisted.

Little did I know in that moment that her pulling away was the first indication that I might lose her before the week was out.

Something caught my eye as it darted among the sparse trees near the edge of the woods to the west of the house. It was too large and colorful to be an animal, unless the local deer were in the habit of wearing yellow dresses or cloaks. Whoever it was didn't move like someone out for a pleasant afternoon walk. They seemed to be trying to hide.

"Who is that?" I asked.

Jerome grunted, and Theresa turned from her window.

"What is it, Mama?"

The yellow figure was gone.

"Does Mrs. Trewlove take walks in the afternoon?"

"Used to," Jerome answered. "But she's not so well now."

"It's nothing," I told Theresa, not wanting to explain. Had it been a person at all? "Maybe just a trick of the light." How easy it was to lie to a child.

✤

"Well, aren't you a precious thing?"

Theresa gripped my hand tightly—or was it that I was gripping hers?—as we stood side by side on the portico steps. Behind us, Jerome was noisily liberating our trunks from their perch on the back of the car. I'd imagined us being let out at the imposing set of front doors, but the car had passed them without slowing and pulled into a carriage entry at the east side of the house. I wondered if it was a sign of our low position. We certainly were not guests.

The woman smiling down at Theresa wore a starched apron over her simple black dress, and a white linen dust cap covered much of her nutmeg hair. Her broad hips stuck out on either side, but her shoulders were narrow, giving her the shape of a pear. Her bright eyes, fixed on my Theresa, were friendly and warm. I was skeptical, but if such a pleasant woman lived in the house then maybe my first impression—that it was an unfriendly, forbidding place, indeed, possibly the last house I would ever see—was wrong. My dear husband, Allan, had often teased that I was overdramatic.

"Cat got your tongue?" The woman grinned broadly, and I saw that her canine teeth were just that much narrower and longer than the others, indeed like a cat's. She leaned down to give Theresa's nose a familiar tweak.

To my surprise Theresa smiled in response. She was a much sweeter child than I felt I deserved. "Mama is the new teacher. My name is Theresa—really Theresa Marie."

"My daughter is overexcited," I said hurriedly. "I'm Susannah Ross. Mrs. Trewlove?"

The woman reared back with unexpected laughter. Was she mad? Would she lean down and try to tweak my nose as well? "Lord, no! Wouldn't Mrs. Trewlove have a laugh at that? Come inside, come inside." She stepped back, indicating we should enter. "Jerome, Miss Susannah's to be in the Blue Room in the main gallery in the front, and Miss Theresa's in the east wing, the Bouquet Room, next to Miss Lilith."

As her words sank in, I realized I would be separated from Theresa for the first time in our lives. Always, she had slept in her small bed in the room next to ours. Allan and I would lie in our own bed and listen, smiling, as she sang to herself or told herself stories. The songs and stories had eventually stopped, but still, she was nearby. And now she wouldn't be. Did I dare say something? But at least we were to have rooms in the main parts of the house, not in the servants' quarters, and that was something.

Without a word, Jerome lifted my larger trunk onto his shoulder, then picked up Theresa's by a leather strap. Theresa and I followed the woman—who finally told us her name was Molly—into the house.

The carriage entry led directly into a long dining room hung with medieval hunting tapestries, and then we entered the dim central hall. Captivated as a child, I marveled at room after magnificent room. Perhaps *magnificent* is too extravagant a word. They were stately rooms, filled with highly polished furniture, paintings, and precious bronzes and sculptures. Before we went up the stairs, Jerome huffing behind us, I noticed that the front doors, which were lacquered with shiny ebony paint, were barred with a substantial iron bolt.

Molly read my thoughts. "You'd be surprised how many travelers think this is some kind of hotel or public house. They just open the front door and let themselves in."

It seemed a poor explanation. Were we in some kind of misplaced Tudor fortress? And if so, what were we guarding against?

Theresa was delighted with her surprisingly sunny bedroom, which was papered with enormous bouquets of tulips and jonquils, and immediately ran to the cushioned seat beneath the window to look outside. When she had calmed down a bit, I opened her trunk, and helped her change out of her traveling boots.

"I'll come back and unpack your things in a few minutes," I said.

"I can do it myself. It's my own new room!"

When Molly suggested that it was good for Theresa

to get used to her surroundings, I looked around the cheerful room. There was a small student's desk, and a wardrobe with a step beside it that she could use to reach the rack inside. Several new-looking dolls rested against the bed pillows. It was perfect.

"All right. I'll come back in an hour. Have fun." I kissed her cheek, and she ran to open the wardrobe to get started.

As I followed Molly through the broad hallways to my own room, she pointed out the other bedrooms and told me a little about the paintings lining the walls. There were a number of moody European landscapes in blues and golds and greens, but most were portraits of past Trewloves: forbidding, older women in fashionable dresses of the past two centuries. It wasn't until we reached my room that I silently noted the absence of any men in the portraits.

"Believe me, you'll be happy to be in the middle of the house, away from the girls," Molly said, opening the door to a spacious room that was, indeed, done in contrasting shades of blue. "When they get to playing nonsense, they drive a body to distraction." I wondered just how active my new charge would be. And what if Lilith and Theresa didn't get along? It was a question that had already caused me many hours' worry.

When Molly was gone, I stood at the window, rather stunned to finally be alone. From there, the front gardens didn't look quite so vast, but rather like a quaint private park.

Now I could see how the stone animals stood out in a

kind of pattern, arranged like spokes in a wheel. And at their center, surrounded by tall blue irises, was the statue of a girl sculpted in creamy marble, strung through with seams of ochre. Her delicate face was lifted to stare at the house, and I couldn't help but think how lonely she looked there, all alone.

⚜

I opened my eyes in twilight, my cheek pressed against a deep velvet-covered pillow. If the sound of giggling hadn't awakened me, who knows how long I might have slept? Remembering where I was, my heart quickened. I'd only meant to rest my eyes for a few moments before unpacking my trunk.

Where was Theresa? If the giggling was any indication, she was out in the hallway, and not in the room where I'd left her. I went to the door. More soft laughter, and whispering. I turned the key, but opened the door to receding, running footsteps and more laughter. In the dim light of the hallway, I saw a swath of blue linen and the heel of a black patent leather shoe disappear into the next doorway.

"Theresa!" Something about the quiet of the hall kept me from raising my voice above a loud whisper. I waited another moment and called her again.

"Here we are." Theresa was the first to emerge from the room beside mine, but it was the smaller girl behind her who spoke. "Is Theresa in trouble? Have we done something wrong?"

This could only be my student, Lilith. Even in the scarce light I could see the intelligence her grandmother had written of in her dark eyes, "a wisdom beyond her years." I hadn't expected it to be true. In the two years since I'd certified as a teacher, I'd heard too many mothers and grandmothers rhapsodize about perfectly stupid little girls as though they were the next Madame Curie. But as wise as she looked, Lilith was still a young girl, not quite eight years old, and two inches shorter than my Theresa. Her black hair was cropped short in a fashionable bob, just like that of nearly every other little girl her age, and her dress and stockings were as spotless as her gleaming shoes. There was one more thing: Lilith was quite the most beautiful child I had ever seen. Her features were perfectly even, her nose and lips finely drawn, but still childish. And her skin was like the fairest part of luminous mother-of-pearl.

Feeling like a traitor to have thought another child more beautiful than my own, I looked more closely at Lilith for some flaw, some excuse to think less of her appearance. All I found were hints of hunger and need in her appealing eyes. But those weren't really flaws, were they? No one could fault a child for being hungry for affection—especially a lonely child living out in the country with her grandmother.

"Mama?" Theresa's voice was anxious, and I drew my gaze from Lilith's face to hers. "Did we wake you?"

Unsettled, realizing I'd been staring at Lilith, I stammered out, "I-I didn't mean to sleep."

"Mary *always* sleeps in the afternoon because she's as old as that big beech tree in the woods. She thinks I need to nap, too. But I never do." Lilith reached for Theresa's hand, and looked up at her adoringly. "Now that *you're* here, Theresa, I shan't have to take a nap!"

It was a cheeky thing to say in front of another adult—particularly one who was going to have charge over her, but I didn't correct her. How spoiled a child was she? And how shocking it was that she should refer to her grandmother, Mary Trewlove, by her Christian name.

"Is your grandmother downstairs?"

"Oh, she'll be down when Molly rings the dinner bell at seven-thirty. She never comes down between lunch and dinner. We have to get dressed up. Mary is very particular about sitting at table." With that, she tugged at Theresa's hand. "Let's go." Theresa gave me a guilty, excited glance, and let Lilith lead her down the hall.

I went to my nicely fitted bathroom to splash water on my face, and then changed into one of the two dinner dresses I owned. Outside the window, evening was falling quickly. I checked my appearance in the veined and murky vanity mirror and carefully re-pinned my low bun. No modern bob for me. But what did it matter how I looked? I only needed to be presentable to a company of women and girls.

On the playful jingling of Molly's silver bell, we gathered in the medieval dining room. Two electric lamps were lit in the nearest corners, but most of the shadowy light came from two floor candelabras and a row of candles on the table. Our introductions were brief, but I was glad to see that on meeting Theresa, Mary Trewlove's haggard features broke into a look of pure pleasure. It was unusual for a tutor to bring a child along to a family position, and I'd been worried how Theresa would be received.

From the strength of her neat handwriting on the letters we exchanged, I had supposed Mary Trewlove to be in her fifties. But the hunched curves of her spine and shoulders, and the dullness of her cataract-glazed eyes told me she was certainly in her late seventies or eighties. She had obviously once been a handsome woman, but the years had given her sagging jowls and made her slightly hooked nose prominent in her thin face. Her gauzy vanilla dress did no favors for her jaundiced skin, rheumy eyes, and wispy white, close-trimmed hair. Both the dress and hairstyle were far too modern and youthful for her, but it was the jaundice that most concerned me. My father had been a doctor, and I suspected that Mary Trewlove was suffering some advanced form of liver disease.

Dear God, what if she dies soon? What will happen to us then? It would mean another difficult search for work. We had no family to return to, and we couldn't survive on my meager widow's pension. I had been lucky that a former colleague of my late father's had told me of this position.

"Will you start your classes tomorrow?" Mary Trewlove asked.

Molly stood at her left, holding a china tureen in the shape of a turtle, so that Mrs. Trewlove could ladle the soup into her own bowl.

"It's turtle soup!" said Lilith, interrupting my answer. "We have it every Sunday, Monday and Tuesday. That lazy Jerome only catches turtles on Saturday. *I* wish we could have it every night." Mrs. Trewlove said nothing, gave the child no admonishment.

Obviously, the old woman was too indulgent. I glanced at Theresa, who looked appropriately chagrined at Lilith's outburst, and vowed silently that she would not be corrupted.

"You do *like* turtle soup, don't you?" Lilith inclined her head toward Theresa, who she had insisted sit beside her.

Theresa hesitated, and looked back at me. I nodded. "I'm sure I will," she said.

Such a good girl, my Theresa.

"Jerome only catches those big old snappers that bite." Lilith smacked her hands together. Mrs. Trewlove flinched. "Not the cute little painted turtles. He's not allowed to catch those."

We were quiet while Molly took the tureen around the table. I noticed that Theresa only took one small ladle of the thick soup.

Determined to take back the conversation from the children, I told Mrs. Trewlove that we would begin classes at 9:00 a.m., and that I hoped she and Lilith could show us the schoolroom after dinner.

Lilith didn't answer but, with no small amount of drama, loudly slurped her soup from her spoon and closed her eyes, savoring it.

"That won't do, I'm afraid." Mary Trewlove put down

her spoon. "We never start lessons until after 11:00 a.m. Children need their sleep, and Lilith requires more than average."

"Perhaps an earlier bedtime, then," I suggested. Lilith paused in lifting the spoon to her mouth, but then continued, slurping even louder.

Mary Trewlove gave me a vague smile. "We're very set in our habits, I'm afraid, Mrs. Ross. Please understand. I'm sure you and Theresa will adjust nicely. It's a very civilized schedule." She turned to Theresa, dismissing me. "How is your soup, dear? Do you find it agreeable?"

Theresa nodded. "It's delicious." I knew she was lying, but I doubted that anyone else would guess.

An 11:00 a.m. beginning to the school day was a ridiculous proposition. Laziness in children should not be encouraged, and I was beginning to get the idea that not only was Lilith lazy, but she was also spoiled and demanding.

After dinner—roasted potatoes, a standing beef roast with brown gravy, and Floating Island for dessert—Mary Trewlove, pleading a headache, said she would retire to her bedroom. She told Lilith to show us the schoolroom, and encouraged me to explore the house and gardens in the morning, but to stay out of the walled garden behind the yews because the entryway was crumbling and Jerome had blocked it with a sawhorse. "No doubt he'll get around to repairing it within the year." She gave me a wry, knowing look that said Jerome was unreliable with his estimates.

Lilith stood on tiptoe to give her grandmother an

affectionate kiss on the cheek.

"Rest well, dearest," she said. Despite her spoiled behavior, she still looked like an angel. "We have to plan for my birthday on Saturday. You know we have so many things to do. You *must* feel better."

Watching Mary Trewlove make her halting way up the front staircase, I wondered what she did with herself all day in her room. *Dying,* came the unbidden answer.

⚜

At eight in the morning, I half-awoke to the ringing of the small alarm clock I'd packed in my trunk, but, strangely weary, I fell back asleep. When I awoke again, it was almost nine o'clock. Just a month earlier, I would've already been in my classroom, faced with two dozen girls and boys who would rather have been outdoors or in their own beds than listening to me.

After hurrying through the long hallways to wake Theresa, I found her bed empty. But when I listened at Lilith's door, I heard the girls talking and laughing. I knocked lightly before opening it. The only open window shade in the room cast a rectangle of sunlight on the enormous four-poster bed where the girls, in their nightdresses, sat playing with dolls. Otherwise the room had a gloomy aspect. It was not the sunny boudoir of a spoiled child that I expected, and was far less cheerful than Theresa's room. Lilith's might have been the bedroom of an old, wealthy spinster who was overly fond of dolls. For dolls of all sorts and sizes covered nearly every available surface, crowding close and tilting eagerly forward like a Lilliputian army at the ready.

"Time to dress and have breakfast, girls. We begin class directly at eleven."

Theresa answered with a prompt, "Yes, Mother." But Lilith only gave a faint nod and went back to her dolls.

I closed the door feeling unsettled. What a strange child Lilith was.

After a light breakfast in the dining room—an egg with toast and a small bowl of canned peaches—I made sure all was ready in the schoolroom in the east wing, then set off to explore the grounds.

The grass was damp with dew, and even the leaves on the freshly leafed trees looked glossy and wet. In the distant pasture, the Percherons stood at the fence, solemn and motionless, except for the flicking of their ears and massive tails. I thought about approaching them, but then noticed the obtuse Jerome near the stable door. I doubted the truth of his claim that the horses would injure someone, but didn't want to test the man.

I can't say that I was terribly unhappy in that moment. It was a pleasure to be so far from the city. We were even three or four miles out of tiny Carystown. Because I was so distracted and overcome by the unfamiliarity of the place, I hadn't yet begun to miss the few friends we'd left behind. Everything was new and strange. Uncertain, yet not unpleasant. But even as I heard the faint chimes of the closest church mark the ten o'clock hour, I still felt we had somehow been lifted out of time the moment the car started up the winding drive to Trewlove Hall.

Thinking I might find my way back in through the kitchen, I skirted the west end of the house—the end where the woods seemed to be slowly encroaching. At the far corner of the building, I came upon a dense row of yews running along the edge of the woods. The yews were over twenty feet tall, and packed so tightly together they seemed an impenetrable wall. Just beyond, a few oaks and beeches towered above them, but they looked old and sickly. Perhaps the yews were stealing all their water? In the distance, I saw the decrepit sawhorse marking the crumbling entry to the old garden, but I could see nothing of the garden wall.

I confess I was curious about the walled garden, and imagined it to be very mysterious, but told myself there would be plenty of mornings for exploring. Perhaps there was even another way inside. But right then I was anxious to make sure the girls were dressed and breakfasted and ready for lessons.

Before I could walk even a dozen feet, I heard an alarming rustling sound from the hedge. For some reason, my mind immediately went to bears. I knew there were still a few black bears up in Ohio. Surely there were some here, as well.

The rustling was followed by a woman's anguished voice. "Let go, let go of me!" I took a hesitant step back, uncertain whether to run away or assist whoever was coming.

A moment later, the woman broke through the hedge, alone, her eyes squeezed protectively shut as she fought the dense branches. Her face was broad and homely, and her ragged hair stuck out at all angles. Her cheeks and half-bare arms were scratched and lightly bloodied, and her shabby gray dress and yellow cloak were snagged and looked as though they hadn't been washed in weeks. When she opened her eyes and finally noticed me, she fell back a step, shocked into silence. But then she rushed forward, grabbing me by the arms.

"What did you do to her? I want her back!" She tried to shake me, but her skeletal hands were weak, and I stood my ground. "Why won't you give her back to me?" Her words came at me with a gust of foul breath.

She was mad, but I didn't fear for my life. Surely she was the woman I'd seen running through the woods the day before, and she obviously needed help.

"Come with me. Come inside the house." I tried to sound comforting. "I'll get you some food. Some water." Her lips were cracked and showed signs of bleeding. "You must be terribly thirsty."

Finally she broke away, cowering as though afraid I might strike her.

"You won't trap me," she said. "You ain't going to do to me what you did to my girl. I know Satan's work!" She sidled away slowly, then broke into a run, going the way I had come.

"Wait!" I ran after her, but she was too quick. Her feet were bare and gripped the ground firmly, as though she actually *were* an animal. My own shoes were unsure on the slick grass, and I nearly fell more than once. "Let me help you!" I cried. She veered into the woods and disappeared.

✤

"Surely someone can catch her. Have the police done nothing?" I looked up at Molly from my seat at the kitchen table. "What about her family?"

Molly put a steaming cup of milky tea on a saucer in front of me, and stirred a mounded spoonful of sugar into it. I hadn't asked for milk or sugar, but was too flustered to complain. "She started banging on our front door a few weeks ago, raving about her daughter being missing. These beggars. They don't last long around here. She'll move on."

The tea was just the right temperature, and I welcomed the sweetness. "She's obviously mad. The authorities should take her to a hospital or asylum. And what if she really *does* have a daughter? She could be out there as well." I could only think of Theresa being lost in the woods—hungry, cold, and alone.

When Lilith and Theresa came running in from the dining room a few minutes later, we closed the subject immediately. My attention was quickly drawn to Theresa, and the clothes she was wearing.

"Where did you get that dress?" I stared at the navy-blue sailor dress, with its broad collar and scarlet tie. The dress hung loose on her thin frame, making her look thinner and more fragile than usual.

"Mary always sends for clothes for me, and she gets my favorites in a bigger size, too, so I can have them later." Lilith was holding Theresa's hand again, but Theresa looked worried.

"You two *did* ask Mrs. Trewlove?" I didn't want this to be the start of some misunderstanding. The clothes were expensive, and certainly privately made.

"They were in my closet," Theresa said. "Lilith made me put them on. I didn't want to, Mama. Lilith said I had to."

"Is this true, Lilith?" I believed Theresa, but we were in a precarious position.

Lilith dropped Theresa's hand. "That's not the way to accept gifts, Theresa. You hurt my feelings." Tears started in her eyes. "I suppose now you don't want to be my friend. I guess you want to leave."

"I didn't say that." Theresa gave me a look that said she was feeling confused and helpless. "Mama?"

Before I could respond, Molly interrupted.

"Let's have none of this foolishness. You look very nice, Miss Theresa. Mrs. Trewlove will be so pleased the dress fits you. Now, isn't it time for lessons?"

At that moment, the case clock on the wall struck eleven. Molly's admonition obviously included us all, and I didn't see how I could continue without appearing contentious. That Lilith was upset was distressing enough.

⚜

Lilith proved to be an able student. If anything, despite the difference in their ages, she was well ahead of Theresa in mathematics. She also spoke French like a native—

something that surprised me—though she said she had never lived in France.

"Maybe your mother taught you?" I asked.

Lilith shook her head, a violent *no*. "Not my mother. I don't want to remember my mother."

That was exactly what she said, that she didn't want to remember her mother. How strange it sounded.

"Well, perhaps your grandmother, or one of your other tutors, then?" I wondered how many tutors had come before me.

"Mary speaks French like me. Mary loves me." She cocked her head to one side, and gave me a sweet smile.

There was no getting a straight answer out of her.

By the time lessons were over, I was relieved to see that she and Theresa had forgotten their disagreement.

"Je vais t'apprendre à parler en français." Lilith leaned her head against Theresa's shoulder, and Theresa giggled.

When Lilith said they would play outside in the garden after lunch, I remembered the madwoman. What might she do to the girls?

"Why don't you stay in this afternoon and make plans for your birthday, Lilith? And Theresa, please pick a special song to practice on the piano to play at the party. Do you both know what you want to wear?"

It was the right thing to say. As they left the schoolroom for the kitchen, where Molly would give them a late lunch, they talked excitedly over one another.

I went to the far window that overlooked the yews, and could just see the top edge of a pale red brick wall behind them. But I wasn't high enough to see what was beneath the trees inside. Both times I'd seen the woman, she hadn't been far from the garden.

✤

For those first few days, Mary Trewlove showed little interest in getting to know me. After three days of lessons, I asked her if she would like to review the academic plans I'd made, based on what I'd learned about Lilith's skills. But she replied that she was sure whatever I came up with in the way of lessons would be fine, and only insisted that lessons continue through the summer, rather than be interrupted by a long break. It suited me because I had no money for summer travel, and it meant our daily lessons needn't be too arduous.

Molly, though, was friendlier. I sat in the kitchen with her often in the mornings or late afternoons. I quickly became used to the strong tea, and enjoyed her stories about the gossip in town. I thought it odd that she knew so much gossip despite rarely leaving the grounds of Trewlove Hall. She sent Jerome out with a shopping list every other day, and I could only imagine his terse requests at the butcher's and the market. Surely he was no favorite.

The next afternoon it rained, and so I didn't have to worry about the madwoman bothering the girls, because they stayed inside. The other days, I went outside with them, and read in the sunshine while they played and chased each other around the animal statues in the front garden. I kept an eye on the woods, but the madwoman didn't reappear. I hoped she had finally been apprehended, but I couldn't help but remember how thin and disheveled she'd been. When had she eaten last? What if she were already dead?

On Friday, the night before Lilith's eighth birthday, Mary Trewlove didn't come downstairs for dinner.

"She's poorly," Molly said, helping Lilith put mashed potatoes on her plate. Every night we had some variation of potatoes, and beef, chicken, or lamb, with a meringue or Floating Island for dessert. There were never vegetables, or even fruit with dinner. I had never seen Lilith eat anything green, nor had Theresa and I had any fruit outside of breakfast. It was a strange diet, and I didn't know how long I could bear it.

"Shouldn't we send for a doctor?" I asked. Across the table, Theresa looked weary, as though she might fall asleep in her chair. Were her eyes deeply shadowed, or was it a trick of the unreliable candlelight? Beside her, Lilith looked fresh and rested.

"Oh, Mrs. Trewlove is happy to send for a doctor for Lilith, or Jerome, or me, but she doesn't like them for herself. Says they're know-it-all busybodies, and I can't say I blame her."

Nevertheless, after supper I knocked on the old woman's door. I'm sure I heard her tell me to come in, but she looked surprised to see me and struggled to sit up once I was inside.

"Molly says you're not well. Can I bring you something? Tea, perhaps?"

Mary Trewlove wore an old-fashioned lace bedcap over her cropped white hair, making her face and nose look even thinner and narrower. The room smelled of minty ointment and lavender.

"I want to have energy for the party tomorrow. I fear it will be the last birthday of Lilith's I'll see."

She picked at the blanket with one bony hand, not looking at me directly, but at the wall opposite the bed, where there was an enormous mirror hung with a mesh drape. I wondered if I would ever be so appalled at my own aging that I would cover my mirrors. I was twenty-seven years old then, and mirrors are usually kind to the young.

"Molly said you prefer not to have a doctor. But maybe he could help you." I wanted to add *with the pain*. I wasn't so naïve as to think a doctor could much prolong her life.

"I have... medication for the pain." She waved a weak hand toward the tall brown bottle on her bedside table. "We have more if we need it."

I guessed that the bottle must contain a morphine solution.

"I know what you're thinking, Mrs. Ross. I know I'm dying."

It was a stark admission, and my chagrin must have registered on my face. I didn't know what to say.

"Of course you're wondering what to do when I die. You're worried that you'll have to leave and find another job. Another place to live." I tried to demur, but she raised a finger to shush me as though I were a child. "I want to reassure you that you and Theresa will always have a home here. I've already spoken to Molly. I learned all I needed to know about you through your letters and references. You will be an excellent guardian for Lilith, and I know she'll be eternally grateful."

I was stunned. I hadn't thought of staying at Trewlove Hall *forever*, and I wasn't sure I could develop enough affection for Lilith to be her guardian. And as disloyal as it felt to dear Allan, I'd harbored hopes that I would eventually marry another man, someone who would be a father to Theresa, and a companion to me.

"You don't really know me, Mrs. Trewlove. Surely Lilith has other family? People who will want to take care of her themselves?"

And what about that horrible feeling I had when we first saw the house? No, I can't ever forget that.

Mary Trewlove shook her head. "You'd be giving me a great gift if you and Theresa decide to stay. I'm so weary, and I want to make sure Lilith will be taken care of."

I wanted to say no, but the offer implied security, and might suit us until Theresa was married, or went to work on her own. She might even go to college. The pay here was good, and I really could save. I was torn.

"Please come here, my dear. My eyes are bad, you know. Sometimes when I wake I can't tell the difference between morning and evening."

When I reached her bedside, she held out her trembling hands to me. They were ice cold to the point of pain, and she gripped mine with more strength than I thought she could have.

As I watched, her eyes miraculously cleared of their

cataracts and yellow jaundice, and they were the bright blue eyes of a very eager young woman. Moist and pleading, they seemed to hold every emotion: from extreme joy to desperation to hope to resignation.

"Promise me," she whispered. "Promise me you'll stay. You'll take care of them. Don't worry, you'll know what to do."

Them? I didn't need to be reminded to take care of my own daughter. Did she mean Molly and Jerome, as well? "Of course," I said. "I promise." It was the only answer one could give to a dying woman.

A surge of heat passed through our joined hands, as though together we held burning coals. I think I cried out, but my memory isn't clear. After what seemed a lifetime, she relaxed her grip. She blinked, and the jaundice and cataracts returned to her eyes. Closing them, she collapsed against the bank of pillows and dropped into a deep sleep.

⚜

The night was cool, but not cold, and I put an extra blanket on the bed before opening the window. I hoped that the fresh air would cleanse my mind of grim thoughts of Mary Trewlove's impending death. What had happened between us in her room? Everything was moving too fast. We'd barely arrived, and everything was going to change again, in ways I couldn't predict. But if we left, where could we go? I lay, wakeful, missing Allan, miss-

ing our time together as a family before he'd been sent
to war in France. We'd dreamed of going there together
someday, but now he was dead, and all I had left was
Theresa. Living here, in this strange place, there would
be very little chance to make another marriage, little
chance to find a man I could love even half as much as
Allan. We wouldn't starve here, but we wouldn't really
live, either.

Finally, the cool evening air and the sound of the peep-
ers in the woods worked their magic. I slept several hours,
until there was a muted, frantic knock on my door.

"Mama. Mama. Let me in!" Theresa's voice was barely
audible.

I hurried from my bed to let her in, reflexively locking
the door as soon as she was inside. She threw her small
arms around my waist, and hid her face in my nightgown, breathing hard. I stroked her head.

"Shhhhhh. Shhhhhh, darling. What's wrong?"

"I want to leave here. I want to go home!" She sobbed,
her shoulders shaking.

I held her close for a moment and, with a little diffi-
culty, picked her up and carried her to the bed. We lay
there for a long while as she cried. How could I reassure
her? There was no *home* for us to go to.

"What is it, love? Is it the house? I know everything
feels different here."

Theresa shook her head.

"Is it Lilith? Did you have a fight?"

"I don't like it here, Mama. Why can't we go? We
could go into town and take the train home again. It's

not right here. Nothing's right. Molly's not right, and Lilith…" She didn't finish.

"I'm sorry, darling. We have to stay here for now." I couldn't make her any promises. I couldn't give her what she wanted. If anything, I felt like I was lying to her because I knew we wouldn't be going anywhere for a long, long time.

At last her tears stopped.

"I wish I could make it different," I said.

Dissatisfied, she moved away, and turned her back to me. The nightgown she wore was unfamiliar, and I realized it must have come from Lilith. More often than not, she and Lilith wore matching outfits, dressing like twins. After a few minutes, Theresa's breathing slowed, and I knew she was falling asleep.

"Sleep well, darling." I kissed her soft cheek.

"Molly and Lilith never sleep," she murmured. "Lilith only wants to play."

What could she have meant? I lay back on my own pillows, wondering. But I didn't dare wake her to ask. Finally, I felt the bonds of sleep pull me under as well.

Sometime near dawn, I dreamed of an animal running through the nearby woods, sporadic moonbeams illuminating its feathered yellow back like flashing lights. The scene was out of focus, but I could hear something roaring down from the sky, crashing through the upper branches of several trees, and I knew the yellow animal was in danger. It turned its shaggy, oversized head toward the oncoming sound and screamed in terror. In the dream, I looked away, but there was only darkness.

Understanding I was in a dream, I knew I must wake to get away from the grisly tragedy. I opened my eyes to a pearly dawn, but the screaming continued outside the window, and its last anguished notes were terrifying. Worse was the brief silence that followed, a silence that was momentarily filled with faint notes of childish laughter. My heart was pounding, and I wanted to get up to look out the window. Had I been awake or asleep? The laughter stopped as suddenly as it started.

I lay in bed, Theresa breathing softly beside me. There would be no more sleep for me—at least I can't remember that I slept. When a clock in the hall struck five, I suspected I would not sleep for many nights to come.

At last I rose from the bed, careful not to wake Theresa. As I completed my toilette and pinned up my hair, something oddly bright in the dull mirror caught my eye. I leaned closer. Was that a streak of gray in my hair? It didn't seem possible.

⚜

In the morning, as Molly put chocolate icing on the chocolate cake she'd made the day before, I asked her if she'd heard the screaming in the night.

"Bless you, no I didn't," she said. "That must have been a fright. Those coyotes sound very like babies screaming. Maybe you didn't have coyotes in the city."

"I can tell the difference between a human and a coyote," I said. "It was definitely human. What if it was that

woman? She might be hurt." Something made me ret-
icent to mention the laughter. "Maybe I should go into
the woods and look. There's a path, yes?"

Molly shook her head. "I wouldn't do it. But if it will
ease your mind, you should go. I'm certain it was coyotes. Either way you might wait until after the party."

The birthday party started badly, and ended quickly.

Oh, there were so many plans. Lilith and Theresa had
made up a list of activities to take place after a lunch,
which was to feature a special Saturday turtle soup, and
a chocolate cake with strawberry ice cream that the girls
helped Molly churn after breakfast. When they came
down for lunch, they wore matching party dresses: white
silk frocks that hung to just below their knees, with sky-
blue satin sashes and bows of the same blue in their hair.
I held out the white rose garland I'd made for Lilith, and
seeing it, she snatched out her bow, and begged me to
secure the flowers in her hair. When I was finished, she
hugged me, looking up with adoring eyes.

"I do love you, my Miss Susannah! You'll be my friend
forever and ever, won't you?"

I hugged her and laughed, but it felt forced and insin-
cere. Theresa stared at Lilith from behind. The shadows
beneath her eyes were deeper now. She'd slept hard and
long that morning, as though she hadn't slept in weeks.
But it hadn't refreshed her. If anything, she looked worse.

I never learned what happened between the two girls.
If only I had pressed Theresa the night before. But I'd
felt too guilty, knowing we would be staying on. I hadn't
really wanted to know the truth, because I might have to

choose between my daughter's happiness and our security. Of course, that was exactly what I'd done.

If only I'd been braver. If only I'd been the mother she deserved.

Lilith turned around, gently touching her garland. "Look, Theresa! I'm like a flower fairy in a book."

Before that day, Theresa would have brightened or even agreed. Now, she scowled, and walked stiffly to her place at the table. Lilith watched her, then turned back to me.

"We made place cards, so you have to find yours at the table, Miss Susannah. I mixed up everyone's seats!" She looked at Theresa. "You are in the wrong place. You have to move."

Theresa picked up the place card in front of her, and traded it with the card at the next place. She gave Lilith a smile that I could only describe as cold.

"You're in *Mary's* chair, Theresa Ross. You have to move."

"Your grandmother should get to sit at the head of the table, like she always does. Just because it's your birthday doesn't mean you get to tell everyone what to do, *Lilith*." Theresa crossed her arms in front of her.

Now it was Lilith's turn to scowl, but she was looking at me.

"Make her move, Miss Susannah. It *is* my birthday, and she's being horrible. She's been horrible to me all day." Her pale skin flushed with a shade that was more lilac than pink.

I sighed, wishing I were anywhere but in this dining room, in this house.

"Theresa, if you can't be nice, then please go upstairs until I tell you to come down."

"I won't!" She pointed at Lilith. "I hate her, and I hate this awful house. I want to go home!"

There was a heavy silence that seemed to last for a long time.

My head—indeed, I think, the entire room—began to fill with a strange, pounding pressure. I couldn't move, and could barely breathe. Lilith was staring at Theresa, and Theresa stared back, defiant. But her defiance quickly fell away. Slowly lifting her hands in front of her face, she began to scream. The room's faint sunlight changed to the cool blue light of a full moon, and Theresa's hands slowly began to turn a mottled gray. First her fingertips, and then her palms, down to her wrists. Tears trickled down her cheeks. I still couldn't move or speak, but my heart screamed for her.

There was a loud clatter, and Molly shouted from the butler's entrance to the dining room: "Miss Lilith!"

The spell was broken and the sunlight returned. Theresa's skin was no longer gray, and she sank back into her chair, sobbing.

"My cake! Look at my cake!" Lilith ran to where Molly stood over the shattered platter and clumps of chocolate cake.

When Lilith raised one hand, I was certain she was about to strike Molly, but a dreadful glint flashed in Molly's eyes. Lilith must have seen it, too, because her hand dropped to her side and her whole body wilted.

I realized that since I'd arrived I'd seen her as something

more than a little girl, because she was so well-spoken and confident. Imperious. A second spell was broken now, and I saw that she was just a young child.

What kind of child can make the sun turn cold and the air stand still? What kind of demon or witch torments another child so, causing her such pain?

We have to leave here.

"I don't think I want to have any more birthday today," Lilith said.

⚜

I wish I had listened to that part of myself that told me we should leave that moment, and not even take our things, but just run out the front door. But I didn't listen. The strange occurrence frightened me, but what had I really seen? Both girls had been overwrought, and Lilith was freakishly intimidating for a little girl. Theresa was exhausted, but uninjured.

I could almost hear Allan laughing. *Demons don't exist, my darling. You have such imagination.*

Theresa and I would avoid Lilith, pack our things properly, and leave the next morning. I was owed a week's wages, and though Mary Trewlove had obviously been too ill to come downstairs for the party, paying me would only take a few moments, and wouldn't be much of a strain. The next day wasn't so far off. If Jerome refused to drive us to the station, we would drag our trunks to the end of the long drive, walk the three miles into Carystown, and hire a car to pick up the luggage.

Having some semblance of a plan calmed me. I prepared a lunch tray for both Theresa and myself, and took it up to my bedroom. I had no concerns about Lilith's comfort. Molly would have to take care of her.

Theresa lay blanketed in sunlight on the long couch beneath the window overlooking the drive. "I shouldn't have made her angry. I'm so sorry, Mama." Tears gathered in her eyes. She looked so much like Allan. Sometimes I wished she didn't, because it hurt too much.

"Everything's going to be fine," I lied. I didn't really believe everything was going to be fine, but I didn't want her to be more worried than she already was. "We'll leave here tomorrow morning. I promise."

She nodded and gave me a faint smile through her tears.

"Now. Let me see your hands."

There was no sign that they had been any different for even a moment.

"They don't hurt anymore."

"I'm glad." I took her hands in mine, and was much more gentle than Mary Trewlove had been with me.

After lunch, I read to Theresa from *Understood Betsy* as she snuggled against me. It was the last time we would ever truly be together.

When she fell asleep, I lay down and tried to nap as well, but I was too restless. What about the lost woman in the woods? Theresa and I could leave, but I was convinced that she must also somehow be a victim of the strange Trewloves. How could I go, knowing she might be out there, injured or dying?

✢

There was no answer when I knocked on Mary Trewlove's door, and when I peeked inside, I saw her bed was empty and her cane was missing. If she hadn't been well enough to come down to lunch, what was she doing out of her room?

Downstairs, Molly was nowhere to be found.

With Theresa still deeply asleep, and Mary Trewlove gone—where?—I decided I had time to take a quick look in the woods for the woman. I was still dressed for the party, and so put on a pair of overshoes I found in the kitchen breezeway. The kitchen itself was filled with the scent of vanilla and cocoa, and I followed the scent to a table where three layers of another chocolate cake were cooling. I resisted the urge to upend them all onto the floor. Lilith needed to be punished, but taking my frustrations out on the cake would simply be childish.

Outside, the sunshine waned, disappearing behind thick, Spanish gray clouds that threatened rain. At the head of the rough path into the woods, I picked up a large stick, broken from a tree limb, and carried it into the woods with me.

The weeds and wildflowers in the woods were twice as thick as they had been on our arrival. Spring was alarmingly fecund here, as though its greenery wanted to swallow and stifle everything in its path. I imagined the madwoman trapped by the young poison ivy vines, or buried by burdock or the ferns growing along the path.

I searched for more than twenty minutes, staying

within view of the path, and didn't find the lost woman. But on the way back to the house, I followed a smaller, almost hidden path, and discovered another entrance to the walled garden: a battered, sagging door mounted with rusted ironwork. The long grass and weeds around it were bent and broken. Someone else had recently come in or out this way.

I went inside.

"Hello?" A web of lilac branches blocked my view, but I sensed that someone was nearby. Pushing the branches aside, I gasped at the scene before me. This was no overgrown, forgotten place. There were the ragged, spindly trees, but everything else looked healthy and neatly trimmed: apple and, I thought, peach trees; white peonies in long bushy banks along the wall; neat plots of roses in pink and red; a circular bed of zinnias surrounding a concrete fountain that was topped by the figure of a young girl in medieval dress. The child's unseeing eyes were downcast, fixed on the constantly spilling stream of water coming from her ewer.

The fountain girl was not alone. There were a dozen other stone figures scattered around the garden—all young girls, in every manner of dress popular over perhaps the last hundred years. It felt like a Victorian scene, something that might be set up in an old folly. Or in a graveyard. I wandered from one statue to another, marveling at the details of their clothing and their faces. I had the strangest feeling that if I were to touch one, it might come alive.

I recalled the sense of loneliness I'd felt when I first saw the girl in the gardens in front of Trewlove Hall. There were so many others here, together, but they each looked lonely. Lost.

Near one end of the garden stood a figure of a plump little girl with round cheeks. She was charming, with her textured basket and enormous bow, but something else drew me toward her: the dirty, yellow mound lying at her feet.

"She's dead. We can't help her now." I turned my head at the familiar voice to see Mary Trewlove leaning on her cane beneath a tall, drooping lilac bush.

"How do you know?" I asked. She'd startled me at first, but she looked somehow *right* there in the garden.

"You're welcome to look for yourself."

From the shape of the mound, I could discern the outline of a human figure beneath the filthy cloak. I lifted up the cloak's edge.

Sure enough, the woman I'd seen near the yews was curled beneath it, her matted hair loose, her hands layered beneath her head as though she had lain down to sleep. Though I was afraid, I gripped her shoulder to shake her awake. But there was no warmth in her rigid body.

"We'll have to notify the police. What about her family?" I stood slowly.

"She has no family. Jerome will bury her."

I was shocked. "We can't just bury her. The authorities… we don't even know who she is. What about her daughter?"

Mary Trewlove, as weak as she was, gave a sharp bark

of a laugh. "Her name is Alma, and there is no daughter to find."

At that moment I knew Theresa and I had to leave immediately. I would go to the police to tell them what I'd seen, and that Mary Trewlove knew who the dead woman was. I told her what I planned, and that I wouldn't let her keep us there. She was old and fragile. What could she do?

When I finished speaking, her shoulders sagged, and I thought she might collapse. As wicked as I thought her, I didn't want her to die here in this strange garden, so near the dead woman at my feet.

"Susannah, you promised," she whispered.

"I can't raise Theresa here. That you would even suggest that we bury this poor woman in unhallowed ground without notifying someone sickens me. And I'm sorry to tell you that Lilith is a spoiled, unpleasant child. Theresa needs to get away from her. We can't stay."

Mary Trewlove grabbed my arm. "Don't let her hear you say that. Not ever. If you want your daughter to live, you must stay. And never, ever mention to Lilith that you are thinking of leaving." Her filmy eyes were wide with alarm. "Don't you understand?"

I almost laughed, but she was too serious. Had her illness driven her mad?

"Let go of me."

"Do you think I'm joking? Look at Alma."

Now I did laugh, but nervously. "What does this have to do with her? Let go!" I jerked away.

"If you won't look at Alma, look at me, Susannah.

Look at *my* daughter!" She pointed to a nearby statue of a little girl who looked six or seven years old. She was bent over slightly at the waist, one hand extended, as though to pick a flower. The skirt of her drop-waist dress fanned out around in the style of dresses I'd worn as a child, and her hair was done in two plaits neatly caught with a bow at the back. I touched my own hair, thinking of how similar it had looked when I was young.

"I don't know what you mean." I was genuinely confused. Was this really a statue of Mary Trewlove's daughter?

"Look at her! Look at my Annabelle! Six years old, and cast forever in stone. I don't even know if she can hear or feel. She has no heartbeat. Stone. My daughter is stone."

The poor woman was surely as mad as the dead woman had been. "You're not well. I'll go into town and get help." I started for the main garden door. Its entry was—unsurprisingly—not crumbling at all.

"Stop, Susannah. Please. I'm telling you the truth. I came here fifteen years ago, with Annabelle, because I needed work, just like you. The last Mary Trewlove hired me to be Lilith's governess. But when I realized the horror of this place, and of—that *child*…" Her voice shook. "I tried to get us out of here, but I was too late. Lilith caught us. To punish me, she made my Annabelle into that *thing*."

"Lilith is only eight years old today. What are you saying? *You're* Mary Trewlove. How could you have had a six-year-old daughter fifteen years ago?" I knew it was cruel, but I said, "Look at you! That's impossible."

Her hands shaking, Mary Trewlove felt her way to the marble bench beneath the lilac and collapsed onto it.

"Tell me the real truth! Stop trying to frighten me," I said. The presence of the strange stone children and Alma's body filled me with dread.

Trewlove Hall will be the last house I'll ever see.

"I'm forty-two years old, and my name was Margaret Troyer." She looked up at me. "That is the real truth. It's living with Lilith that has taken my life. She feeds on love. A mother's love. She's an abomination."

My knees felt weak. "That's not possible."

"Alma and her daughter were unsuitable. The daughter attacked Lilith. I thought I'd calmed Lilith down, but she tricked the girl into coming out here the next morning. Alma went mad when she saw the statue. Jerome was supposed to make Alma disappear, but he does things in his own time. She must have just died here near her daughter."

I remembered Alma's words: "I know Satan's work!"

Dear God, there really are demons, Allan.

"There have been many Mary Trewloves at Trewlove Hall, but only one Lilith," she said quietly. "I believe Lilith came from a family of devils that abandoned her, and left that creature, Molly, to guard her. Now Lilith can't bear for anyone to leave her. She never grows older. She never sleeps. The only one who has any control over her is Molly. They're just alike. They never change. Evil never changes."

"This can't be happening. I won't let it happen." I ran for the garden door.

"I'm dying," she called after me. "I'll be dead before morning. If you try to leave with Theresa, Theresa will die, too. Just like all the other little girls."

⚜

I ran.

It can't be too late. God, don't let it be too late!

In the kitchen, Molly stood working at one of the enormous sinks, but she didn't even turn around as I hurried through. Neither did she call after me.

Molly and Lilith never sleep. I hadn't listened to Theresa. I hadn't paid attention. She'd tried to tell me they weren't normal. *Abominations.*

Molly and I understand each other, now, but we will never be friends.

I kept the image of Theresa lying asleep on the blue velvet lounge in my room in the front of my mind. That was where I'd left her an hour before, and there was no reason she should have gone anywhere else.

As I ran up the stairs and through the halls, I gasped for breath, my head pounding with sudden pain. The air had turned noxiously thick and oppressive—just as it had in the dining room at lunchtime—and the wan daylight was replaced with chilling moonlight.

It can't be too late!

I tried to scream Theresa's name, but the only sound that came out of my mouth was a pathetic mewling. It didn't matter, because Theresa was no longer in my bedroom: The velvet lounge was empty.

As thick as the air was, I kept moving, clawing my way along the wall and grabbing portrait frames to steady myself. There seemed to be hundreds of portraits now, all bearing the same name on their identical brass plaques: *Mary Trewlove*.

When I reached the hallway leading to Theresa's and Lilith's rooms, the pressure grew to a crescendo that caused me to cover my ears. I was sure my head would shatter from pain.

And then the pain was gone.

No, it can't be. Please, no!

I opened the door to Theresa's room. Lilith stood beside the bed, her back to me, one hand resting on the edge of Theresa's open trunk, which was half-filled with clothes. Only when Lilith turned around did I see Theresa, standing forever still and silent behind her. I couldn't bear to look at my daughter's precious face, only her rough, gray hands, her gray traveling boots, and the stiff, stone folds of her dress.

A sob broke from me, and I covered my mouth.

Lilith's dark eyes were wet and full of sadness. "Theresa told me you were going to take her away, and leave me all alone," she said. "You won't leave me, will you, Mary?"

THE BODY ELECTRIC

BRYON QUERTERMOUS

BRINDY DYE NEEDED TO GO get her baby. The rain was coming down in thick sheets and NeNe was out there in the swampy weeds, exposed and alone.

Brindy'd never gotten used to drinking in this weather. Give her a blizzard and a fifth of something brown and she was a happy girl. This humidity was bullshit, and whiskey did weird stuff to her head during hurricane season. Not as weird as the shit Dusty did to her head when he hit her, but weird enough to make her wonder if she was even awake.

The window in her bedroom looked out over the back of the trailer park to the field where her baby liked to play.

Where NeNe liked to play.

She still had a name. She'd never grow old or get married or have babies, but she had her name: Navayah Nelody Dye-Accord. Dusty and his jap car last name made her baby sound like a foreign peace law, but he'd given her a few clean needles and some good pills to make her add the name, him being a proud dad and all.

Goddamn this weather.

Her hip was tricky from Dusty throwing her down the steps of their first trailer outside of Detroit, and her knee was blown out from when he hit her with the car her last day of work at the nursing home before moving to New Orleans to take care of Pop. She rolled the fingers on her left hand into a gimpy fist and tried to push herself up from her bed. Two lite beer cans and a bottle of pills fell to the floor when she moved, but she didn't notice the needle still in her arm until she tried to scratch the back of her head.

The rain poured from the sky and blew against her window like God was trying to sink the trailer. That might be a nice way to go. She'd heard good things about drowning in her suicide support group. Supposed to make you feel heavy and tired and light, and then you woke up in heaven or hell or just passed on to whatever was next. She wanted to pass on, but not without her baby. If Brindy could get to her before the water took her away, they could pass on together. Maybe get another shot in a better place.

Her reflection in the window's rainy splatter made it hard to see what was going on outside, but it sure looked like someone else was sneaking around where her baby was. One of the perverts who lived in the park, probably. She didn't have a problem with perverts so much, God knows she was no good girl, and they'd been kind to her and NeNe, but nobody needed to be passing a baby on to heaven but her momma.

Pulling out the needle made her bleed and made her head spin. She remembered for a second having the same feeling before and that's why she'd left it in. Needles were bullshit, like the weather and the sugary booze in the summer, but they were easier to come by than pills. The TV was getting louder, or maybe she was just remembering it was there, but she liked her odds with the TV in her head. TV'd been good to her and NeNe, and would never steer them wrong. She made a final push out of bed toward the sound. There were more cans on the floor and another needle she almost stepped on in the bathroom, but she made it to the TV and the *Wheel of Fortune*.

"Panama Canal," was the last thing she said before she passed out again.

⚜

The pervert from across the way woke her up the next morning. His name was really Matthew or something white and Biblical like that, but everybody in the whole goddamn park had names that sounded the same, so she got used to thinking of them as the pervert from across the way, the pervert with the nice van, the pervert with the head scab, the pervert with the good grill. Despite his name, the pervert from across the way was a black guy with a lumpy head and slimy hair, but she was too Christian to think of him as the black pervert, and he really was across the way. Always across the way, watching her and NeNe, but never saying anything or making them feel creepy or whatever. Just watching.

He said, "She didn't blow away or nuthin', so you know, or whatever."

Brindy swatted at the air between them, but didn't make a move to get out of bed. Her head was thick with something other than booze, and she was having trouble shaking it clear.

"Why am I... Jesus, pervert, what'd you do?"

"I ain't no pervert where you're concerned, and you know that. You and your pop and that girl of yours are family like my blood is family."

"I'm just foggy is all. No offense meant."

"Family don't always mean friend, though."

She nodded, not sure what to say to that, and horked up a thick wad of phlegm. The room spun when she spit off the side of her bed, and she was aware of her mouth opening and her tongue moving and some kind of sound coming out, but the specifics were gooey. When she woke up again, the pervert was gone, her head was clear, and she had a decade's worth of mourning to do.

⚜

Brindy read the coupon circulars with a cigarette and a coffee mug full of DayQuil. The storm that had blown through took some trees and some trailers with it but left behind the shitty weather and oppressive heat. She'd taken a walk around the park when she woke the second time, hoping everything she remembered was a dream, or her imagination. But nobody was outside, and she wasn't ready to go talk to people until she cleared her head and made a plan. A picture of her baby from a birthday party last year was on her phone and reminded her that at least some of it was real. She had a daughter and her daughter was gone.

Nine years old. How had that happened? Brindy tried, she really did. The minutes and hours had gone so wrong, but the years, they'd been okay. The birthday party at the skating rink. Church camp. Even days around the park with Pop. She'd done what she could. Weren't a lot of men in her life to look to, and the women weren't much for role modeling, either, but she didn't hit her baby, didn't touch her with anything but motherly love. And she fed her carrots and whole milk and made her read real books without pictures. Her baby was smart.

Brindy rubbed her thumb across the cracked phone. Even through the webbing of broken glass, NeNe's aura shone brightly through the decrepit trailer. Framed photos on the wall across the room, moist with rancid condensation, anchored Brindy's nerves and kept the worst of her... the worst of everything... in check. Without her baby, whatever was left, Brindy would be left with the rot of her world, the rot of her life, the rot of forever.

"I saw you in the window when it happened," Matthew

said, touching her arm lightly. in the kitchen sink, and put on enough clothes to keep temptation away from her neighbors, but not so much she'd suffocate from the heat. She'd strut across the park in her rain boots and a smile if she weren't too Christian to cause her fellow man to stumble. She settled for a linen dress and steel-toed boots—bought on credit for a week's work in a factory—in case she had to kick off a snake or swamp rat, and carried Pop's old cane just in case.

The pervert across the way saw her coming and met her on the porch. She waved and dug her boot toe into the ground in front of her. It was spongy and clung to her boot like her grandma's Jell-O salad clung to their old dog one year at Christmas, when he was being an ass and knocked over the dinner table.

"You look better," he said. "So we can go see the preacher now."

"That man ain't no preacher," Brindy said. "Don't care how many crosses he wears or prayers he says."

"You want that precious girl of yours to pass on the right way, you got to get a man of God to—"

"I'll pass my baby on myself. Don't need no *preacher man* to hold my baby and ask God not to send her to hell."

"But the preacher says—"

Brindy kicked him in the balls and smacked him across

the back with Pop's cane. He fell to the ground, gasping.

"'Less you want this cane somewhere even the preacher can't reach it to bless, you'll keep your mouth shut and help me find my baby."

He nodded, and when he was breathing again, she helped him up. They walked around to the back of the park where Brindy remembered seeing someone pick up her daughter. *Park* was too ambitious a word for where they lived, she thought, as they slowly marked their steps along the outer edge of the dozen trailers that made up their little compound. It was far enough away from schools and playgrounds and pools to be safe for anyone on the sex offender registry, including her father, who was dying of lung cancer and didn't have anyone else to take care of him. Her baby was supposed to spend time with Pop in his last days and build memories and a family tree, then go on and live a life Brindy couldn't provide her alone. Pop and his rotting lungs weren't supposed to outlive her baby.

Brindy and Matthew the pervert walked together toward the spot she'd seen NeNe's body last night. Regrets from a life of shitty living piled deep in her head, but the big regret was not being with her baby when she... well, during her last few... truth was, she'd been drinking whiskey at Pop's bedside when NeNe was outside. He'd been a vegetable for a month now, but she couldn't bring herself to pull the plug. She kept hoping someone from the homecare agency would come for the equipment and make the decision for her, but they never did, so she spent an hour every afternoon drinking and watching *Judge Judy* with him and an hour every night reading to him from the Bible.

"I saw you in the window when it happened," Matthew said, touching her arm lightly.

A creepy tingle slithered up her arm like a leech and she shook his hand away. Had he touched her baby like that? She'd never thought of that. The perverts in the trailer park, they were family. They bought her a turkey at Christmas and NeNe a Barbie doll Jeep to drive around the park in the summer.

Brindy swung Pop's cane at him and missed his head by an inch or so, which sent Matthew to the ground again. She stood over him.

"Did you touch my baby?"

The pervert shook his head and curled into a fetal ball.

"I was just looking out for her. You let her bob around here like a piece a chum for these others... these other... we don't want to touch nobody's babies. We living right, and staying away, and you can't just keep putting us in position to... you can't just—"

Brindy poked the cane into the pervert's throat.

"Didn't say I cared about anybody else 'round here. You the only one watching us every day."

"You ain't watching your own baby, so somebody should, and that somebody's me."

She eased the cane off his neck and helped him back up again.

"Already feel bad enough about my mothering," she said. "Don't need a pervert like you making me feel worse."

Matthew nodded and took her hand. The creepy tingle was still there, but faded a bit. She turned her hand so she was shaking his instead of holding it.

"Tell me what you saw."

"I always been worried about them wires over there," he said, grabbing the cane and pointing toward a mess of jumper cables and circuit boxes and wires wrapped around a small tree. "Think maybe one person in the entire park pays for electricity and everyone else taps into that... mess."

Brindy tried to take the cane back, but Matthew pushed her off with his shoulder and kept pointing at the tree as he walked toward it.

"Your girl was a climber," he said. "Reminded me of my own Ruby back in the day. But you look around and it's all swamp and no good climbing trees."

"Except that one," Brindy said.

"Except that one."

"I don't even think she cared about climbing. She liked the jumping. Wanted me to put her in gymnastics. Can't afford food without bugs in it, but expects me to find money for gymnastics."

"Every day I seen her over there looking at that tree like she had a plan. Couldn't do nothing from my house while I watched her. Kept hoping she'd turn back, but... well, I don't think she suffered any, if that makes any difference."

Brindy thought about yesterday. One of her worst days of the year, even before this. The weather. The whiskey. The everything. She'd done some things with Dusty she hoped would relax her, but the whiskey got to him, too, and pissed 'em both off even more.

"You shoulda come and told me," she said softly.

"Knocked quite a bit when she was in the tree," he said. "Heard some moaning that sounded private, so I kept on walking."

"Jesus," Brindy whispered, then silently said a prayer asking for forgiveness.

"I went around back, too, but didn't want to get too close to her. We're doing life right this time. Best we can, you know? And that means stayin' away from what haunts us."

"You saw her fall?"

"Like it was one of them slow motion replays on television," he said. "Even remember reaching my arms out, like maybe I could catch her or something from all the way over here. But all I caught was a vision I can't shake from my dreams and a nasty eye from you."

"And she was dead?"

"Wasn't moving, and that scream... being dead's the best thing for her after that scream."

The combination of memories and guilt and the creeping wetness in the air made Brindy sick to her stomach. She put her hand out to hold herself up with the cane before remembering she didn't have it, and fell face first into the swampy ground. Matthew crouched down next to her and pulled her face out of a puddle by her hair.

"You seen where it happened. You made me hear that scream again. So now we goin' to the preacher to make sure that baby passes on the right way."

She nodded the best she could with her movement restricted by Matthew's grip on her hair, and he pushed her face back into the mud.

✤

The preacher had a trailer in the park, but he never stayed there more than a few hours on Sundays, to watch football or play cards with the other perverts after reading something to them from his old crusty Bible and saying a prayer for their souls. A quick walk around the trailer confirmed no one was there, so Brindy and Matthew set off on the walk to the bigger house. That's where the preacher spent his days with his families, and did God knows what else in the small house out back.

Brindy had been to the big house with its giant, decaying steel gate once before, when she first arrived at the park with NeNe. The preacher, no name ever given, was the one who ran the park, and he'd tried several times to talk her out of staying. Toward the end of that meeting, he even hinted that something awful would happen to Pop if she stayed and corrupted the perfect balance of healing intent he said he'd created. But Brindy insisted, he relented, and they drank two bottles of wine by the fire while NeNe played with the preacher's wife.

"Never understood where this place came from," Matthew said as they approached the gate. "Looks like it should be up north in New York or Massachusetts as a school for preppy kids or horse riders or something, not out here in this swampy hell."

"Fits in around here about as well as that preacher man."

"I had a dream once, the first time I came out here," Matthew said. "Drank a beer with the preacher and fell asleep on his couch. I remember seeing him in this old black wool coat standing out by these gates right here trying to get in. Dancing around, putting a hand or a foot through the bars, but never walking through the gates. Went on like that for a time before these big ol' gates turned blue and zapped that preacher man right in the heart."

"Like my baby."

"Never did believe him when he said I had more than one drink, but who am I to argue with a man of God, right?"

"We shouldn't be here."

Brindy turned to walk away, successfully grabbing the cane from Matthew this time.

"You walk away, you'll always wonder," Matthew said.

"Better than seeing whatever he's done to her in there."

"Ain't nothing bad in that house. Too cold and stone and barren."

"Not the one out back."

The small carriage house out back fit the area better. Sagging wood that had once been elaborately engraved and trimmed held up a roof with enough peaks and turrets to make the whole thing look like a giant wooden birthday cake. The red and yellow paint had long ago peeled away in most places, replaced with cobwebs and climbing vines, and the walkway to the front door was clouded in a hazy red mist Brindy imagined was from brimstone. She reached out for Matthew's hand, but hesitated, remembering the creepy tingling she got each time they touched earlier.

Matthew knocked once before the preacher appeared at the door. He had a wide smile full of yellow teeth and puffy gums. His hair was messy and electrified with static. The black wool coat Matthew mentioned from his dream was draped over the preacher's shoulders, even though Brindy's old weather thermometer on her porch had shown the temperature nearing ninety that morning.

"It was wet last night, or you would have been here sooner, I reckon," he said, waving them inside.

The smell inside matched the rest of the house. The air was still and flat, musty, rotting, and vaguely electric. Brindy wished she'd worn something more concealing and protective than her thin linen dress. She felt the spirits of the house move through the flat air and through her body and up her legs.

"I want my baby. I want her to... You need to help me—"

"All in good time," the preacher said. "Would you like a drink first?"

"I don't want a drink. I want my baby. I want to know what you did to my baby and I want to take her home."

"The Earth is not our home, my dear Miss Dye. We are but temporary—"

"I don't need your mumbo jumbo bullshit, preacher man. I *want* to see my daughter."

The sharp smile turned quickly to a menacing leer.
"Yes. Let's go see your daughter."

Brindy prepared herself mentally for many outcomes. She wanted to be strong in the face of tragedy and strong in the face of even the worst possible outcomes. What she wasn't prepared for was to hear her daughter say hello.

"Mommy," NeNe said, her voice floating from a small nook off the entrance to the house. "I missed you."

Brindy took her daughter in her arms and spun her around joyously, but the mood remained somber. The air remained flat and putrid. Her daughter was not smiling.

"It's so good to see you, baby. I missed you, too."

Brindy hugged her daughter again. She expected NeNe to nuzzle her chest, like she did when she was a baby, but NeNe kept her head turned toward the preacher. When the hug was over, Brindy fell back against Matthew in exhaustion and relief.

NeNe said, "Why did you let me die?"

❖

The three walked back to the trailer park in silence. Brindy was confused and horrified by her daughter's cold demeanor, and Matthew was twitchy and awkward around NeNe, which made Brindy even more nervous.

That night, she decided the time had come for Pop to pass on properly, so she made his favorite spicy chili for dinner and ate three bowls of it in his room. Together, they watched the evening news. Her daughter was spacey and reserved, and every attempt Brindy made at fixing things sent them both into a depressing spiral.

When Pop took his final breath, Brindy kissed his forehead, then dialed the number for the funeral home to come and get him. NeNe was in the other room, but she appeared in Brindy's side view and quickly swatted Brindy's phone out of her hand.

"Bury him by the tree," she said. "Or they'll come for me, too."

The corner of NeNe's mouth wiggled as she stared at Brindy. Her eyes were unfocused, lazing so far apart they seemed to be splitting off from each other. She wobbled around for a few seconds before falling to the floor. Brindy bent down to make sure her daughter was breathing. When she leaned in close to NeNe's face to listen for a breath, her daughter's eyes opened, and she snapped at Brindy's throat with her teeth.

NeNe continued snapping at her mother, even as Brindy scrambled away from the bedroom and slammed the door shut.

"Make him electric," NeNe said through the door. "We'll live forever."

Brindy ran to the kitchen and reached around on top of the icebox until she found the revolver she kept up there for emergencies. She held the gun away from her body as she approached the bedroom door. There were no more sounds coming from the room, so Brindy relaxed her gun hand and ran to Matthew's house.

"That preacher man did something to my baby," she said. "I need you to stop me before I do something ungodly."

She could see Matthew looking down at the gun and waited for him to invite her inside. The invitation never came, and Matthew seemed more off than normal. A salty film of sweat and liquor hung in the air, and each breath Matthew took smelled like the underside of her liquor shelf.

"It's dark times for you both," he said, slowly. "You're edgy and ripe with visions and demons, and that ain't no time to be grabbing no gun or visiting no preacher man."

"I need you to watch her for a bit."

"No, no, no," he said on the verge of tears. "You can't be doin' something like that to me. It's not right. It's not right. It's not right."

"I don't have anyone else, and I need to know what he did to her."

"You thought she was dead, now she's alive. Rejecting a miracle can only bring you more pain."

"She's not alive, and that's not my daughter. I brought a corpse in my home and the preacher man needs to pay."

Matthew shut the door and turned the dead bolt.

"I'm living life right. You can't make me do this."

"I know you're always watching her," Brindy said. "This time I won't be there, is all."

She'd taken a few steps away from his trailer, when Matthew opened his door slightly.

"Just wait till morning and I'll do whatever you want."

"I can't sleep with that *thing* in my house. She's always liked you. Maybe you can fix her."

✤

Brindy's plan was to shoot the preacher man between the
eyes and then search his house. She couldn't do either,
though, because he wasn't there, so she ended up having a
glass of sweet tea with his wife. They talked about family
and God and heaven and how much sugar was enough
for a good sweet tea. As the evening wore on, Brindy felt
comfortable enough to confess her original intentions for
her visit. The preacher's wife smiled and shook her head.

"That would have been a sight to see," she said.

"My husband… my Dusty… uh, her father always said
I was like a stick of dynamite full of stupid, just waiting
for someone to light me."

"That's quite a colorful way to say you've got the servant's heart."

"I wish I had my daughter's heart. I wish I knew she'd
get through whatever this is. Whatever he did to her."

"He did it *for* her. And for you. For all of us."

"I just don't know."

"Go home to your baby. Give her some space and some
time. She'll come back to you."

Brindy stood to leave and awkwardly held herself
between a hug and a handshake before the preacher's
wife grabbed her and embraced her heartily. Tears and
sweat weren't enough to break Brindy's growing feelings
of comfort and happiness, feelings that she would never
have again. At the very end of the hug, the preacher's

wife pulled Brindy in closer, gripping her painfully tight.

"When it's time, we'll have you both."

✣

Brindy stood at the gates, stunned. Her instinct told her to run as fast as she could back to her baby and to Matthew. Something was wrong, but she was too afraid to face it. She wanted to go around back to the carriage house as well, but she knew what she would find back there, too. So she stood at the gates to the out-of-place, East Coast-style mansion and hoped to be struck dead by a blast of electricity.

"I can show you the others," the preacher said from behind her. "I can't imagine anyone you'd tell would believe you."

The others turned out to be the bodies of ten young girls, all within a year or so of NeNe, who the preacher said was special because she survived.

As he opened the cellar door where the bodies lay, the preacher began to recite in a hushed, hollow voice:

> *"I sing the body electric,*
> *The armies of those I love engirth me and I engirth them,*
> *They will not let me off till I go with them, respond to them,*
> *And discorrupt them, and charge them full with the charge of the soul."*

"Oh my God," Brindy said, when she saw the empty

faces of the small bodies piled on top of one another.

The preacher kept going.

> *"Was it doubted that those who corrupt their own bodies conceal themselves?*
> *And if those who defile the living are as bad as they who defile the dead?*
> *And if the body does not do fully as much as the soul?*
> *And if the body were not the soul, what is the soul?"*

The preacher kept speaking, getting louder with every verse, and she recognized it was the Whitman poem from the English class where she met Dusty. Seeing so many bodies of other mothers' babies was too much. She wanted to go to her own baby, whatever she looked like, however she acted.

Brindy decided they'd leave that night. Pop didn't need them anymore. He'd left his life savings for them, she knew where. And then they'd drive. Away from the swamp, the whiskey, and the perverts. They'd drive together and become something new together. She was as dead inside as she thought her daughter was, they both needed a revival. They'd find God, or something like him, on their own, without a preacher, the way her grandma said man was meant to find God.

She heard music as she approached her trailer and wondered if maybe they'd take a minute to dance before they left. NeNe loved to dance when she was a baby and before gymnastics, and before the reality of cost set in, Brindy had dreamed of her daughter being a dancer on Broadway. The music sounded like a show tune, something from the eighties, if the synthesizers were any indication. The song was building as she opened the front door. She saw Matthew's body lying through her bedroom doorway the same time she heard the lyric from the song.

I sing the body electric.

She rushed into the bedroom and saw NeNe lying next to Matthew, both of them undressed and bleeding from their wrists. NeNe's eyes were closed. Matthew's were open, his mouth still gurgling and his chest slowly rising.

"What did you do to my baby?"

He shook his head and pointed to a note on the dresser. Brindy picked it up and read Matthew's scrawl:

You were too concerned with the daughter you wanted and forgot about the one you had. You made me do this.

She grabbed her baby's body and wrapped it in a blanket before running as fast as she could back to the preacher's gates. He was waiting in the carriage house with his wife when she arrived, and took NeNe's body when she offered.

"Whatever you did to her, I don't care. You know? The first time? Whatever you did. Do it again."

The preacher shook his head slowly and ran his hands up and down NeNe's body. Brindy cringed, but kept her eyes on the preacher. She'd do whatever he wanted to bring her baby back.

"I'm not sure that's possible," he said.

"That pervert killed her and it's my fault. I didn't believe in you and what you can do here, but I do now."

"Where is Matthew now?"

"Rotting on my bed."

"You… took care of him?"

"Did it himself. Killed my baby then killed himself like a coward."

"So they passed on… together?"

"You said she's special. Show me."

"For a miracle of this… intensity… we need more. You say you believe in what we do here. You need to show me."

"I'll do anything," Brindy said.

The preacher's wife smiled and handed Brindy a knife.

"If any thing is sacred the human body is sacred,
And the glory and sweet of a man is the token of manhood untainted,
And in man or woman a clean, strong, firm-fibred body, is more beautiful than the most beautiful face."

IN HOME VISIT

DAVE WHITE

*A*S HE LINED UP THE *free throw, Alex eyed the back of the rim.*

Balance, eyes, elbow, follow through. Do that and the ball wouldn't touch iron, just swish through the net. His coach always told him free throws were a great way to pad the stats. He knew when he became a coach, he would repeat that phrase over and over.

If he could only let the go of the goblin that stared him down.

Alicia stood on the porch, leaning against the pillar. Their house wasn't big—it wasn't one of the mansions erected just a few blocks away. They'd had goals to get to that neighborhood one day. Before Mom and Dad tried to take on the flood.

But for now, they stayed in the rickety house, and Alex shot free throws in the driveway. He was doing everything he could to follow his sister's advice and forget.

"Ha-ha!"

As usual, the goblin sat atop the backboard, just out of his peripheral vision, an opposing crowd. He wasn't really there. He was an illusion trying to distract him. A reason to hang on another year and then get the hell out of Dodge.

Alicia stepped off the porch the moment Alex released the ball. He knew it was intentional. She'd say she was just going to get the empty garbage can on the curb, but she was also trying to distract him. Keep his eye off the rim. Make him miss the shot.

He didn't. It swished.

"Good one," Alicia said. "Eyes on the prize, right?"

The goblin chuckled again. Alex went and got the ball. He'd broached the idea of seeing a therapist about the voice with Alicia, but they didn't have the insurance. She told him it was all in his mind. Not to worry. She was going to raise him right. Get him into a good college. Get him on a team. And then get him into coaching.

It was all about forgetting and working hard.

Alex went back to the crack in the asphalt and lined up to take another shot.

"Oh, this is good." The goblin's voice was a croak. He'd never spoken before.

Alex hesitated.

"You take this shot, and your life will go one way." The goblin's voice was like an ocean at high tide. "If you pay attention to everything else, you will be a hero. Right?"

Alex blinked the goblin away and lined up the shot. He could feel Alicia walking toward the curb. Like a car pulling into a blind spot, he knew she was there, but couldn't see her.

He heard the engine of the van. Then the squealing brakes. He lifted the ball up to his forehead.

Balance.

The squealing grew louder.

Eyes.

"Ha-ha!"

Elbow.

"You have to choose, Alex."

Follow through.

"Choose now."

The ball swished through the net just as he heard the crunch of metal and bone.

⚜

Alex Stepian hated the heat. Especially the oppressive sauna-like sweat box he stood in now, in Southern Mississippi. If there was a sign he needed to get in better shape, it was his green polo shirt marred with sweat stains underneath the line of his chest. Walking through the small town just to grab coffee, just barely off the plane, and he was drenched.

This was why New Jersey was for him. It's why he moved away from here. There were seasons. It was late October and this felt like the last days of July.

But recruiting is what it is, and landing the top talent for a rebuilding college basketball team meant scouring the world for players. Including small-town Mississippi.

There was a 6'9" kid down here, long and lanky, who could do it all. Block shots, play with his back to the basket, then step out beyond the arc and swish the three.

The tape on this kid was unreal, and as far as Alex knew, no one had heard of him. Alex just happened to come across his highlight tape one late Friday night when—after four whiskeys—he checked his e-mail. A link to the clip was there and he watched it once.

When he woke up the next morning, he was sure he'd imagined it. But when he checked his e-mail, it was there. He watched the highlight tape—ten minutes of dunks, blocks, and threes—eighteen times, looking for any clue this kid wasn't the real deal.

Internet search after Internet search, and he couldn't find anything bad about the kid. Of course, he couldn't find anyone else talking about Lonzo Childs, either. Alex had to meet him.

Alex immediately followed NCAA procedure, making sure the student was a senior since it was too early to visit any other class year student, and then booked a flight and was on his way to Ocean Springs, Mississippi, just outside of Biloxi. He had an address for the school the kid played for.

But first, coffee.

And, hopefully, some goddamn air-conditioning.

He stepped through the door, and a little bell rang above him. He was hit with a swath of hot but moving air. Alex took a breath and realized there were only ceiling fans. No AC. He exhaled and went to the counter. He ordered a hot coffee anyway. Iced coffees didn't click with him, and he'd read somewhere hot coffee makes you sweat more and that keeps you cooler. Even if he didn't need more pit stains, being cooler was a good option. He bought a Gatorade as well.

After fixing the coffee with cream and sugar, he took a seat at an open table. The first sip burned his tongue. Maybe he should have gone with the iced coffee. He pulled out his phone and started to scroll through e-mails. His assistants were handling practice today, but he expected updates.

"You're not from around here, are you?"

Alex looked up and saw a clean-cut military guy standing over him, arms crossed. A tremor went through Alex, and he wasn't sure why.

"What gave it away? The sweat?"

The guy grinned. "Nah. The insignia on your shirt. That's a Yankee school, ain't it?"

Alex looked down at the Ben Franklin University insignia, an intertwined BFU, and said, "Yeah. I'm the hoops coach."

The guy nodded and pulled out the chair across from Alex. "Do you mind?"

"I'm only going to be here a few minutes." Alex leaned back in his chair. "I grew up here, actually. But I moved away a long time ago."

The guy grinned. "Southern hospitality. I won't take up much of your time. I'm Nate Fredricks."

Alex stuck out his hand and they shook. For a second, Nate's face went static and then faded into a shade of green. Alex blinked it away. He could forget.

"What you doing all the way back down here? Miss the temperatures? Ha-ha." Nate grinned.

"Coming back was never my first choice, but it's the

job." Alex sighed. "Going to scout a kid, maybe convince him to come to my school. You ever see Lonzo Childs play? He plays for the local high school."

Nate shook his head. "Man, you came all the way down here for that?"

Alex shrugged. "It's the job. And you never answered my question."

He took another sip of coffee. It was at a palatable temperature now. The coffee shop was nearly empty, and it felt like the baristas were watching him. He'd never felt that up north. He hated being back here.

Nate shook his head. "I'm a football fan. Everyone is down here."

Alex remembered. The Friday Night Lights, where the town made it out to the high school game, the breeze coming off the ocean. Further into town there was no breeze, but that's why the football stadium was near the shore. Got to keep the fans happy.

Another reason to leave town.

"I know," Alex said. "But what can you do in the winter? Watch hoops."

"How does recruiting work?"

"Well, you try to sell a kid on your school and why he would be a great fit."

"And this kid is a great fit?"

Alex nodded.

"And if he says yes?"

"That would be awesome. He then signs something called a National Letter of Intent, which binds him to the school."

Nate shook his head. "You look kind of familiar."

"I played here in high school."

"I guess so." Nate tapped on the top of the table. "Well, I better get going. You have a nice day. Good luck with your basketball player."

Alex nodded and Nate walked away, the bell to the door ringing behind him. Alex finished his coffee, tipped the barista, and headed toward Ocean Grove High School. As he laughed, he heard the barista laugh. Sounded familiar. He'd only been back a few hours, too.

"Ha-ha."

⚜

The school was huge, almost like a college campus. Nothing like what he remembered when he went here. There were four buildings—one for sophomores, one for juniors, and one for seniors. To the right of that was the administration complex, which looked like the size of the entire school when Alex had attended. All were connected to a huge gym.

Money makes the world—even public education—move.

He pressed the buzzer and looked up toward the security camera above the door. He grinned.

"May I help you?" The static voice of an older woman came through the intercom.

"Alex Stepian from Ben Franklin University? I'm here to see Coach Cobb about Lonzo Childs."

"Come to the main office, please."

The door buzzed and Alex pulled it open. A wash of air-conditioned air rushed over him and he exhaled. Finally.

The office was to his right. A few teachers talked to each other in the hallway. One sucked down water from a plastic bottle, while the other pointed at lesson plans. Alex didn't give them a nod, he just turned and entered the office.

A secretary as old as the sun ambled over to the counter and put a binder in front of him. She opened it and the flap snapped against the countertop. She scratched her white hair, and placed a pen down.

"Sign in, please. Dr. Leafwich will want to see you."

Alex signed the pad in front of him. At the same time, he said, "But I'm here to see Coach Cobb."

The old woman shook her head. "Leafwich first. Those are the rules."

She pointed toward the office of the principal. Alex thanked her and walked over to the door. He knocked out of habit, then crossed the threshold.

Dr. Leafwich sat behind his desk, leg crossed over his knee. To his right a computer screen shined an Excel spreadsheet. On his desk was a picture of his family. Leafwich stood up, came around the desk, and offered his hand. Alex took it.

"A big, bad Power Five basketball coach in our neck of the woods? Doesn't happen often. Welcome, sir."

"You always get the football coaches, I bet."

"Nick Saban was in just the other day. But hoops? Never happens. We're terrible." Leafwich reached over and turned off his computer monitor.

"But you have a good player. I'd love to meet Lonzo Childs."

Leafwich squinted at him. "His mother said to expect your call."

"I notified the school I was coming." Alex shifted his weight. "I'm trying to help kids in my area. Get them out of their neighborhoods and teach them a skill. Teach them basketball. Give them and their family a better life. But if I don't land Lonzo, I will lose my job. My team hasn't been good yet. We need a break. We need Lonzo. I need to see him."

"Well, I didn't get the message from you."

That was odd.

"But it's a busy school, and Thanksgiving is coming, so we're dealing with that and—well—this is the weird part."

Alex's stomach took a turn. Everything in the room felt off. Maybe it was the quick change in temperature, but he felt slightly faint.

"You are an alum of OCHS, right?"

Alex nodded. He was supposed to be in sell mode, but he could barely utter a word. Everything about the principal and this room felt off. Almost like a dream, and he couldn't figure out why. Maybe it was just Leafwich's cold demeanor. Haughty. Alex couldn't put the charm on someone like that.

"It didn't end well, I see."

Alex swallowed and found his voice. "It was time to leave."

Leafwich nodded. "That's the weird part. The same thing happened to Lonzo Childs."

Alex tilted his head.

"He doesn't go to this school."

"But the e-mail I got..."

"He never went here." Leafwich's eyes dimmed to a yellow. "Ha-ha."

The room tilted for Alex just a hair. "I don't understand."

Leafwich shook his head. "Neither do I. But Childs' mother called me and told me to expect you. She said that after I gave you the tour, you could go visit her and her son. But she was very specific, I had to give you the tour first."

Alex put his hands on the arms of the chair to steady himself. This wasn't a normal old recruiting trip.

Leafwich marched him out of the office, back into the heat. They trudged along the sidewalk, next to the browning grass and trees that seemed to wave in a nonexistent breeze. He could see kids in class though open windows. Some snuck on their cell phones, some wrote in notebooks, and some actually made eye contact with their teachers.

"None of this was here when you were here, right?"

Alex looked at him. He didn't really want Leafwich to know about his alumni status. He was going to drop that on Childs first.

"I do my research." Leafwich pulled a door open and let Alex step in. The AC washed over them again.

"When I was here, it was like a little brick schoolhouse.

No air-conditioning. Closer to a brick oven. I hated it."

"And when you played basketball?"

"I'm lucky we didn't suffocate."

"You only played suffocating defense." Leafwich smiled.

Alex didn't. "Uh huh."

The hallways were spotless, save for one stray, crumpled-up piece of paper. Leafwich leaned over, picked it up, and with a smooth hook shot, he swished it into a nearby garbage can. He looked at Alex for a comment, but Alex didn't bite.

"Why are you taking me around?"

"Because, Mr. Stepian, we need alumni like you to come back and help out. You know all about fundraising, you're a college coach. Shouldn't you want to help the people who brought you here? It takes a lot to keep a building like this up."

Alex chewed on his lip. "You know why I left this place, right?"

"Your parents and your sister died."

Alex nodded. "They both died trying to help. My parents were trying to get people out when the floods came after the hurricane. I was just a boy. My sister, she was eighteen and she was trying to help me grow up and get into a good school. But she was gone a few years later, too."

Leafwich licked his own lips and seemed to be searching for an answer. His face flickered green. Finally, he said, "This is a great school. The past is past. Help us out. It would be a good way to make amends."

Alex closed his eyes for a moment and forced himself to forget what he just saw. "I would like to speak to Lonzo Childs. That's the reason I came down here. If I'm not going to meet him here, perhaps you can tell me where to find him."

Leafwich pushed the door of the gym open. The space was huge, and arena-like. Bleachers extended from the walls on all four sides. There was a giant scoreboard with a video system on the far wall. A gym class did jumping jacks.

Alex's jaw dropped open.

"Impressive, right?"

Alex looked. "This is a high school, correct?"

The principal laughed. "You don't remember me, do you? Maybe you don't want to."

A shiver went through Alex. He looked Leafwich up and down, hoping for his brain to signal some form of recognition. It didn't. Alex shook his head.

"I was there that day, Alex. You owe us. You owe us all."

Alex froze in his tracks. Despite the air-conditioning, the sweat came rushing back. He took a long gulp of air.

The principal turned on his heel and left the gym.

"Now," he said. "If you'll follow me, I'll get you the address for Mr. Childs."

⚜

Alex had to double-check the address. The further they moved away from the school and the water, the bigger the houses got. That wasn't the problem, however. The problem was the house that matched the address didn't look like someone lived there.

The house was a tall, brick mansion, with a wide porch and four columns holding up an overhang. It was gated, but the iron bars had started to rust over and the front gate had fallen off its hinges. The grass and two trees were overgrown. The grass was knee-high, and the branches of the trees seemed to sag under the weight of the air.

Speaking of, the air was heavier now, a lump of water in gas form, leaning on Alex's shoulders and infecting his lungs. Like breathing through a straw. He understood why the trees could hardly stand.

The paper with the address matched the number on the brick column that used to hold up the gate. Alex stepped over the gate and onto the asphalt driveway. He walked slowly toward the front door, praying for a breeze.

When he was a kid, he lived less than ten blocks from here in a house with a shorter driveway and a basketball hoop at the end of it. When the visions came, they came above the hoop. He used those visions like a crowd trying to distract him from making the free throw. The people shouting, cursing at him, wishing him dead.

Those visions had stopped once he moved away.

In the back of his brain, a little voice told him to keep walking. Find Lonzo Childs. He hadn't heard the voice in ages. His chest tightened and he blinked the sound away, like turning down a car radio to focus on if the brakes were working. The movement made little sense, but it worked.

Approaching the front door, his hands started shaking. Not like a caffeinated tremor, but full-on shivers. What the hell was going on? He closed them into fists and flexed the muscles in his wrist. The shaking slowed, but didn't stop. The first time he tried to press the doorbell, he missed. On target the second time. Bells chimed like Big Ben hitting the top of the hour.

As he waited, Alex considered walking past his old home after he met Lonzo, seeing where he lived and if he could battle the demons away one more time. Grit. That's what he preached to his team. The ability to withstand and keep getting up.

It's what Lonzo Childs had. He could see it in the video highlights.

Alex took another deep breath and drank in the air.

The door opened, and the sight of the woman standing in front of him froze Alex to the ground.

"What is this?" Alex asked, backpedaling away from the door. "What the hell?"

The woman stepped onto the porch and held out her hand. She was tall, waiflike, and looked remarkably like Alex's sister.

Alex's dead sister.

"Come with me, Alex."

He shook his head and recoiled as she reached out for him.

"I don't understand. I don't—"

He gasped for air and remembered that day long ago, the one that left him wanting to run from here, run from the South, run from the house where he was raised.

"Come inside, Alex. We must talk."

"No," he said. "Lonzo Childs. I came for Lonzo Childs."

The woman—it couldn't be Alicia—tilted her head at him.

"There is no Lonzo."

The air hung over him like an anvil, and sweat poured down the back of his neck. Stars crowded the edges of his vision. And then he felt himself moving toward her as if he were floating. His hand moved, unattached to his brain, a reflex instead of a conscious action. He intertwined his fingers with hers.

She took him inside.

❖

Alex lined up the free throw. He was guesstimating the distance, but instinct and muscle memory told him he was at the line, a small crack in the driveway the marker for his foot.

The tricky part about shooting outside was the breeze. Inside, it was a factor he never had to worry about. Crowd noise, pressure because of the score, and tired legs? Yeah, those were problems. But he could force that out. The breeze, no, that was a different sort of factor.

Just like the voice.

He took the shot just as a gust of air passed through. The ball shanked left, just slightly, ricocheting off the rim and then the side of the house.

"Ha-ha!"

He retrieved the ball, shutting the noise out. The goblin that sat atop the backboard wasn't real. It was just his anxiety getting to him. The worry. The fear. Of letting people down. Of not working hard enough.

That's what his therapist told him. The one the school mandated after he caved John Samuel's face in. He'd missed the game-winning free throw last season. One that would have sent them to the State Championships. The next day, in English class, John Samuel laughed at him. The same "Ha-ha" the goblin sent his way.

So Alex punched him. A lot. Punched him so much, the teacher had to tear him off the nearly-unconscious body.

They wanted to expel him. And if not for his sister, if not for Alicia, now eighteen and his legal guardian, begging and pleading, they would have. The therapist was the compromise.

And he'd learned from the talks. How to box it out. Keep the fear away.

But the goblin still hung around, like the breeze, throwing him off his game just a hair. The voice was always whispering that he'd never be anything, that he'd be a failure day after day. And the voice invited him to embrace it.

"Is it laughing at you again?"

Alex looked to the front door, as he dribbled the ball between his legs.

Standing there, arms crossed and a crooked grin on her face, Alicia watched him.

He nodded. "It's nothing, though."

"I know. You've gotten so much better."

"I'm trying."

Alicia skipped down the front steps and took the ball from Alex. She shot without hesitating and swished it.

"Sometimes it's better to not think and just do."

"It's not that easy."

Alicia retrieved the ball and swished another shot.

"No, it is exactly that easy. I line it up and let it go. You think too much. Ever since you missed that shot."

It was Alex's turn to get the ball now. He sprinted for it, picked it up off the first bounce, and laid it into the hoop.

"The best athletes can forget the past," Alicia said. "That's what you need to do."

That was the first hint it was time to leave the South.

⚜

The door swung shut behind him, and there was a hiss of air from somewhere above. The house's temperature was oppressive, like a sauna whose door had just been opened.

Alicia looked like she hadn't aged a day.

"I don't understand," Alex said. "You're—"

She shook her head. "No, I never was."

"But your funeral..."

Again, the headshake. "You never attended it. Did you?"

Alex closed his eyes tightly and tried to imagine the funeral. He couldn't find the memory. Was she right? No. He would have stayed. No matter how badly he wanted to escape, go somewhere cold and start over—he would have stayed for Alicia.

She led him down the hallway, past wooden tables and over red carpet that hadn't been vacuumed in ages.

"Ha-ha."

Alex's head snapped up and he looked around. The laugh. He hadn't heard it in so long. He looked at Alicia. She nodded.

"He's here, too," she said.

"I don't understand. Why did you bring me here?" Then he rephrased. "I don't understand how you're even alive."

Alicia smiled and it was like she'd never been gone. She reached out, her arm moving like it was in slow motion, gliding through air, and touched one of the wood-paneled walls. The wall slid into the panel beside it like a pocket door. That led into a smoking room, with full bookshelves and large padded chairs with wooden frames.

And in one of the chairs was the goblin.

"Welcome," it said. It steepled its fingers, elbows resting on the arms of the chair. His index fingers touched his nose.

"No," Alex said. "This isn't happening. How did we get here? I forgot all of this. Alicia, you told me to forget. You said the best forgot."

The goblin laughed again. It wore a suit, and the knot of his tie bobbed against its throat as he cackled.

"Maybe," it finally said, the words coming out of its mouth like white noise static, "it's time you join me. Join Alicia."

Alex stepped back, but the pocket door slammed shut behind him. Alicia stood off to the side.

"Don't you remember?" she asked.

The fog swirled around his mind and it came back to him. Like it always did.

❧

The van wheeled around the corner, rubber burning on the asphalt. The drop of sweat fell from his eyebrow. He lined up the free throw.

Alicia walked toward the curb to grab the empty garbage can.

The goblin sat on the backboard and said, "Choose."

❧

Alex blinked himself back to the present. The goblin pointed toward a table. There was paper and a pen.

"That's your letter of intent," the goblin said.

Alex blinked.

"Sign it," Alicia said. "Join us. I miss you."

A National Letter of Intent was what a recruit signed when they decided to join a university. It bound them to the school they wanted to attend. It helped get them their scholarship.

"What is this?" Alex asked.

"Consider this our recruitment of you. We want you back. You owe us." The goblin cackled.

Alex closed his eyes. "Back?"

"I tried to get you that first time. I asked you to choose and you took your shot. You didn't join Alicia. She came with me, and you ended up with your life. You ran from me, didn't you? Left here and went north. Got away as far as you can. To where I couldn't reach you. But I can get others to do my work for me. Send e-mails."

The table sizzled. It was an odd sound, like it was being fried. But as far as Alex could tell, it wasn't on fire. It just shook—on its own, it shook. The pen rattled against the top of the table and suddenly turned his way, the tip pointed at his chest. He could pick it up and sign the paper in one sweeping motion. No hesitation.

Why did he want to?

The realization washed over him.

He turned to Alicia.

"Is this all in my head?" he asked.

The goblin leaned forward, its mouth curling into a grin.

Alicia asked, "What do you mean?"

"You really are dead, Alicia. Long dead. But you just told me you weren't."

"I needed you to follow me." Alicia looked toward the goblin, then back to Alex. "We summoned you here with promises of making your dreams come true. I miss you. Mom and Dad miss you, too. Come with us, Alex, and let's start over. Mom and Dad are there, too. You can free all of us. Just sign."

Alex opened and closed his hand. The pen was calling to him. He wanted it. He wanted to sign it. But not without more answers.

He turned toward the goblin. It raised its eyebrows.

"Why me?" He pointed to Alicia. "Why us?"

The white-static voice of the goblin hurt his ears. "Your parents. They died as they tried to help the victims of the floods. Do you remember? They tried to drag those children out of the flood. I couldn't have that. So they drowned. And Alicia, she took care of you after. Kept you alive. Fed you. Tried to give you a life. And she failed after I intervened."

The goblin shook its head, the pointy green chin going back and forth.

"You took your shot, too. And a good one. You moved to New Jersey. Started recruiting those kids from Camden and Paterson. 'The bad neighborhoods,' you called them. Tried to give them good lives. Tried to save them, right? Like you couldn't save your parents and Alicia."

Alex felt bile burn at the back of his throat.

"But you failed without my help, actually. You just weren't good enough. The kids you helped, you thought that was great. But you couldn't help more. Because you didn't win. Lonzo Childs was your savior, right?"

The room was so hot. The walls started to drip with water.

"And now you came down here. That's all it took, some trickery by me. It's so much easier to fool people these days. Don't you think? With technology, they fall for anything. In the old days, I had to turn into a snake."

Alex's eyes went wide.

The goblin said, "Sign it and we can fix all this. You

can be mine and the world will be right. But it has to be you. You have to choose. The fewer people trying to help all the time makes my job easier. Tips the scales."

Alicia looked at Alex and smiled. He thought of Mom and Dad. He could barely envision them, just a silhouette of Dad with his arm around Mom. He wanted to know what they looked like again.

He reached out and picked up the pen.

"Good," Alicia said.

He signed.

The goblin cackled.

Alex finished signing. Put the pen down. Closed his eyes.

He heard thunder.

⚜

Alex lined up the free throw. He opened his eyes. He was here again and didn't know how. But he knew what he had to do.

Alicia stepped off the porch as he released the ball. Swish.

"Good one. Eyes on the prize."

Alicia walked toward the garbage can on the curb. Alex went and got the ball. He felt the bumpy rubber against his hands.

And then he heard the van round the corner. He looked toward Alicia. He'd never seen this before. She was always to his back.

He looked away for an instant, toward the basket. The goblin was sitting on the rim now. His fingers were steepled again.

"I will follow you forever," he said. "You'll try to forget, but you can't. You have another chance now. You signed. Remember that. You signed."

Alex looked toward Alicia.

"Choose."

Alex dropped the basketball and ran toward Alicia. Out of the corner of his eye, he saw the van. The brakes squealed.

He ran toward Alicia. She didn't see the van. Her fingers wrapped around the handle of the garbage can.

Maybe he could push her out of the way. Save her. He was only feet away now.

The van fishtailed and he knew what was going to happen. The driver had lost control.

The last thing he heard was the goblin cackling.

"You're mine now. I won you."

And the world went dark.

THE PERFECT HOUSE

LISA MORTON

"YOU SURE YOU WANNA GO to the old Ducommun place?"

If this had been a horror movie, the person asking that would have been a creepy old dude with one bad, milky eye, missing teeth, and a grizzled beard that might or might not have bits of flesh stuck in it. But this wasn't a horror movie—at least not yet—and so the inquirer was a chunky teenager with a dyed blond ponytail who chewed gum while she talked (with an Alabama accent) and eyed me as if I'd just spoken in tongues.

"Uh, yeah, I'm sure. Why? Not like there's anybody living there."

The girl, who was maybe eighteen, finished bagging my protein bars and coffee drinks as she squinted at me.

"Who told you that?"

"The woman who owns the house."

She shrugged, handed me the bag. "You'd think she would know."

"Are you saying there *are* people living there?"

"There's lots of folks 'round here who come into town once a month, pick up a few things, and don't nobody know exactly where they live. Maybe they live there, maybe they don't."

The transaction was done. I thanked the girl, picked up my bag, and walked out of the Piggly Wiggly.

I got into my rented SUV, unwrapped one of the protein bars, and shoved it into my mouth as I glanced around the small town of Jackson's Corners. I'm a city boy by birth and preference; I wasn't used to places where you could see half the town from one intersection. In fact, this was my first trip scouting a location in the South. When they'd told me what they needed—medium-budget horror picture set in a huge, broken-down mansion in the middle of an endless field of weeds—I'd known I wouldn't find anything like that in L.A. I'd gone through websites and notebooks for days, I'd talked to other location managers and scouts. Finally, someone in Mobile, Alabama, told me about a new property that had just come up on a local website as being available for a shoot. He sent me the link, I checked it out, and heard that delicious inner "Bingo!" call the instant I laid eyes on the Ducommun house. It was strangely designed for the South—less plantation style and more edge-of-the-sinister-moors style, two stories with a lot of stonework, but that made it even more perfect. The movie, *Haunted*, was actually set in Britain in the 1880s; the production team had offices in Charleston. They only needed the house for a few days' worth of exteriors, so going to Britain was too expensive. If the Ducommun place worked out, I'd be *Haunted*'s hero.

I finished my protein bar, swigged some of the coffee, and checked my notes again before starting up the SUV. The house should be no more than twenty minutes away. If it worked out, the residents of Jackson's Corner would get a nice little economic boost for a few days, although I wasn't sure they'd appreciate it.

The house's current owner, MaryEllen Loewe, lived in upstate New York and wanted nothing to do with either her family estate or Jackson's Corners. She said no one had lived in the house since the 1970s, and in fact she'd only visited it once, as a child on a family vacation. She'd put it on the market a few times, but it was apparently too isolated and too run-down to fetch any real money. One day she'd seen a ghost movie with a house that she thought was far less frightening, so she'd come up with the idea of offering the place as a location.

As I drove out of Jackson's Corners, I thought back to my phone conversation with her. When I'd asked her how long it had been since anyone had been out to check on the place, she'd been evasive, told me she'd had a local friend take the photos I'd seen. Now it made me wonder if the grocery store clerk could've been right—might it have picked up some squatters along the way? If it had... well, as great as it looked in the photos, there were always other houses. I'd come up against squatters in the past, even had to work with the local sheriff once to oust them when the director had fallen so in love with the place that he just couldn't have any other house in east L.A. The squatters had been a down-on-her-luck mother and three kids. I'm enough of a Hollywood Liberal to have felt guilty as hell about tossing them out, even though they'd trashed the joint. I would never do that again.

After leaving Jackson's Corners, the two-lane county road wound through low, untamed fields punctuated by outbreaks of trees, clustered so thickly you'd think you could barely walk between them... and yet some of those dense gatherings held old structures, set so far back in the growth they were barely visible. Surely no one still lived out here... but there were dirt lanes leading back from the main road that looked well-traveled. Back in L.A., I lived in a Valley condo that I thought was wild because it backed onto a concrete-lined wash and I'd once seen a coyote down there. Living out here just seemed unimaginable to me.

Thank God for GPS, or I'm sure I would've missed the overgrown driveway that led to the Ducommun place. The house itself wasn't visible from the road, although there was a crumbling brick pedestal with a mailbox on which the name could barely be made out.

The dirt drive was pitted and bumpy. I crawled over it at barely five miles per hour, thinking that the last thing I wanted was to destroy a rental miles from civilization. At some places the drive was little more than a path, so thoroughly overgrown that brush scraped against the windshield and the sides of the car. If anyone lived out here, they weren't much on landscaping.

Finally, the woods cleared out and the house was revealed, lurking just beyond a tumbledown wrought-iron fence and gate. I parked, checked my phone, pocketed my keys, and got out.

The gate consisted of two doors that resisted my first push slightly—the hinges were rusted into place—but finally gave with a nerve-jangling screech. Beyond, an unpaved path led between knee-high weeds to the house itself.

The photos I'd already seen hadn't lied—one look at it raised goose bumps. The house was built in a U-shape, with two wings that flanked a central courtyard and entryway. The wings had steeply pitched roofs with thick chimneys, while the house between was flat, with dormers jutting from the shingled roof. The center feature of the house was an entryway with a roof that was oddly reminiscent of a steeple, tall and narrow with a pitched roof that curved down on both sides. It was impossible to tell what the house had been built from—whether it was stone or wood, it was so aged and discolored that its grayish-brown walls looked ancient and even alien.

Rodrigo Alfaro, the young director of *Haunted*, was going to fucking *love* this place.

It was the perfect house.

Even the weather was ideal—an overcast day that shed a dull, flat light on the Ducommun house. I brought my phone up and started snapping pictures. I paused just once to review the photos on the phone's screen, then continued to shoot.

Walking up closer to the house did nothing to dispel its aura of decay and mystery. The place just looked cold, even dead; no vegetation grew next to the house, where the air smelled of mold. Astonishingly, the windows were still intact, as were the interior draperies, making it impossible to spy into the house.

I walked around to the side, shooting as I went. I was still looking up at the house as I circled around to the back—but when I brought my eyes down, I stopped dead in my tracks.

I was staring at a clothesline, complete with freshly washed clothes flapping in the slight breeze. These weren't old castoffs, hung out half a century ago and forgotten—one was a black T-shirt featuring the logo of a metal band that had been hot about ten years ago. Beyond the clothesline was a field that had obviously been tended—rows of corn ran straight, tomatoes clung to cages, potato vines were green and leafy.

Suddenly anxious, I turned and looked up at the house and saw something I'd missed—black solar panels, so the house had an off-the-grid power supply. Of course I'd missed them from the front—they were only placed on the rear of the house, hidden from the view of anyone casually approaching from the front. A few feet to my left was a pump handle with a fresh puddle around the base.

On the bottom floor of the house, a drapery swung back into place.

Someone *was* in the house. And they were watching me.

Heart hammering, I turned to head back to my rented

car. I kept my head down, tried not to seem obviously alarmed and rushed, even though my throat was dry and my palms were sweaty.

I never even felt someone behind me. At least I think they came up behind me. I only know that there was a sound like a cannon blast, one brief flash of pain in my head, and then nothing.

⚜

Pain. Dark. Unable to move.

Those were the first three things that came when I woke up. My head hurt and I was nauseous. I'd been hit on the head. I hoped I didn't have a concussion.

Once my eyes adjusted, I saw I was inside. My arms were behind me, the wrists tied together; my feet couldn't move, either. Weak sunlight filtered in around floor-to-ceiling draperies, making dust motes dance in broad shafts. Something glittered on my chest, and I saw that several necklaces had been draped around my neck. One had a crucifix dangling from the end, but I couldn't make sense of the others. The air smelled strange, like a combination of mildew and herbs.

What the fuck?

I had to be in the Ducommun house. The drapes and the windows behind them matched what I'd seen from the outside.

"He's awake."

I jerked against my bonds, startled by the sound of

a feminine voice. Squinting in the gloom, I could just make out a woman squatting on the floor about ten feet away. She sounded middle-aged, her voice husky. She was slender, seemed to be wearing something like a billowy peasant blouse and jeans. She wore the same kinds of necklaces that had been placed on me, and her arms were tattooed with images I couldn't make heads or tails of.

A man strode up behind her. Big, husky guy, long grizzled beard; although I couldn't see anything but shadow, I guessed there was a lot of gray in there. As he paused before one of the curtained windows, I could tell from his silhouette that he was over six feet and two hundred pounds. He also wore the necklaces, which I now guessed were supposed to be amulets or talismans, some kind of folk magic or hoodoo.

This wasn't looking good.

The woman rose and approached me, leaning forward. "Can you hear me?"

I tried to answer, but my throat was dry and I choked.

She asked, "Do you need some water?"

At least they weren't going to kill me. Or at least they weren't going to kill me when I was still thirsty. I nodded.

She approached with a glass mason jar full of water and tilted it to my lips while the man watched carefully. The water was warm but good; I spluttered, but got enough down to loosen up my throat. "Thank you," I said.

"You're welcome." She set the jar aside and stood over me, looking down.

Now I could get a better look at her. She was in her forties, might've been beautiful except that she had some of the telltale signs of hard living—leathery, tanned skin, nails so short they might have all been broken, so skinny that lines once curved had become angular.

My head was still throbbing, although thankfully the queasiness was fading. "Don't suppose you've got an ibuprofen around..."

"Sorry, we don't."

The man stood behind her, scowling, unmoving. It was obvious that he didn't approve of something; I only hoped it was the fact that I was being kept here at all, and not that I was being kept here *alive*.

Something else sprang up in my peripheral vision, something in the shadows behind the man. I turned my head slightly, and for a second I thought I saw a figure crouched there, glaring at me. Then the man shifted his weight, stepping in front of the bent thing with the bared teeth, and I wasn't sure I'd really seen it at all.

I turned my attention to the woman, who peered at me with curiosity and sympathy. "Look, my name's Dustin Mathers, I'm out from L.A. scouting locations—"

The woman cut me off. "What does that mean?"

"It means that somebody wants to make a movie here, and they'll give you a lot of money if I can coordinate it."

My two hosts exchanged a look at that, a shared expression that was one part amusement, one part alarm, and one part excitement. Now the man spoke, and his voice was a heavily-accented rumble. "Ain't no movie gonna be made here."

"I agree, and I know you probably thought I was a trespasser and that's why you knocked me out, so how about we just call it even, you let me go, and you'll never hear from me again—how's that?"

The man stepped forward, and I saw he carried a length of steel pipe—probably what he'd used to hit me with. "So does everybody out in California think all of us down here in the South are just stupid?"

"No. No, of course not, but... well, there are people who know I was coming out here to look at this property. When I don't show up for a while, they'll start checking."

The woman asked, "What people?"

"The woman who owns this place, for one."

At that my two captors exchanged a look and then snorted in derision. "The owner, huh?" The woman barked a harsh laugh. "What else did she say?"

"That the house was unoccupied."

The woman's face turned red. For a moment her mouth hung open, moving a little like a fish on a dock. Then she screamed, "*Bitch!*" as she stormed out of the room.

"SueAnne, honey, wait!" That was the man, going after her. I heard them in another room, arguing about "that *bitch*," and then a door slammed, the voices were muffled, and I thought they'd gone outside.

I was alone. I didn't know for how long, nor did I know what kind of mood they'd be in when they returned—maybe they'd decide that saving me at all had been a mistake, and the next time that pipe came down on my head would be the last.

I had to try something while I could.

I tested the bonds on my wrists and realized it felt like

a simple zip tie. That was good.

Why was that good? Because every experienced location manager carries a lot of shit they might never need. What folks might not realize about the job is that we don't just find cool places where movies can film, we supervise those locations when the work's actually happening. During shooting I wear a safari vest with pockets; those pockets are crammed full of everything from gaffer's tape to phone chargers to power bars to wads of cash. Even when I'm not on a set or wearing that vest, I carry a few extra items with me. I figured my captors had taken my phone and my keys, but they might have missed the little knife I kept in a back pocket.

I seemed to be strapped to an old dining chair with a narrow back. I was able to move my hands to the left side enough to tap my rear pants pocket.

I felt a tiny bulge there and nearly passed out from relief.

It took some maneuvering, but I managed to get two fingers of my left hand into the pocket. Being careful—*so* careful!—not to drop the knife, I pulled it out. Another few seconds and I'd managed to get the knife blade out. Fifteen seconds later, the zip tie fell away from my wrists.

Moving as quickly as possible, I brought the blade down to saw through the tie at my ankles. I got to my feet, nearly stumbling as my vision swirled, but I steadied myself until the world stopped spinning. I shoved the knife away again and got my ass out of there.

The room we'd been in was on the ground floor and led into a central downstairs area. Other rooms opened around the sides. To my left, a big staircase went up to the second floor; to my right, grand double doors led outside.

I heard the couple arguing just beyond the doors. I was still trying to decide which way to go when their voices started to come closer.

I opted for the stairs and ran up them two at a time.

I'd just reached the top landing when I heard the doors open. I sprinted down the hallway to my right, noticing two things right off the bat: There were a lot of closed doors up here; and the way my feet brought up clouds of dust made me think nobody had been up here in ages.

I was near the end of the hallway when I heard the man shout, "Fuck!"

They'd discovered I was gone.

To my right, a narrow flight of stairs led to an attic. Maybe they wouldn't look for me up there. Maybe they wouldn't think to follow the trail I'd probably left in the dust. I had no other choice at this point.

At the top of the stairs was a trapdoor. I pushed on it; it gave. I opened it all the way, climbed up through it, and lowered it as silently as I could.

The attic was pretty much what you'd expect to find in a house this old: Thin light filtered in through a few grimy windows, revealing a long space cluttered with boxes, broken furniture, abandoned toys, old steamer trunks. The roof peaked not far overhead; anyone taller than six feet would have to duck on the sides of the room.

Footsteps were thudding up the main staircase.

I looked around for somewhere to hide. There wasn't

much time. I picked a corner where I could crouch behind a low cabinet with a broken leg.

I positioned myself and listened. They were coming down the hall now. "Can you tell where he went?" called the man.

The woman—SueAnne—said, "I think he stopped here... maybe this way...?"

I tensed.

I peered around the edge of the cabinet, and movement caught my peripheral vision. I turned to look down the length of the attic to my left, and in the distance I saw a man. He had some sort of metal collar around his neck, studded with spikes so he couldn't lower his head; the collar was attached to a length of heavy chain, which was secured around a support post with a padlock. The man was black-skinned, naked, covered in long, thin, horizontal wounds, some of which were fresh enough to ooze blood. He was wide-eyed in terror and agony, his mouth open in a silent scream.

How could I have missed seeing him?

As I watched, paralyzed, he pulled against the chains, writhing as fresh, bloody stripes appeared on his torso.

He was being whipped. By something I couldn't see.

I stumbled back, colliding with an old dressmaker's dummy that tumbled down onto me. I pushed it away, barely stifling my own scream, scrabbling on hands and knees toward the trapdoor, less concerned with what awaited me below than with what I was seeing now.

And then I wasn't seeing anything, because he was gone. I never saw him wink out or fade. He was just...

gone.

The trapdoor was thrown back and I nearly tumbled through it. Strong hands caught me, fixed around me, and dragged me down the stairs to the second-floor hallway. SueAnne was there, eyeing me with concern. "Let's get out of here."

I didn't put up much fight as they dragged me down the hall and the stairs, back to the room on the ground floor I'd escaped from. The man shoved me back into the chair and fished more zip ties out of his pocket, but I held up my hands in what I hoped was a placating manner. "Please, you don't have to tie me. I won't fight you. I promise."

SueAnne asked, "What did you see up there?"

"A man chained, covered in blood… he looked like he was screaming, although I couldn't hear anything... and then he just vanished."

A look passed between the two of them, but it was a look I couldn't understand—relief. The man seemed to have forgotten about the zip ties. The woman spoke up. "Good. That was just a residual."

"A what?"

"A residual. A *ghost*. But residual means it's like a recording—it just goes through the same thing over and over. Usually with residuals they repeat one of their last actions before they died, in the place where they died."

"Why is it good that I saw that?"

"Because the residuals can't hurt you. But the intelligent ones can. Those—" she gestured at the strange necklaces I still wore, "—keep you safe."

Oooohhkaaay... I got it now. These people were nuts. Whether they'd been whack before they came here or squatting in a two-hundred-year-old mansion falling apart around them had driven them insane didn't much matter to me then. What *did* matter was knowing that they were looneytunes. I had to get out of here before they decided to sacrifice me to their Goat God Belial or whatever it was that crazies did with their captives.

I looked back at the man, whose scowl made me think maybe he wasn't nuts but went along with her craziness for whatever reason—love, money, family obligation, who knew.

The woman pulled up another chair closer to me and sat down, eyeing me. "I'm gonna tell you what's really going on here—"

The man growled and stepped forward. "SueAnne, you sure that's such a good idea?"

She appraised me, and I saw compassion there. She might be nuts, but there was also something decent in her. "I think Dustin here deserves to know."

He groaned and turned away, but didn't stop her.

"First of all," she said, "my name is SueAnne Coates, and that big ol' bear over there is my husband, Jeff. My maiden name, though, was Ducommun. The woman you talked to about this house—MaryEllen—is my sister."

Was this just more craziness, or could it be true? I'd never actually met or seen MaryEllen Loewe, but I knew her maiden name had to be Ducommun, and SueAnne was probably about the same age. I said, "And MaryEllen owns the house—"

SueAnne cut me off. "No, she doesn't. When our daddy died ten years ago, he left it to *both* of us. I'm just as much an owner as she is. She has no right to be trying to do things with this house that she hasn't asked me about."

"So why would she?"

"Because she wants to sell it."

"And you don't?"

SueAnne looked around, both wistful and a little angry. "If I could leave here, I would in a heartbeat. It's not a matter of what I want. It's what I *have* to do."

"Which is what?"

She took a deep breath and said, "Keep the things in this house from getting loose in the world."

"What 'things'?"

SueAnne rose and paced as she answered, occasionally glancing anxiously into the room's high corners. "This house was built in 1820 by Jean-Paul Ducommun, a wealthy French landowner who had to flee his native country when he was implicated in the rape and murder of a young servant girl. He came here with his wife, Claudette, who many thought had also been involved in the murder. They built this house, planted the surrounding land, amassed slaves, and soon became even richer.

"They didn't lose their reputation, though. Folks in these parts whispered about parties that went on for days, where both animals and children were offered as sacrifice to gods no one should ever worship. Eventually even Claudette disappeared. Neighbors claimed they'd heard her screaming in the fields one night, but no trace of her was ever found."

SueAnne crossed the room, which was an odd mix of antique furniture in varying stages of decay and more modern living necessities like propane lanterns and a television. The floors were much-polished hardwood, their aged gleam making me wonder if they could have been in use since the house was built. The walls had faded from their original red to the color of a purplish bruise; near a brick fireplace, filled with fresh wood, sat contemporary pots and pans. SueAnne gestured to a large portrait that hung over the fireplace mantel; it showed a man with pale skin, black hair and beard, and piercing green eyes. He wore a nineteenth-century coat and stood next to a tall horse that was so vividly hued it was almost crimson.

"That's Jean-Paul," SueAnne said as she looked up at the painting, "with the only thing he really cared about: his beloved horse, Hellfire. The mare's name derived from her distinctive color. When that horse died, Jean-Paul went into such a fury that he whipped three of his slaves to death."

"Nice guy," I muttered.

SueAnne turned away from the portrait to look at me again. "Do you know the story of Madame LaLaurie in New Orleans?"

I remembered the name from a television show I'd done some location work for. "She mutilated and killed some people working for her, right?"

SueAnne nodded. "They drove her out of New Orleans when they found an attic full of tortured slaves. She eventually made her way back to France, but first she came here. My ancestors welcomed her as a kindred spirit, but when they found her in the attic one day with *their* slaves, they got pissed off at the fact that she'd taken their property without asking... not, mind you, at what she'd done with that 'property.'"

"So what I saw in the attic..."

"One of Madame LaLaurie's victims. A residual spirit, reliving his death over and over."

Now, as I've already mentioned, I'm a city boy, an urban sophisticate, lacking only the beard to be a trendy hipster. I'm a skeptic by nature, as happy to play with a Ouija board at a party as the next guy, but never really believing in ghosts or spirits or life after death. But I *had* seen something in that attic that I couldn't explain, and more than that, I'd also *felt* something—a fear so intense that even the circumstances couldn't completely account for it.

Until I had a better explanation—and because I still thought she had too many bats in her belfry—I decided not to question her beliefs.

"There are other things, though," SueAnne went on, "in this house that are worse. *Much* worse—intelligent spirits that will try to fuck with us. The main one is Jean-Paul Ducommun, the evil man who built this house. He died here of syphilis in 1840, and haunts it to this day."

"So why do you stay here?"

"This is my heritage. Do you think I like knowing how my many-times-great-granddaddy made his fortune and lived his life? No." She gestured at the tattoos on her arms, the talismans around her neck. "I learned about these things so I could protect myself, and Jeff. We stay here now to protect the rest of the world from Jean-Paul. Do you know about elementals?"

I shook my head.

"They're the big bads of the ghost world. Some folks think they're like nature spirits gone bad, but I know they're the ghosts of evil people who are no longer confined to a place. My sister wants to make money from this house, but she doesn't want to deal with how dangerous that is, because Jean-Paul could possess someone who comes in here unawares, and if he escapes into the outside world he could become an elemental. And I don't want that on my conscience. What Jean-Paul did when he was alive is already too much."

She paused, then, her face twisting in emotion. I was waiting for her to continue when a deafening *boom* sounded from overhead.

I jumped about a mile. The only time I'd ever heard anything like that had been when I was on location for an action movie that involved blowing up a building. Then it came again—*boom!*—and again. Three times, so overpowering every time that it was hard to believe the building itself wasn't collapsing.

SueAnne didn't move a muscle, didn't even flinch. After the third sound, she said, "That would be Jean-Paul."

"The ghost?" I asked.

"We're the only three living people in this house, so yes—the ghost."

She may have bought in to that nonsense, but I didn't. I not only thought there was someone else in the house—someone who had played some sort of trick on me in the attic—but I was starting to wonder if the freaky necklaces they'd put on me were somehow drugging me, making me see and feel and hear things that weren't really there.

I had to get out.

"Look," I said, rising to my feet but sitting back down when I saw the husband get twitchy, "why don't you just let me go on my way? I give you my word that I won't say anything to anyone, I'll tell your sister that this place doesn't work as a film location, and you'll never hear from me again. I mean, how long had you planned on keeping me here?"

A look passed between SueAnne and Jeff, and I realized they hadn't really thought about what they'd do with me.

"Why should we believe you?" Jeff asked.

"Because if I try to tell the local police about you, you can tell them I was trespassing and you were just defending your property."

Jeff squinted. I'd scored points. I tried to press my advantage. "Y'know, did it ever occur to you that maybe your sister was hoping you'd knock me out and hold me here, that maybe she thinks she can finally sell the house out from under you if you're both in jail? In fact, maybe she's already called the cops and they're on the way here *right now*."

Jeff groaned. "Oh *fuck*…"

SueAnne looked at him, anxious. "Jeff, you don't

think…?"

He nodded at me. "He could goddamn well be right, SueAnne. That sounds just like something your sister might pull."

"So what do we do?"

He turned and started to pace. "I don't know… I don't know…" He stopped, turned, and shouted at me, "Stay there!"

I held up my hands in surrender.

Jeff strode out. SueAnne ran after him. "Jeff, wait—!"

They went to some other part of the house and slammed a door. I heard them arguing, but I couldn't make out the exact words.

I should've run then, but there was a little problem: I had neither keys nor phone. I wasn't sure how far I'd get on foot; Jeff was a big guy in good shape.

I was about to try it anyway when I heard a door crash open and SueAnne called out, "Jeff, no—!"

Jeff strode into the room where I waited and pointed a hunting rifle at me. "Sorry, man, but this is the only way to be sure."

SueAnne ran up to him and yanked on one arm. He threw her backwards. She collided with the wall, slid to the floor half-conscious.

In that moment, I charged. If the son of a bitch was going to shoot me anyway, I might as well try *something*. We were maybe thirty feet apart and he was still off-balance from dealing with his wife.

The rifle went off. Something thudded into me. There was a flash of pain and I nearly lost my footing, but staggered on.

He was about to fire again. I jumped the last few feet. We collided chest to chest, the impact driving him back. He hit the ground hard, but I rode the fall, reaching for the rifle. I got it in both hands, but he had it, too, and we wrestled that way for a few seconds, me on top of him. Then I managed to drive the butt of the gun down into his chest. He made an *oof* sound and relaxed his hold. I wrenched the rifle free and smacked the side of his head with it. He went limp, his head falling to one side.

They were both out. I patted him down with shaking hands, found my keys and phone in one of his pockets. I stood, my feet nearly going out from under me—something slick was on the floor.

It was blood. *My* blood.

I reached up to my left arm and found it was covered in warm, sticky stuff. I knew I might not have long, that I had to find my car and get out of there before they either came to or I bled out.

I stashed my phone in a pocket and, with the rifle in one hand and the precious keys in the other, I started out of the room. I stopped halfway, however, remembering the necklaces they'd made me wear—the ones that I thought might be drugging me. I tore them off and tossed them to the side, then kept going.

I reached the front door, turned the knob, ready to sprint to my rented car and freedom—

The knob wouldn't turn.

I panicked, trying hard, scanning furiously for something to unlock—a dead bolt, a key, a latch, but there was nothing. The knob refused to budge.

Suddenly I was shivering; the temperature had plum-meted. I felt a presence behind me. I turned, expecting SueAnne or Jeff, but instead what was behind me wasn't human. It was a tall, roughly man-shaped shadow, black, wavering like something glimpsed at a distance through heat waves. It exuded power and intent, and something else...

Evil.

It didn't so much reach out for me as *grow*, expand, until it surrounded me.

I screamed as I felt the first icy touch.

❧

I'm jingling the keys as I step through the door and out into the world. I move quickly, anxious to make my escape. It takes a few seconds to orient myself; I stagger slightly.

Then I see the vehicle and move towards it. I'll have to trust to instinct when it comes to operating it.

I wish I could ride out of here on Hellfire.

But all that really matters is that I'm finally free of that damnable house. The world is waiting. My host is from someplace called Los Angeles. I've never heard of it, but I think it sounds like a city where I'd fit right in.

It's time to make this world mine.

SLEEPING ANGELS

DAVID BELL

"WHAT ARE YOU DOING?" DANIEL asked.

"It's my phone," Emily said.

"But why are you putting it on that little tripod?" he asked. "Why is it out at all?"

Daniel became self-conscious about his appearance. He knew he hadn't shaved for two days, knew his bathrobe was dirty and stained, knew his thinning hair stood up in little wisps. She hadn't said anything about a phone.

"It's a camera, too," she said. She was Emily Francis, and he'd expected her to come over that day, and she did. Right on time. They were supposed to talk, but if she'd told him about the phone and the tripod, he must have forgotten. That happened more and more now that he was past seventy. "See?" She pressed a button, and the phone made a nearly inaudible beeping noise. "We're filming now."

"Filming?" Daniel reached up and pulled the two sides of his robe closer together, hoping to cover up the dingy T-shirt underneath. What was worse on camera? A dirty robe or a T-shirt that used to be white but was now gray? "You didn't say—"

"I think I did, Daniel."

"Look, I'm going to—"

He started out of his seat, reaching for the phone on the tripod. But when he did, Emily held her hand out, blocking him.

"Uh-uh-uh," Emily said. "How do you expect this interview to have any impact unless we film it? How else can people rediscover your work?"

"You said an interview. I thought you meant print, something you'd write down. You know, for a magazine or a newspaper."

"Who reads that stuff anymore?" Emily asked. She was young, mid-twenties, small-boned, almost fragile looking. Slightly pale cheeks, freckles like a child. But when she spoke, her voice was confident, full of steel. "People need to *see* you, Daniel. They need to *hear* you."

"Can I at least change my clothes?" he asked.

"No, this is good. They need to see the *real* you. The way you live now."

Daniel settled back into his chair. He'd trusted her this far, hitched his wagon to her star. And if he really wanted people to rediscover his books, to know who he was again...

"Shall we move on?" Emily asked, but didn't wait for an answer. "Let the record show it's Monday, April twenty-fourth. So, for the sake of our viewers, state your name."

"Daniel Stone."

"Age?"

"Seventy-two."

"Occupation?"

"You know all this."

"It's for the audience. The people watching."

Daniel sighed. "I'm retired. Mostly."

"What did you do before that?" Emily asked.

"I was a writer. A novelist." Daniel heard the pride in his own voice. Yes, it had been a while, but he still felt proud of his work. "I published eight novels many years ago. Some of them did pretty well."

"You made a lot of money?"

"Some."

Emily looked around the room. They were seated at a small kitchen table. The space was cramped, the house unassuming from the outside. Three bedrooms, two baths. A small yard in a middle-class neighborhood.

"Enough to live... well, it's not very glamorous, is it?" Emily asked.

"I'm not married. Not for many years. Never had kids. I live simply and made the money last. You know, Holly-wood optioned a couple of the books. They never made the movies, but I still got some money. Once in a blue moon I get a letter from a reader, someone who found one of my books in a used bookstore or a Goodwill. My editor is dead. My agent still sends me a Christmas card, but that's about it."

"What's the name of your best-known book?" Emily asked.

She wore a little knowing smile on her face. It irritated Daniel. That's what she wanted to talk about. That book, the one that apparently started all of this.

"*The Sleeping Angels.*"

"It was a success?"

"You know it was."

"Tell me." She sounded more insistent. Almost angry.

"It did pretty well. It snuck onto the bestseller lists for a week or so. Translated into a few foreign languages. A little review ran in *Time* magazine."

"Oh. Is that a big deal?" Emily asked.

"It was. Back then."

"And what was that book about?" Emily asked. "Why did it do so well?"

"I didn't know we were—"

"Daniel. *The Sleeping Angels?*"

Daniel shook his head. He clutched at the robe again, pulling it tighter. He felt a draft from under the kitchen door and shivered. "It's a pretty simple story, really. Four girls get murdered in a small town. The police find their bodies in the basement of an abandoned estate, all laid out side by side. The killer ends up being the father of one of the girls, the youngest one. A detective tracks the killer down, brings him to justice, and he is executed, bringing closure to the town. But the detective is changed forever."

"And why is it called *The Sleeping Angels?*" Emily asked.

Daniel shifted in his seat. His feet shuffled below the table. "I thought we weren't going to—people don't always understand."

"Why is it called that, Daniel?" Emily asked.

Daniel paused before answering. He looked around at the dripping faucet, the peeling wallpaper. If people started reading the book again, even a few thousand...

He had so many ideas for new books.

"Okay. Because of the way the dead girls were found. They were laid out side by side in the basement of the mansion. They were all wearing white shrouds." Daniel couldn't help himself. He objected to the direction the conversation was going, but when he started talking about his book—his most famous book—his storyteller's instincts took over. He could see the scene in his mind, the way he'd described it all those years ago. The way he'd imagined it based on—"They were between the ages of fourteen and seventeen. Innocent. All virgins. When they were found, they hadn't been dead very long, so their cheeks still looked rosy, their skin almost warm to the touch. Like they were asleep. Like they were... well, that's where the title comes from."

Emily bent over. Daniel heard her rustling around in a bag she'd carried through the door with her. She popped back up, holding a photograph.

"The girls were found in this house, right?" she asked.

Before Daniel was able to see the photo, Emily turned it around and showed it to the camera. She held it there a long moment, making sure the viewers could see it in detail. She then flipped the photo around and laid it flat on the table, sliding it across to Daniel.

But he didn't need to look at it. He knew what was in the photo.

"That's the house, right, Daniel?" Emily asked.

Daniel kept his eyes on Emily, refusing to look down. He lifted his index finger and tapped it against his temple. "The house is in here. I imagined it. I created it."

"Did you? Really?" She slid the photo closer until it touched Daniel's elbow. "Look at that. You've seen that before, haven't you?"

"I didn't agree to this."

"You agreed to the interview, Daniel."

"I don't think this is the best course of action. A lot of people—"

"Just look at the photo," Emily said. "Okay? It won't bite."

Daniel gave the photo a quick glance, not even bothering to pick it up off the table. His eyes confirmed what he already knew. He'd seen the house before. He knew exactly where it was. He just wasn't sure why Emily insisted on getting him to admit that on camera.

"It's the Hoffman Estate." Daniel recognized the rusted wrought-iron gates, the crumbling masonry and roof tiles, the boarded-up windows, the overgrown yard, the weeds and trees twisted and thick like a jungle. He couldn't say how long ago the photo had been taken, but the house didn't look much different than the last time Daniel had seen it in person. And that was almost forty years earlier. "You knew that before you even asked me."

"Just to be clear," Emily said, "that's the Hoffman Estate in Camp Henry, Ohio. Built in the mid-nineteenth century by rubber magnate Milton Hoffman. For nearly a century considered to be one of the most glorious homes in the Midwest, it eventually fell into disrepair and then bankruptcy by the 1970s. Abandoned and vacant for over forty years. That Hoffman Estate?"

"Yes," Daniel said. "That Hoffman Estate."

"You used to live in Camp Henry? You were a reporter there?"

"Lots of novelists use real-life as inspiration for their novels. You're making it sound like I committed some kind of crime because I was inspired by what happened in that house. I was a reporter, and I covered the case. Then I wrote a novel about it."

"A very successful novel."

"Should I apologize for being a success? For being a good writer?"

Emily smiled. She looked smugly satisfied. "No need to apologize for that." She pulled the photo back and moved it near the base of the tripod. "But let's talk about the man who committed those crimes. The man who murdered the Sleeping Angels."

Daniel pointed at the camera. "Don't we have enough already? You said a short interview. And I'm not dressed."

"Daniel, if you don't like the interview when we're finished, just tell me."

"And we can redo it?" he asked.

"Who committed those crimes?" Emily asked. "The murders of those four girls?"

Daniel tried to feel reassured by her words about the video, about redoing it. He felt like she was hiding something. Or not telling him the full truth. Back in his reporting days, he could easily sniff out a phony. He could spot a liar within three minutes of starting a conversation.

But he feared that living alone had dulled his ability to identify those who intended him harm. After all, no one ever intended him harm anymore. For that matter, no one ever intended him good. He rarely saw anyone, kept few friends, talked mostly to his cats. A few times a year he conversed with his neighbor next door, a retired widower, or a local librarian who knew he'd been a writer and liked to pick his brain when he wandered in to check out the latest magazines. But the interview could change all that. A young journalist, Emily, with a pen and a voice, could bring his work back to some measure of attention.

Wouldn't it feel good to publish just one more book? To get back in the game one more time... before it was too late?

"His name was Michael James Hart," Daniel said. "He wasn't the father of any of the girls, like in the book. He was a local handyman, had done some work in one of the girls' homes. He had a history of violent behavior, but nothing like those murders."

"You interviewed him. On death row."

"A lot of journalists must have."

Emily shook her head. "No, they didn't. He only talked to you. He liked you."

"That was a long time ago," Daniel said. "I don't know who he talked to and who he didn't."

"He was repentant, wasn't he?"

Daniel paused. He leaned forward. "You know, you seem to be asking these questions as though you already know the answers. If you know so much about it, why do you need to ask me? I thought we agreed to just talk about my books, to maybe drum up a little interest so some publishers would see it. This seems out of bounds—"

"He was repentant, wasn't he?" she said again, her face leaning in closer to Daniel's, her voice rising. She didn't wait for Daniel to respond before she said, "He converted to Christianity on death row, expressed his sorrow for the crimes. And he told you he had just one wish, one thing that could be done to honor his memory."

Daniel pushed back from the table. The chair made a loud, scraping sound against the dingy linoleum as he stood up. "Okay, that's enough. You clearly don't want to talk about me—"

"Sit down, Daniel."

"Sit down?" Daniel stared at the young woman. What did she know? She was a child, not even born when he was writing his books, not even aware of how the world worked. And she thought she could push him around? "You need to leave right now. And give me that video or whatever it is. Destroy it. Erase it. I don't want anyone seeing this. I was a fool to think you wanted to help me."

"It's too late," Emily said.

"Too late for what?"

"For that." Emily nodded toward the camera. "You see, Daniel, a lot has changed since you had a writing career. There's this thing called Facebook Live, and you're on it right now. Everything we've said has already gone out to my viewers. And anyone else who happened to come along."

Daniel felt like one of those tribesmen who has lived his entire life in isolation, unaware that the rest of the world was speeding by in cars and on computers and with telephones. He blinked a couple of times at Emily and then turned his head to the camera.

"You're kidding," he said.

"Nope."

Daniel had heard something on the news recently, something about Facebook Live. Had one man killed another on there? Broadcasting the crime for all the world to see?

Was Emily that crazy?

"You're bluffing," he said.

Daniel moved as fast as he could. He took two quick steps around the side of the table, reaching out for the camera.

But he was too slow. As soon as he moved, Emily moved, too, snatching the tripod and camera and scooting back in her chair. She deftly kept the camera pointed at Daniel as he came closer.

"Anything you do to me goes out on the air," she said. "It's going out now. So if you want to attack me or hit me or something, be my guest. But the whole world will see. Well, maybe not the whole world, but a decent number of people."

Emily's face remained obscured by the camera. Daniel
saw the lens, that lone, unblinking eye. His hands were
shaking, but he stood frozen in place. What if she were
telling the truth? Did he want to throttle a woman on a
live broadcast? How would that help his writing career?

"Why don't you sit again?" Emily said. "If you do, we
can wrap this up. You can try to come off a little better.
You haven't exactly made a great impression."

Daniel thought about storming off, but then what? The
world had seen him acting like a crazy old man.

And if there was a live audience, if people were watching him...

Wasn't that what he wanted?

He returned to his seat, sliding it in close to the table.
He folded his hands while Emily gently set the tripod
back down.

"Okay? Ready?"

"I guess so," Daniel said.

"This next part really shouldn't take long. You probably don't want to say much about the promise you made
to Michael James Hart."

Daniel made a half-hearted attempt at getting up again
but stopped himself. He didn't have the energy. And he
looked at that black, all-seeing eye again.

"You did make a promise to Michael James Hart,
didn't you? Michael James Hart. Or as I refer to him...
Great-Uncle Michael."

Daniel felt the cold draft again, but this time it origi-
nated inside of his body, not through the crack under the
door. *Great-Uncle Michael?* He couldn't be.

But how improbable was any of what was happening in his crummy little kitchen already?

Great-Uncle? *Still, what did any of it prove?*

Then Emily was bending down again, rummaging in her bag. She came up with a piece of paper, one yellowed with age and folded in quarters. Gently, as though handling a fragile bird's egg, Emily opened the paper.

"And if you want to grab for this," she said, "thinking you can crumple it up or tear it, there are copies. And at least one other letter that says the same thing."

Emily held the paper up to the camera, just as she did with the photo of the house. She held it there for what felt to Daniel like a long time, long enough for people to at least read some of the words. He did think about reaching out and snatching it, but if she had another one or copies of it…

But he felt his anger rising. He had a pretty good guess about what the letter said.

Emily turned the letter around so she could read it. And she did, into the camera, her voice steady.

"I've been talking to a reporter these days, a nice guy. He listens to me very carefully. And he seems to understand me, sometimes better than I understand myself. I've told him everything, everything about my crimes and all the mistakes I've made. He's agreed to write my story down."

"Stop it," Daniel said. "This isn't fair. It happened forty years—"

Emily continued reading. She didn't even look at Daniel. *"I won't see it in print, of course, because I'll be gone by the time he's finished and the book gets published. I've asked him for one promise, one very sincere promise, and he's agreed to it."*

"Stop this." Daniel stood up again, hoping he would intimidate Emily, put some kind of fear into her that she'd stop.

But again she avoided looking at him. She kept her eyes on the paper.

Daniel felt ignored. Shut out. It was almost as if...

He clenched his fists, felt his face flushing.

Did she want him to grab for the letter? For her?

Did she want him enraged?

"He has promised me that he will give the profits, all the profits from the book, to the families of the victims of my crimes. Split four ways. That is my dying wish—"

Daniel leaped forward. His hip banged against the side of the table as he reached for the camera. Once again, Emily deftly moved out of the way, managing to keep the camera going and pointed at Daniel's face as he scrambled forward.

But Daniel refused to stop. He lunged again, feeling his robe come open. With the grace of a dancer, Emily avoided Daniel's charges at her. He heard her saying, "You're seeing this, right? You're seeing the level of rage at the truth. And I'm not feeling safe. Okay? Okay?"

Daniel stumbled over Emily's vacated chair, banging both his shins and nearly falling over. He steadied himself and again saw the unblinking camera eye. He looked down, saw the open robe, his dirty pajama pants, his ragged slippers. He felt a loose strand of hair on his forehead.

What am I doing?

But then the back door opened. Daniel turned to see a young man, also in his twenties, fit and muscular with a handlebar mustache and tattoos on his forearms. He entered the kitchen with confidence and came directly toward Daniel.

"Don't worry, babe. I've got him."

The young man easily wrestled Daniel to the floor, restraining his arms and pressing his body against the linoleum with his superior strength and weight.

Daniel couldn't tell for certain, even though he tried to crane his head around to see, but he just knew Emily continued to film, making sure to capture every moment of Daniel's humiliation.

She kept filming when the police came through the door a few minutes later and placed handcuffs on Daniel's wrists.

⁜

Daniel puttered around the kitchen. He brewed coffee, fed the cats, cleaned a few dishes from the night before, and then sat down with the daily paper. It had been nearly two months since the day Emily came over with the camera, broadcasting their confrontation to the whole world of social media. Two months since he spent an uncomfortable twelve hours in a jail cell before a cop came back, opened the door, and told him he was free to go.

"You're lucky," the cop said. "She's not pressing charges."

"What about me?" Daniel asked. "Didn't she violate my privacy?"

"You could try to press charges, I guess." The cop chuckled. "But with that video having gone viral..."

So Daniel just went home, retreating into his house and his limited life even more than before. He ordered food from places that delivered. Skipped his trips to the library. Stayed inside during daylight and walked to the mailbox only after dark.

Despite his efforts, he learned what was going on in the world. Information and people slipped through.

Reporters came to the door. Cranks called on the phone until Daniel changed the number.

A delivery guy for the local Chinese restaurant snapped his picture one night when he opened the door. "I knew it was you. I knew it. You're even wearing the robe."

He snapped a few more pictures before Daniel shut the door, neither collecting his food nor paying.

He'd even heard that a hashtag had been made about him, whatever a hashtag was. #bathrobeman

It all died down after a few weeks, and Daniel hoped that one day, maybe in another month or so, he could venture out again, like a bear emerging from slumber.

The phone rang.

Who had the new number? Daniel thought he knew. Telemarketers. People eager to sell him a cruise or a home security system.

Where were you when I needed you? he wanted to say.

He'd been alone so long, he reached for the phone, happy just to hear another voice.

"Daniel?"

"Yes?"

"Daniel Stone? It's me. Charlie Goodyear."

Daniel hadn't heard the voice in... how many years had it been? Twenty?

When did the last rejection letter come? Twenty years ago?

"Oh," Daniel said. "Hi, Charlie. This is rather unexpected."

"I know, I know."

"Are you still working in New York? Still running the agency?"

"Absolutely," Charlie said. His voice sounded thinner, scratchier. How old would Charlie be now? Sixty-five? Just a bit younger than Daniel. "I keep thinking of retiring since the business has changed so much, but I'm still in New York, and only taking on the projects I really love. It gives me time to enjoy a life where I don't have to always read with a deadline. Sometimes I actually read a book for fun. You know?"

"Sure." Daniel looked around. "No deadlines here."

No fun, either, he wanted to add but didn't.

The line fell silent. Daniel thought he might have embarrassed his former agent, made him feel bad for not keeping Daniel's career alive. *Good,* Daniel thought. *You should feel bad.*

"Well, anyway," Charlie said. "I don't want to keep you too long. I just wanted to let you know about something I learned today. I guess you don't... you're not on the Internet much, are you?"

"Not since I became a hashtag. Whatever that is."

"Right. Of course. I saw all of that." Charlie paused. He started to say something and then stopped. Then he said, "And the video. Anyway. I wanted you to hear from a friend, someone who would soften the blow a little."

"Hear what?" Daniel asked. His coffee grew cold. He hated when the coffee grew cold. But he couldn't drink it. Charlie had hooked him.

"It's about that young woman, Emily Francis. Do you know what I'm going to tell you?"

"That she ambushed Joyce Carol Oates? Started a bar brawl with Stephen King? I give up. I've tried to forget about her."

"Well, she's written a book."

Daniel considered the news for a moment. He knew she was a writer, a journalist. Didn't every journalist want to be a novelist? Isn't that the path he once took?

"Okay," Daniel said. "I guess that makes sense."

When Charlie started talking again, Daniel understood even more.

"Well," Charlie said, "it's really quite fantastic. It's part memoir, part true crime. She must have been working on it for years, given the level of research into her great-uncle's crimes. But then she must have finished it... I mean, just in the last month or so."

"After she came to my house," Daniel said, starting to understand.

"Yes," Charlie said. "You figure prominently in the final chapter, of course."

Daniel reached out and sipped his coffee. Lukewarm.

The day kept getting worse. "Why are you telling me all of this?" *As if I don't know...*

"We're taking it out for offers today. I expect to get quite a few. I think the amount could go into the high six figures. Movie interest is there as well. With her public profile... I mean, ever since the thing with you. The viral video and everything. And it doesn't hurt that she's easy on the eyes. She'll look great in photos and on TV. She's great on social media." Charlie laughed a little. "Why, she's already thought to give a portion of the profits from the books to the victims' families. She thought of that all on her own. The kid's golden."

"Again, why are you telling me this?" Daniel stood up and carried his coffee across the kitchen before splashing it into the sink. It made a dark mess. "Are you rubbing it in?"

"No," Charlie said. "Look, this is all going to break soon. And the book's going to be everywhere. I guess I wanted you to hear it from a friend, so you could prepare for what's going to come. I know you had a bad time before with her, and I don't want that to happen again. I fear it could."

Charlie dropped the mug into the sink. It clattered so loudly it hurt his ears. "Maybe I'll sue you. Maybe I'll sue her. And the publisher. Maybe I'll bring you all down for slander."

"But it's all public, Daniel. The letters, the video. Hell, Emily's grandmother is quoted in the book. You should see her. She's as good on camera as her granddaughter." He paused. "I'm sorry, Daniel. Like I said, I wanted to tell you this way, friend to friend."

Daniel stared out the window above the sink and into the backyard. The grass was high and needed to be cut. The weeds were thick and hearty. Daniel's knees ached, his back ached. He wasn't sure how long he could live in the house and maintain it. But to get into assisted living cost money he didn't have. He remembered his own father after his stroke, wasting away in a nursing home all those years ago, surrounded by screaming, dirty, broken people.

Daniel's future. A one-way trip.

"Let me ask you something, Charlie. Okay, so this Emily kid hit the jackpot. Great story. Great writing."

"The writing's just okay," Charlie said. "The story's great. Actually, the hook is great. That's what gets me. That's what I can sell."

Daniel paused, took that in. Then said, "Okay, so she's set because of this video, because of what she did to me. The social media and the hashtags and whatever else."

"Bathrobe Man," Charlie said.

"Right. Okay." Daniel felt his blood pumping, felt himself getting excited about what he was ready to say. "Look, if she's hot because of that, then isn't the same true of me? I was just as much a part of the story as she was. And you know me, I've got seven manuscripts ready to go. I've been writing all along, the same kind of stuff I wrote all those years ago. They may need a little polishing, but you can help me with that, just like you always did. Now, do you want me to send something your way—"

"Daniel, wait." Charlie's voice was firm, cutting him off before he could go any further into his spiel. "Maybe now isn't the right time."

"Not the right time? Look, I don't know much about anything, certainly not about the way publishing works now, but I understand the idea of striking when the iron is hot. I'm Bathrobe Man. I'm hot now. Why not get the books out while the getting is good? Do you want me to write another one, something new? I can do that. I'm full of ideas. I have outlines and ideas. That's all I think of all day."

Charlie was slow to answer. When he did speak, the words came out reluctantly. "Yeah, you see, you're a different kind of hot right now. To be honest, Daniel, you're kind of radioactive. No one wants to touch you. The combination of the way you went after her on that video and what you did to the families of those murder victims… it's just a tough pill for everyone to swallow."

"But she goaded me," Daniel said. "Yes, I was supposed to share that money, but my father was ill and I… Okay, what if we do it under a pen name?"

"That kind of defeats the purpose of being hot, doesn't it?" Charlie paused and let out a long sigh. "Can I be honest with you, Daniel? You know why your career dried up back then? After you wrote *Sleeping Angels*, you just started to repeat yourself. Sure, the stories were compelling, but it was just the same thing, over and over."

"That's what the publisher wanted. You, too. They all wanted that. Another hit. Another one just like the last."

"But you repeated yourself too much," Charlie said.

"Daniel, I really think you just holed up and wrote. You didn't get out, you didn't engage with the world. I think you lacked any real experiences to write about at some point. So you repeated yourself. And now we all know *Sleeping Angels* wasn't your story, either. I guess I don't know who you are as a writer."

"Okay, what about—"

"Daniel, I have a busy day here. Real busy. But let's say we'll check back in with each other in a few months or so. Okay? That sounds like a good idea. Maybe by then…"

Daniel hung up. He knew he'd never hear from Charlie again.

✚

The lights in the TV studio were bright. Emily tried to concentrate on the host, a handsome middle-aged man with a shaved head. He sat with his legs crossed knee over knee and held papers in his hand, as well as a copy of her book.

"We're back this morning with author Emily Francis. Her newly released book is called *The Sleeping Angels and Me: My Journey to Understand My Family's Past.* Critics are saying this book is part memoir, part true crime hybrid. Emily, the book isn't without controversy. Some of your critics have already pointed out that you have claimed in the past, most notably on that famous Facebook Live video, that you are the great-niece of Michael James

Hart, the man who committed these horrible crimes. You wanted to provide some clarification on that point. You're not actually his great-niece."

Emily maintained her smile. "Not by blood. But our families were very close. My mother was friends with Michael, so we've always referred to him as Uncle Michael. It just felt that way to me growing up."

"But some of the victims' families have objected to your use of the word 'family' in the title of the book."

The lights were hot. Emily felt the heat brushing her face. "Right, but don't we all agree family is more than just blood?"

"And it should be noted that you *are* giving a portion of the profits from this book to the families of the victims. Not a small gesture, considering how well the book is expected to do."

"I didn't want to forget those girls. That's really what this journey has been about for me. Remembering them."

The host looked impressed by her answer. Emily delivered it exactly as the publicist had told her.

"You did quite a bit of research on this," the host said. "It's always impressive when a writer digs in and throws herself into the research process on a book. You also did something interesting to fully understand the story of these girls. Can you tell us about that?"

"I wanted to know everything I could, of course. So I arranged to have myself locked inside the basement of the Hoffman Estate where the girls were killed. I spent the night alone in there just so I could experience some measure of the terror they did."

"Not many writers would go to such lengths."

"That's just part of my process," Emily said. "I needed to know I could get the details right, and then I could give myself permission to write the book."

"And there's a movie in the works," the host said, his voice brightening. "Any details you can give us about that?"

Emily tried to look coy. "Well, it's awfully early for details, but I'm very excited by it."

"Not even a hint about the stars—"

"Well—"

"I'm sorry, Emily." The host lifted a finger, pressing it against the device in his ear. "We're getting some breaking news now. Are we going to cut over to that?" He waited a moment. "You want to do it side by side? Do we have that?"

Emily wasn't sure what to do. She worried that something awful had happened, that a plane had crashed or a school had been shot up by a crazed gunman. She looked to the host for guidance.

"Can you see that monitor right there, Emily?"

The host pointed off camera, and it took a moment for her to locate it, the live shot of the interview. When she saw it, she couldn't really process what she was seeing.

She saw herself, sitting on the nicely appointed set in her new dress. But next to her she saw an image of Daniel Stone. He was speaking into a camera.

"I know you recognize that man, Emily," the host said. "That's Daniel Stone, the infamous Bathrobe Man from your viral Facebook video. Our viewers will note that he's dressed in a nice suit today and seems to have mastered the use of a smartphone. He appears to be on Facebook Live. Is that where that feed is from?" He listened. "Yes, it is. Facebook Live. Do you know where he is, Emily?"

Emily studied the screen. She felt a small surge of anger rising inside her. Was he really doing this on the day of her release?

"He's... He's at the Hoffman Estate. He's standing in front of the house."

"The Hoffman Estate, that's the house where the Sleeping Angels were found murdered. The frightening house where you spent the night in order to research your book."

"Why is he there?" Emily asked. "What is he saying?"

"We've got the audio coming up... right now. Listen."

"...understand why I didn't honor that promise I made to Michael James Hart. It's true I agreed to share that money with the families because it was based on those horrible murders." Daniel paused. He lifted a whiskey bottle and took a long drink. And then another. He stumbled a little. A number of thumb icons started floating across the screen, indicating the approval of viewers. "Just before the book came out, my father suffered a debilitating stroke. I'm an only child, and my father needed a lot of care, so I used the money I received to take care of him. I always intended to make up for it later. I always thought I'd be making much more money from my writing than I ever did. I quit my job to chase the dream of being a bestselling novelist, but it didn't quite work out. I never honored the promise, and people mostly forgot about me." He took another long drink, let out a mild belch. "Until I became Bathrobe Man."

"He's obviously disturbed," Emily said, unable to take her eyes off the spectacle. "He's trying to take advantage of my big day."

"I wish we could talk to him," the host said. "Is someone working on that?"

"So I'm here to fulfill that promise," Daniel said. The number of floating thumb icons increased. "Back at the place where it all began." He reached into his pocket and brought out a bottle of pills, rattling them in front of the camera. "Sometimes people, like houses, outlive their use. And it's best to tear them down and make way for something new. I'm going to do that today. But consider this my last will and testament. I want all proceeds from my literary estate to go toward the families of the victims of the Sleeping Angels murders. In perpetuity. I don't know if that will help them or not, but if this video goes as viral as the last one starring me, maybe it will."

He opened the pill bottle and filled his palm.

"Cheers!" he said, and threw the pills into his mouth.

Emily looked at the host. He watched the screen with his mouth open.

"Oh yes," the host finally said. "We're not going to show this disturbing content."

The screen became obscured by an avalanche of floating thumbs just before the feed was cut, leaving half the screen in darkness before it shifted back to the full shot of the set.

For a moment, Emily and the host sat stunned, staring at their own images reflected back at them. Then the host moved into action, turning to Emily.

"Well, okay... uh...." He pointed at her.

"Emily."

"Thank you, Emily," he said. "And we'll be right back."

❖

Charlie Goodyear sat in his office in Greenwich Village. He wore his half-moon reading glasses as he flipped through a newly submitted manuscript from an unknown author. He liked the voice and the story but wasn't sure if he could sell it.

The truth was he really couldn't focus on the work before him. He anticipated getting news and so kept looking at his watch and then the closed door of his office.

Come on, he thought. *Come on.*

As if she heard his unspoken urging, Charlie's assistant, a twenty-something with a bright smile named Rachel, knocked and came through the door. Her smile was even brighter than usual.

Charlie looked up. "You got the call?"

"I just got off the phone," Rachel said. "We're on the list!"

Charlie let out a tremendous sigh of relief. He jumped out of his chair and came around the desk. For an awkward moment, he and Rachel stared at each other, unsure if they should shake hands or hug. But Charlie decided to go in for the hug. It wasn't every day one of his clients hit the bestseller list.

When he let go of Rachel, he started making plans. "Get the rest of the staff. Have them meet in the conference room. You know where I keep the champagne and the glasses, right?"

"Yes, sir."

"Good, good. I'll give a little toast, say a few words. And, of course, say something in memory of good old Daniel, the man who made all of this possible."

"Indeed."

"Can you imagine, Rachel?" Charlie said. "We've got six more manuscripts of his. And the price just went up. Way up. I have to think about how often to dole them out. Maybe we can get a cowriter to step in. I bet he has some outlines we could use in all of that paper he left behind."

"You don't even need the outlines," Rachel said. "Just use Daniel's name."

"Of course. But don't say that out loud." Charlie clapped his hands together with joy. "That champagne is going to taste so good. Okay, get going."

But before Rachel was out the door, Charlie thought of something.

"Oh, wait, what did they say about Emily's book? Any good news on the paperback?"

Some of the happiness leaked from Rachel's face. "It didn't make the list again. Sorry."

"Shit," Charlie said, but he wasn't that surprised. Daniel's suicide had come on top of the revelations about her fudging her family connection to Michael James Hart. And then when it came out that she really hadn't spent the night in the Hoffman Estate but instead just walked around the grounds for fifteen minutes... well, the worm really turned. The hardcover made the extended list briefly, and then tanked. The paperback looked to be dead on arrival.

"You still want the champagne, right?" Rachel asked.

"Of course, of course. I was just thinking... you know, maybe we could get Emily Francis to do one of those tearful apology videos. Maybe we can get her back on one of the morning shows..."

"Sounds good, sir." Rachel left the room.

Charlie turned and looked out the window, taking in the expanse of the city below him.

He was starting to understand this new world quite well.

It felt good to be back.

CATWOOD

J.T. ELLISON

I had forgotten how the frogs must sound
After a year of silence, else I think
I should not so have ventured forth alone
At dusk upon this unfrequented road.
—Edna St. Vincent Millay

SHE FLOATS, FACEDOWN, HER BROWN hair a fan around her head. Her red sweater has a hole in it; She still wears her sneakers. The water is murky and shallow, reeds and stems poke up around the edges. Dragonflies flit among the stalks. The early morning air is chilly, crickets and cicadas rumble in the thicket. A lone frog cries his frustration. The trees stand guard over the scene, a gentle breeze passing through them, making them shiver and drop their leaves in horror at the sight below.

A fly lights on her shoulder. I should call the police. I'll have to take the car and drive out. There is no service here, which is why we chose it. No wireless, no cell service, no interruptions. Where is everyone? The silence is overwhelming. Why did it have to be me who found her? Why?

I watch her bob there, the water holding her in its gentle embrace, kinder and better than anything she got from the rest of the world, and think, *It couldn't have ended any other way,* and start to scream her name.

⚜

There are five of us heading to the lake, a long-overdue get-together to commiserate, drink, and in general, catch up. Oh, we are supposed to be working—that's what we've told our better halves. A working weekend with the girls. No Internet, no phones. We'll be unreachable, in a small cabin in the woods, only the house and lake and laptops as our companions.

Justifications abound.

We have plans. (There is enough wine to drown a regiment.) We have an agenda. (I've brought all of my Harry Potter discs.) We're going to alternate writing with business discussions. (We're going to gossip until our lips bleed.)

The better halves help us pack—most, at least; there's one who stormed out and didn't come back until after she was gone, so she left a note with the caretaker's phone number, just in case—fill up our gas tanks, carry the bags to the car, kiss our pretty little heads goodbye, assure us they will be just fine, it is only three days, after all, and wave as we drive away.

I remember thinking, *It's a retreat. It will be a few days to gossip and eat and drink and hopefully write. What can possibly go wrong?*

We meet up at a travel gas station on I-65 South. Five cars—that's silly, so we park and all get into mine. No sense wasting all that gas; like I said, we're writers, which means we're all on a budget. I drive—I have control issues and anxiety issues and the idea of not having my own car on a road trip is enough to send me into paroxysms, so everyone agreed in advance that it will fall upon me to take the wheel. They're good friends. They make it sound like it is their idea.

The drive is four hours, south, into the mountains between Tennessee and Georgia. We stop for road trip supplies. We sing to the radio. There is the sharp scent of rum from the backseat—Ellie has her tiny flask out already. I glance in the rearview and to the side. Ellie, Tess, and Carter are in the backseat, Frances is up front with me.

Ellie, Tess, Carter, Frances, and me. Rebecca. The dream team. The five musketeers. My besties, my team, my crowd, my peeps. The girls who get me through every high and low of my career, as I do for them. Everyone in town is jealous of our bond. We came into publishing around the same time, met at a local author event at the local bookstore, and have been thick as thieves since.

I can't imagine my life without any of them.

It's hard to believe that before the weekend is out, one of us will be dead.

✢

It is dark when we arrive, dusk, really, the sky a light gray, but the forest is thick around us and it's dim enough that we have to break out flashlights to find the front door and the keys that were left by the owner for us. This is my fault, though no one wants to blame me. I took a wrong turn, and we got lost on top of this strange mountain, where the trees reach over the road and stop the perspective views we had from the highway. The GPS stopped working halfway up, as the rental company warned us would happen. The paper map they provided, though, is worthless. Later, we will find out the sign has fallen, rotted out from the heavy winter weather, but at the time, it is downright creepy driving up and down the small country roads trying to find our way in.

That's why I missed the house at the end of the lane.

Once our supplies are hauled in from the car under cover of flashlight, we drink some of the wine and tell a few stories, but the mood is ruined by our late arrival, and eventually, we peel off, one by one, to the various bedrooms and nooks and Murphy beds responsible for our weekend rest. Carter and Francie take the bunk beds—they've always been in each other's pockets and don't mind sharing—and Tess claims the small room behind the kitchen. Ellie climbs the stairs to the loft. Once I straighten the kitchen and lock the doors, I head to the master suite, the biggest room, with the private bathroom. I am paying more than the others so I can have this privacy. They understand. I am not holding myself apart. I am simply uncomfortable around people for long, even my dearest friends.

The sky is darker than anything I've ever seen. I pull the curtains, suddenly uncomfortable with the idea of someone being able to look in on me as I sleep. I hate first-floor bedrooms. Someone can watch, someone can climb right in while you're sleeping and you wouldn't ever know. On a second floor, or even a third, there are stairs that creak, hallways with floorboards that pop and crack, so no one can sneak up on you. When my floor, my bed, my most vulnerable self is accessible by anyone—

Stop.

Don't do this.

You're safe.

You're fine.

Quit acting like a child. There are no bogeymen in the woods waiting to take you away.

But as I stand in my pajamas in front of the spotted mirror, brush my teeth and hair, the little voice that lives in my lower spine says, "You should have taken the loft."

❖

I wake early (I never really slept) and decide a walk is in order. No one else is awake yet, though I hear small sounds from the loft, Ellie is dreaming.

I leave through the back door. I press five feet into the brush down a tiny path, and a charming lake appears.

There is a dock, canoes, seats. We saw none of this last night. The girls will be thrilled. I am already envisioning yoga on the faded wood, the cool night air caressing our unblemished skin. There is a path that I assume goes around the lake, which is rather small. Probably two miles around; I can see the other side. I know from the website there are four houses that share the acreage. I set off, grabbing a large stick to use as a shillelagh in case of snakes, or bears.

Most of the path is choked by brush; no one has tended it. But after a few minutes, the track widens, and I walk freely. I'm beginning to feel the sun on my bare shoulders when I see it.

There is a house at the end of the lane.

We must have driven by it as we wound our way into the woods last night, because as the crow flies it's on the opposite side of the lake, but it's not in plain view. There is only one road, which means it's either the first driveway or the last, but I wasn't paying attention.

The house is gargantuan. Symmetrical. Stately stone chimneys rise from either side, fronted by a three-peaked roof. Cream stone blocks are overlaid with crawling ivy; there are ten mullioned windows. A mansion in the middle of the woods. So incongruous! It is the kind of house people build to be admired, not to be hidden away. But it looks as if no one has lived there for a very long time.

Maybe this land belonged to the owners of this majestic place, and they were forced to sell it off to pay the taxes. Or does that only happen in England? It is an English house, one that would suit the countryside in the Lake

District or Devonshire perfectly. It is not what I'd expect in Rising Fawn, Georgia.

I realize I am still, staring, one hand wound around the wrought iron gate. The gates themselves are huge, too, well above my head, and stand open in readiness.

For what?

Impressed, I drag myself away to finish my walk. There is much writing to be done, and I am pleasantly hungry. The house stands guard behind me, watching. Waiting.

I turn at the curve of the lake. It sparkles serenely, catching the light above. The trees are a shroud, but the sun is strong this early morning, and the water rises up to meet it happily.

I feel good. This is going to be a fun few days. I love being with my friends, I love being in a new place. Yesterday's frustrations are beat out of my body as my feet pound the path. I check my steps: 4,500. Excellent. Well on the way to my goal.

I am so fixated on my wrist that I almost miss it.

The sign is crooked, a pointed arrow, and weathered gray.

COME SEE THE CAVE AT CATWOOD

Catwood? Is that the name of the house? Or the land here? And there is a cave? I love caves. I like how each one is a microcosm of the world, living unto itself, not at all concerned with the outer world. Like blood in a vein, doing its business regardless of the external forces driving it. Nourishing and restorative.

I follow the tiny offshoot path deeper into the woods,

mindful to check myself for ticks when I get back,
though it's early in the season, they might not be out yet.
I don't usually pick up ticks or mosquito bites, some odd,
freak-of-nature genetic lottery that makes me untasty to
the seeking bugs. But these long grasses are full of them,
so check I must.

Who was it that lived in a cave in Greek myth? Pan
to the nymph of the Corycian Cave? Or am I thinking
more of Plato and the allegory with which I've always
been fascinated?

I'm upon the cave with almost no warning. The mouth
is jagged, the grass waist-high. There have been no visitors here for some time. It is untended, and that makes
me sad. Perhaps an animal or two make a nest inside,
but I sense great emptiness and loneliness. The disuse is
a shame, really. It's a perfectly good cave, and not at all
far from the house and the lake. It feels friendly, as if it
would like to be rediscovered.

I step to the edge—I'm not so stupid as to go deep
inside without supplies—and stick in my head, using the
flashlight on my phone to assess the state of things. I see
nothing to fear, so I move inside, carefully.

The wind sounds different in here. The walls are cool
and lined with lichen and moss. I imagine what it would
be like to live in this quietude, day in and day out, alone,
a hermit, and find the thought suits me. I'm a great
romantic when it comes to the idea of solitude—I crave
it, seek it out, and yet always find myself surrounded by
people. I've never understood this.

I stand in the darkness and breathe deeply.

It is a good cave.

Happy and sated, I walk back to the cabin. Ellie is making breakfast; there are mimosas and friends whom I love waiting for me. I will write a story for them, my friends, and do yoga with them on the dock, and feel the breeze rustle the leaves and our hair and fill us, and tonight we will drink wine and talk more about our dreams and our fears.

And that is how our day goes.

⚜

There is a hole in the side of the mountain. People are lined up to go inside. It is a cave, my cave, clearly, and it must be a very deep one, because all the people disappear inside but don't come out again for a very long time.

A natural wonder of the world.

A small lady with wildly curly gray hair and blue cat eyes stands outside, waving the people in. I get in line. I move closer, ever closer, until I am face-to-face with the woman. Her pupils are vertical, her skin unlined. Her face is years younger than her body.

"Leave your fear behind. It will only cost you a dime."

"But I have no money."

"Then give me your hand."

I do, anxious now. I need to get inside. I feel the wind begin, deep in the valley behind me, and I know I must be inside the cave when the wind comes or I will be in serious trouble.

"Ah," she says, standing over my hand, stroking and caressing. "You are one of us. You have been chosen. You may go inside."

I scurry in before she changes her mind so the wind will not get me. I am the last person in line. The woman steps to the entrance of the cave behind me, and screams.

My hair stands on end. The pitch hits a note inside me and I want to wail and rend my clothes in response.

Her cry carries into the valley, and the wind rushes faster to greet her. It is shrieking and screaming, moaning as it tries to get inside, wanting, so wanting. But she holds firm, standing with arms up and legs spread, a barrier between us and the soul stealer.

I was in a hurricane once. The wind blew and blew, the trees bent sideways, the fences came down, and the birds were all killed because they were caught in the eye for hours and couldn't land. Exhausted, they dropped like stones, and washed up on the beach a few days later, littering the sand with their plump, bloated bodies.

I sense the birds in the wind, caught in the maelstrom. They are coming, closer and closer, and the old woman stands firm in the face of their fury and screams, "Catwood!" at them. We stand shoulder to shoulder in the cave, screaming the word with her. Chanting over and over.

Catwood.

Catwood.

Catwood.

The wind stops with an unearthly howl of anguish, gushing up against the invisible barrier the woman has cast between us. The birds drop dead at her feet, hundreds of them, all different kinds, and she lies down and dies with them.

✤

I come awake with a start. My heart is pounding in my chest, so hard it hurts, and I realize I've been screaming aloud, because Ellie is standing over the bed with her cell phone flashlight on saying, "Rebecca, Rebecca, it's okay, it's just a dream."

Oh God. It's just a dream.

But when are my dreams only dreams?

"I'm okay, Ellie. I'm so sorry. I didn't mean to wake you."

"It's okay, sweetie." She hugs me, and her breath smells like piña coladas, like the beach. "I had a strange one, too. Must be this cabin. So many creatives have stayed here, they left some of their crazy behind."

"What was yours about?"

Her face drops. "Vera left me."

"Oh, that's harsh. I hate dreams like that."

"No, I mean she left me, for real. She's moving on. She took a job in Seattle, and didn't invite me to come with."

"Oh, Ellie." This explains the heavy drinking that's been going on. I wrap my arms around her, and hold on tight, waiting for the tears. They don't come. No sobbing, no shaking. She's stiff as a board with tension, but otherwise, resigned.

"You okay?"

"I think so. I'm all cried out. Maybe I'll kill her in a story. Might make me feel better." She stands up. "You want me to shut your curtains, so the morning sun won't wake you up?"

"It's all right. I'll do it. Good night, honey. Thanks for waking me up. I really am sorry about Vera."

"Don't tell the others. I'm not ready to be dissected."

"I won't. I promise."

She tiptoes away, and I look to the windows, dread filling me. The curtains *are* all wide open.

⚜

The next morning, to shake off the dream and the sad news of Ellie and Vera's demise, I set off on another walk.

I go the opposite direction this time. The words I've written the previous day—what few there were; we talked as much as we wrote—glow brightly in my mind. They are good words. I am on to a new story, something challenging and exciting. I don't normally write about happy things, my work tends toward the dark and dramatic, but I was hit with the idea as we drank our wine and ate our chicken salad and talked about how we like to be loved.

Love. Why not write a story about love for once? A happy love, with a happy ending. Can I do it? Can I write something that isn't so dark?

I am consumed by darkness. There is a reason, I'm not

being dramatic. I'm over my Goth years. Mostly.

When I was in my early twenties, a friend had a party, and hired a palm reader to entertain.

I had no interest in joining the fun. I didn't want to know my fate, even one custom-made to please by a house medium.

One by one, friends and acquaintances and strangers disappeared into a dark corner of the ballroom, separated from the rest by a long, silver curtain. One by one, they came out again, eyes wide, smiles huge. *I'm going to be rich, I'm going to be famous, I'm going to marry Tad!*

Simply ridiculous, I thought to myself, having another drink. Who would waste their time on such frivolities?

I was the only one in the room who didn't disappear behind the curtain, though my friends egged me on. Finally, the hostess, being a royal canine bitch, tracked me down. "You're being a spoilsport. Everyone else did it."

"If everyone else jumped off a bridge, would you expect me to follow suit?"

"No, Rebecca. I'd expect you to have the good manners to go along with something utterly harmless so people will stop talking about you. Why do you always have to be the center of attention?"

Now, that last was unfair of her. Being the center of attention was the very last thing I wanted. It was not my fault that I stood out from the crowd—tall women always do.

"I'm not doing anything."

"Yes, you are. You're ruining my party," she cried, flouncing off to be ministered to by her minions.

Oh, for God's sake. Drama queen much?

So now everyone *was* paying attention to me, and I had no choice but to slip behind the damn curtain myself.

The woman was older, not plain but not pretty. She would be easily forgotten if you bumped into her on the street, if you didn't look closely. But when I stepped in, she raised her face to mine curiously, her eyes violet, as dark as a midnight sun, with an eerie gold ring around the irises.

"I've been waiting for you."

"Why? Why didn't you just leave?"

"I promised the hostess I'd read all the guests' palms. It was in our contract. You're my only holdout."

"Great."

"Not into fortune-telling?" The hint of a laugh in her melodic voice made me take a breath. I relaxed.

"No, I'm not. My friend guilted me into it."

"You don't want to know your future?"

"No. A—I don't believe in it. B—I want to live my life without some random prediction hanging over me. I believe we manifest our own destinies. If you look at my hand and tell me I'm going to die of cancer in three months, then I'll spend three months worrying about dying, instead of living. I'd rather be ignorant and have bliss."

"Commendable. How's this? I'll make you a deal. If I see something bad, I won't tell you. Promise."

"Whatever." I sat down and thrust out my hand. "Let's just get this over with."

She hesitated only a moment, then took my hand in

hers. She didn't look at it, simply ran her palm against mine, as intimate and startling as a lover's kiss. She turned my hand over in hers; cool and soft, it was a gentle caress, careless even.

Her brows knitted, and she turned my hand palm up, tracing her fingers lightly over my skin. Her hand tightened on mine.

"Oh, honey. You're one of us."

"What? What do you mean?"

"You can see death. You can see it coming. You've been doing this since you were a child, you poor thing. You must be…"

"Stop. This is ridiculous."

But I knew it wasn't. She spoke the truth. I had a weird sort of knack for predicting death. It had been with me as long as I could remember, and it was something I never, ever discussed. With anyone. No one knew.

Her violet-and-gold eyes were empathetic and kind, the slight horror she'd shown when she first took my hand gone now, replaced with understanding. "We can teach you how to control it. So you can shut them out. You don't have to live with the fear and chaos anymore. You don't need to be their conduit."

I jerked my hand away. "I have no idea what you're talking about."

"Please. Take my card. Call me. I have people I can introduce you to…"

But I was gone, out the curtained wall, out of the party and the simpering gazes of my gullible friends.

Back at the house, I sip my morning tea, watching my

friends goof off at the breakfast table, Ellie slightly quieter than the others, and wonder—if I had listened to the medium back then, would anything have been different?

✢

We have each found our place in the house. I prefer a view of the water, and so the deck couch is mine. It is under a pitched cedar roof, and it's early spring, so I'm a bit chilly in the shade. I light a fire, and it warms things up nicely. I write my love story, praying it won't take a turn for the worse. It's hard for me to write anything that doesn't have a death in it. Thanks a lot, fortune-teller, for manifesting *that* destiny for me. Though maybe it's better. Since my run-in with her, I've learned things. How to shield myself. How to look away when the small movements begin out of the corner of my eye. How to protect my dreams from the dead. It almost always works. Almost always. Last night's bizarre dream aside, I haven't had a dream about death in months.

So far today, none of my characters have died, so there's a bonus.

For our afternoon break, I tell the girls I want to show them something special, and they faithfully troop out the door with me, down the path, to the mansion.

The gates still stand open and welcoming.

"What a wonderful house," they cry.

"Let's go inside," I reply.

"Rebecca," Francie says, "we'll get in trouble if we do."

"No, we won't. It will be fun. I promise. No one's here, it's clearly abandoned."

"Not a good idea, sugar," Tess says. "We might get hurt, you never know if there's a floorboard loose, or something else. We'd be trespassing." Tess, the mother of the group, always looking for hidden dangers.

Ellie shushes her. "Come on, don't be a baby. I think it's a great idea. Here's what we should do. Let's go in and check things out, and tonight, as a writing exercise, we can all write a short story about the house. Something quick and easy, but it will be a fun exercise. I like writing about inanimate objects."

"All right, Ellie, I think that's a great idea," Tess says, fluffing her hair off her shoulders. "God, it's hot right here. The breeze has died." She manhandles the mass into a ponytail, fans her neck. "Ah, that's better."

Francie is still staring at the house, unmoving, but I set off toward the drive, and Tess and Ellie follow.

Carter, though, shakes her head. "I'll see you guys later. I'm not one for ghosts and haunted houses."

"It's not haunted, silly. It's just someone's lake house," I reply.

"If that's the case, then you're going to be trespassing. You and Tess and Ellie go on ahead. I think Francie and I are going to go back. We'll make lunch, have it all ready for y'all when you come back with the details of what's inside. Right, Francie?"

Francie, who is reluctantly stepping toward the house, sighs in relief and hangs back. "Great idea. Do be careful, ladies. Come on, Carter, I'll race you."

They run off giggling like schoolgirls, and Ellie shakes her head, takes a wee nip from her flask, offers it to me. I take a sip gratefully, the sting of the harsh alcohol rising up in my sinuses and warming my stomach.

"Those two are wimps," Ellie says.

"Come on," I reply, surging forward, emboldened by the drink. "Let's see what's what."

The front door is conveniently unlocked. I have no idea why I thought it would be, but am relieved to find it so.

The house itself is empty. No one has been here, or lived here, in quite some time. Not weeks, not months. Years. It has an abandoned air. A thick coating of dust lies on all the tables in the foyer. We leave footprints as we make our way in.

"Who would just leave a place like this?" Ellie wonders aloud. Her voice rings in the hallway, and the house seems to sigh in relief.

Someone is home.

It doesn't like being deserted. It is a place to laugh, and to love. To be cherished. Not to be left alone with an encroaching wood and an empty cave.

I don't realize I am speaking out loud until Tess says, "You speak like it has feelings, Rebecca. It's just an old house."

I clear my throat. "You know me, always spinning stories. I can't see a cloud without wanting to write its tale."

"You really are weird," she replies, fondly, and wanders toward the stairs.

I take the left parlor, Ellie takes the right. The furniture sits uncovered. Mice have taken up residence in the damask chairs, birds in the fireplace chimney, a scattering of feathers below on the marble. The thought of birds trapped in the chimney brings back my strange dream, and I shudder. I do not like dead things.

Through the formal parlor is a ballroom. I feel like I am spying on a moment in time, frozen in amber, unchanging all these years.

It was clearly a grand ball. The vestiges are left, champagne flutes on the mantels, as if their owners were called away to dance and left them, forgotten, in the detritus of the party. Silver trays, now darkened to black with bits of ancient mold stuck to them, balance on small tables. A grand piano stands open, with four other seats to its right—a cello, two violins, and a harp sit abandoned.

It is as if the party ended, all the people left mid-dance, disappearing entirely, including the servants and the owners.

"Rebecca, let's get out of here. I'm getting creeped out." Ellie is standing at my elbow, whispering to me, and I nod. I'm getting creeped out, too. "Where's Tess?"

"Here."

She is standing on the opposite side of the room, holding something in her hands.

"What do you have there?"

"A guest book. The last entry is from 1929. Seems there was a big party, everyone's name is listed. The Rookwoods, the Wrights, the O'Connells, the Archers, the Bouchers. It goes on and on. There must have been a hundred people here for this party."

The paper is old and crumbling. I take a photo of the pages so we won't disturb it more.

"It's so strange, isn't it? Something clearly happened to everyone."

"Something wicked happened here," Ellie says. "It feels all wrong. There must be something in the papers about it. We can look it up when we get home. Come on. Let's bolt. This place is giving me the willies."

As we are walking to the front door, a portrait in the hallway catches my eye. There are several portraits in a row, the family, clearly. But only one holds the visage of a woman with cat eyes and wiry gray hair. Looking at her, I can almost feel her breath on my face. She seems so alive, so annoyed to be stuck in the painting. Like she wants to walk out of the house with us. To be free.

I don't realize I've stopped in my tracks until the girls beckon me, and with a last glance at the woman who saved the valley from the wind, I go with them gladly, closing the door gently behind me.

⚜

That night, we decide to go out to dinner. I think everyone feels disconcerted by the story we bring back from the house, and want a moment to connect with the real world.

The restaurant is ten minutes away, on top of the rise, with a view of the valley below. It is a BBQ joint, and the smells of hickory and vinegar permeate the air of the parking lot and make my mouth water. It feels odd to be back in civilization; though we've only been gone two days, we've become accustomed to the quiet rhythm of the lakeside cottage. It has a magical air around it, a perfect spot for creatives. We've all been writing up a storm, and now it is time to celebrate.

And maybe check our e-mail. Or even do a quick bit of research on who belonged to the lost house in the woods.

Both prove fruitless to me. I have a few e-mails but nothing of import, and I can't find anything about the house.

The food is delicious, though, and we eat until our sides creak, and drink two bottles of wine. I steer clear after the first glass, I'll have more when we get back to the house. Someone has to see us safely home.

When the waitress comes over to hand out the checks, Ellie asks what we've all been wondering about.

"Are you familiar with the history of this area?"

"Well, sure. Y'all visiting?"

I only want to stab out her eyes for a moment—clearly we are strangers, and as such are visiting—but I refrain. "We're in a cabin nearby for a few days."

"Ah. Girls' weekend," she says with a knowing smile, and I don't correct her. I don't like strangers knowing my business.

"There a big abandoned house across the lake from our cabin. Do you know anything about it?" Carter asks, her words a challenge.

"The old Atwood place?"

We're silent. We don't know what it's called.

"It's abandoned," she adds helpfully.

"That's the one," Ellie says, and I hear the laugh she's biting back. "Do you know anything about it, or the people who used to live there?"

The waitress has been friendly until now, but her face grows wary. "The Atwoods, they owned all the land in this town. Used to be mill owners, I think. But they all left decades ago."

"Who owns the house?" I ask.

"I don't know. No one really goes up there. It's kind of scary, and it's private property. I wouldn't want to get caught snooping around."

A man I take to be her boss walks by at that exact moment, giving her a *hurry up* look—a line has begun to form outside, the chairs in the restaurant's porch and foyer are full. A popular place. The only restaurant on top of the mountain, I suspect.

When he turns away, she gives us a pasted-on grin. "Y'all have fun with your computers. Come back and see us."

It's not until we are searching again for the drive in that I realize what she said. We never said anything about working or writing.

I can't shake the eerie feeling that parades down my spine.

They are watching us.

⚜

The Atwoods.

The name rings a bell with Carter, who is our resident historian. The small cabin has a small library, which she took apart the day we arrived, and there is a little book on the area that she found the first night. She pulls it off the shelf, sits at the battered kitchen table, and reads.

"The Atwoods made their money logging the mountains around here," she announces, pushing her glasses up on her nose and taking a sip of wine. "The family settled in Rising Fawn in the 1800s. They were carpetbaggers, from Maine originally, drawn down to the South by the promise of large tracts of land and good prices on the logging. Caused all sorts of a stir when they bought the mountain and built their house."

"Maybe they were tired of being cold in the winter. Can you imagine Maine in the 1800s? Brr," Ellie says, shivering. She pours us each another glass of wine. I've lost count now, but it is our last night, and we're planning to sleep in, and clean the cabin in the morning instead of working, then get on the road by early afternoon. I am pleasantly tipsy.

"Does it say what happened to them?" Tess calls from the kitchen, where she is manhandling open another bottle with a wine key.

"Nope." Carter flips a few more pages. "Worthless piece of crap book. All it says is that the house has been kept in trust since the '30s, and the whereabouts of the family remains a mystery."

Tess cracks the bottle. We hear her giggling and saying, "Oops," then she appears in the door, wavering slightly, the bottle clutched in her hand.

Francie takes it from here. "We'll just have to do some more research on it when we get back, I guess. Who wants to watch a movie?"

The mysterious house is forgotten then, as we sail away to lands unknown on the back of a writer we all admire.

But I can't help myself. Ten minutes in, I get up and draw all the curtains in the house.

✤

A storm rattles through overnight. Rattles, literally: We are under a tin roof, and the acorns fall from the trees with a clatter, waking everyone up. They sound like gunshots, and we cower, laughing nervously, as they ping and pong off the roof. Lightning flares, and the lights flicker.

"Make a fire," I tell Carter, who listens without arguing, for once. We don't want to be left in the dark entirely.

The moment the flames go up, the lights go out, and Carter gives me a thankful look. We look for candles, find a few, line them up on the table. No one can sleep now, the wind and rain are howling, howling, up from the valley, and I can't help myself, chills crawl up and down my arms. That wind feels familiar. It feels malevolent.

We huddle together in front of the fire, hoping for the lights to come back on. I debate telling them about my dream, about the wind and the cave, but decide against

it. I fear I will manifest something if I speak it aloud.
It's one of the reasons I never speak my dreams. Maybe
I should have talked more to the palm reader all those
years ago. As it is, all I do is write them down and pray
death does not come knocking.

We huddle together, telling jokes and stories. Eventually, Ellie admits her secret, and the rest of the night is
passed in drunken anger toward a woman we all love.
But we'll side with Ellie. She is ours. Fuck Vera.

⚜

We wake early by the still-warm ashes of the fire. The
electricity remains out, which means no way to run the
dishwasher or clean the sheets and towels. Everyone is
exhausted. I am in favor of packing up and paying the
fine for leaving the house as is, but I am overruled. In a
huff, I take another early morning walk.

The lake seems so much less ominous when the sun is
out.

I want to go to the cave again, but I can't find the sign.
The storm must have knocked it down. Standing on the
edge of the lake, I realize much of the thicket has been
cleared out, the grasses lying flat against the still-steam-
ing earth. The landscape looks different. I can see small
gray lumps in the distance.

I find the graveyard in a squashed copse beside the lake.

The Atwoods are heavily represented, but there are
other names, older names. Names that match the guest

book we found in the house.

I wander quietly, until I see a grave with a Gothic marble angel perched on top.

CHARLISE ELEANORA ATWOOD

1898–1929

BELOVED

C. Atwood.

Catwood.

The word we screamed in my dream at the mouth of the missing cave. This must be the woman from the portrait.

"She was a great woman."

The voice comes from my right, and I startle like a hare from the brush. The waitress from last night is standing on the edge of the cemetery. She is wearing shorts and running shoes, her long brown hair done up in a ponytail, earbuds in.

"Out for a run?" I ask, proud that my voice only wavers slightly.

"Day off. Finally. I've been stuck pulling doubles all week. Hey, sorry if I was rude the other night. I couldn't tell you more about the Atwood house, my boss doesn't like us talking about it. He's worried people will start gathering again, like they did the last time. He's an O'Connell, you see."

"The last time? O'Connell?"

"Devon O'Connell was Charlise's betrothed. They never got a chance to marry, their daddies hated each other, and wouldn't consent to the match. So they ran off together, and a year later, Charlise came home alone, pregnant, looking like she'd been through a war. Only twenty, but her hair was as gray as my granny's. She would never say what happened, would never tell where Devon was. The families were already at odds, it drove a spike right through them. Legend has it the Atwoods threw a party, a big party, to welcome her home, and the O'Connells showed up en masse to find out once and for all what happened, and killed every one of them Atwood folk."

"Good God, that's horrible."

"It surely was. Charlise, she got away, they say, managed to hide out in a cave somewhere on the land up around here, had her baby in secret by herself. She wandered, alone, raised that baby, sent her off into the world, then lay down and died."

"How sad."

The girl looks into the distance, shading her eyes. "She was touched, in a way, when she came back. Some say she had the sight, some say she could talk to ghosts. I don't know the real truth, but whatever happened that night, after the massacre, there were no bodies. All the Atwoods disappeared, along with everyone at that party. A whole community, gone. No one knows what happened. Only a few people from the families survived, the children who were home with their nannies while their parents died, and disappeared. This whole place is populated by strangers now."

She spits out the word and I feel it as strongly as if an arrow has been shot into my heart.

"If everyone disappeared, where did they go?"

She shakes her head, plays with the cord of her earbuds. "I don't know. No one knows. The wind took them, that's what the legend says. But that's silly. Old wives' tale. You have a good day. Be safe getting back up to Nashville, you hear?" She starts to jog away, but I yell, "Wait!"

She stops, jogging in place.

"If there aren't any bodies, why is there a graveyard?"

She shrugs. "Gotta honor the dead somehow. Besides," and she grins, "you never know who might come along to tend it."

❖

I try to make sense of this tale as I hurry back to the cabin. This is the second time that girl has said something about us that we haven't shared, and I am damn good and ready to get out of here as quickly as possible. The bucolic pond has suddenly become alive and hateful, and I fear we are not safe.

I shouldn't have gone to the cave.

We shouldn't have gone into the house.

My dreams are letting in something old, something evil, and I must stop it, I must stop them.

They are watching. They are waiting.

I round the last curve and realize the path has been washed out. I am forced to turn around, go back the way I came, toward the running girl and the graveyard. The idea fills me with so much dread I decide to cut across the marshy thicket, knowing if I head toward the sun I will run into the cabin.

But I am disoriented, and as the reeds part in front of me, I realize I have gone in a circle and have ended up back at the cave.

"Rebecca," a gentle, mother's voice calls, the words a whisper on the wind. "Come and see."

The rushes begin to move, the breeze settling in, the updraft from the valley below growing stronger. I am powerless against it. My feet move without my consent.

The maw opens to welcome me back, and I begin to shake. I am inside now, deeper than before, the light flickering on my phone. The smell is different, rancid, wrong. I know it's only mud kicked up by the storm, by the rain, by the wind, but something is stirring in my primordial brain, and I stumble. I go down hard, on both knees, falling forward into the muck.

I land awkwardly. Something juts into my ribs, and the pain makes me lurch to the side.

I see the faces then, the skulls, the mouths agape, the bones of their lost bodies white in the darkness.

The family is here. The Atwood family is inside the cave. The rising water has unearthed their bones. The wind can't get them anymore.

*

I run until I can run no more. I am covered in mud and muck and the dust of a nearly century-old grave. I still have no real idea what happened in the cave, how I have manifested this horror, but if I can make it back to the lake, make it back to the girls, all will be forgiven. We will leave, and never come back.

The girl is standing in the trees. She has approached silently, sneaking up behind me. When she steps from behind the trunk of the ash, I no longer see the modern running shorts and bra top, nor earbuds, but an odd black dress, a braid, the glint of silver eyeglasses, all in a blur because she scares me and I run. It's the only reasonable thing to do, considering there is a strange woman approaching me. I run as fast as I can back toward the house. The girls will save me. The girls will shelter me.

"You there. You. Girl. Stop! What are you doing? That woman needs help. What have you done? My God, is she…?"

She stops her pursuit to stare into the lake. *It's a trick,* my mind says. *Keep running.* But I look back once, in time to see her face clearly in the reflection of the lake light. Her face changes, brows coming together as if she's just had a thought. It is shaded in blue.

And then she smiles. And I feel the wind begin to stir beneath her hands.

Shit. Oh, this is not good. Not good at all.

I am fast but she runs me down easily, her feet pounding on the hard earth behind me, closer and closer, until I am down in the dirt on my knees, and she rolls on top of me, breathing heavily.

"Stop fighting. This is your destiny. You have to come with me. Mother wants you."

On the ridge, I see her, standing, arms up, as if she is beckoning me home.

"Catwood," I whisper.

Charlise smiles benevolently, and her words float down from the hill. "You are chosen. You are one of us."

My face is in the water before I can draw a breath. The girl holds me there until I can see the small things crawling in the mud below, small silver fish come to explore my nose, my mouth, my eyes and ears. And then I am adrift. The fear and horror have fled. It is a beautiful place, green and gold and silver. I love looking at the microcosm. It is like the cave, but wet, and willowy.

When I am fully relaxed, the girl helps me from the water, and together, side by side, we march up the hill to protect the land below.

From a distance, I hear my friends, crying, calling, and one voice above the rest, Ellie, shrieking my name over and over, as if I am a lost dog.

I glance back over my shoulder as we walk away.

Ellie is pulling the body from the water.

My body.

Why did it have to be her who found me? She will never recover from this. She will always blame herself.

My friends gather on the muddy bank, crooning my name, speaking as one, a chant being taken up by the hillside and the crickets and the birds and the frogs, and the wind catches the tune and whistles along. It starts as one word, then becomes another, one more sibilant, more cunning, more familiar to the fallow fields.

"Rebecca *Catwood*, Rebecca *Catwood*, Rebecca *Catwood*."

LOOKING FOR THE LOST

ARIEL LAWHON

Phelipeaux Inlet
An hour's boat ride from New Orleans
3:00 a.m. today

AFTERWARD, I THOUGHT OF WAYS to save her. It's an old man's fantasy, you see. Going back. Playing *what if.* A way to keep yourself sane during the long unending years that follow losing a woman like that. But if I've learned anything, it's that you can't go back. You can't do things over. There is only, ever, right now.

And in this particular moment I'm standing at the edge of a mass grave, at three in the morning, flanked by adolescent boys. I paid them to bring me here. Half up front and half when we're back at the Orleans Marina. And if they aren't stoned already, I'm certain they will be by lunchtime. Two hundred dollars goes a long way on Bourbon Street.

As for me, I came here to find a body. But I can't find the body until I find the burial manifest. And that will require a number of felonious acts, not the least of which includes breaking and entering. Thus the boys. Two of them. Carlos and Wyatt. Or Piss and Vinegar, as I came to think of them on our choppy ride up the Mississippi.

"It's dark as shit," Piss says behind me.

"It's the middle of the night, dumbass." Vinegar is scared, and that makes him loud. Brash. It also makes him dangerous, but beggars can't be choosers.

"Vinny," I say, searching out his tall, arrogant form in the darkness. "I'm calling you Vinny from now on. Vinegar is a stupid name."

"My name's Carlos," Vinny says, and then turns to Piss. "Old man's gone batshit crazy."

I'm not so old that I don't enjoy the hint of fear in his voice—a stutter at the end of each hard consonant.

Piss shrugs beside me. "Old man has the money. Who cares?"

"Old man has a name," I say.

Neither of them asks.

Baker. Henri Baker. Detective Henri Baker, thank-you-very-goddamn-much-for-asking.

Vinny turns this way and that, peering into the varying shades of blackness, and asks, "Where we going?"

"That way." I point toward the deeper shadows. Beyond them lie a road and a church, a building filled with decaying shoes, and our destination: an abandoned chateau turned insane asylum turned records depository.

Two things I required of Piss: that he secure the motor-boat, and that he bring the flashlights. He passes them out now, handing mine to me rather than tossing it like he does to Vinny. I resent this and I yank it out of his hand. Then I turn and lead the way, carefully skirting the open trench that lies to our right.

I've grown accustomed to death over the last four decades, but still the bodies make me nervous. A row of coffins is stacked three deep and two wide at the bottom of the hole. Names are scrawled on the side of each pine box in the off chance that someone comes to claim them. They are covered, loosely, by sheets of plywood, waiting for a few more dearly departed to fill the trench so it can be covered over with the loamy soil. A work detail from the Louisiana State Penitentiary—or the Potter's Navy, as they call themselves—won't fill in the trench until it's full, most likely tomorrow by the look of things.

Vinny makes the sign of the cross as he passes the coffins, and my heart clenches. Suddenly June is beside me. I can feel her as I navigate all this death. I can almost see her long, thin fingers flutter across her chest as she tiptoes through this eerie place, praying for the dead. *God, our father, your power brings us to birth.* My beautiful wife—nothing more than ghost and memory. *Your providence guides our lives, by your command we return to dust.* Pronounces blessing on the nameless dead beneath my feet. *Lord, those who die still live in your presence, their lives change but do not end.* Petitions for all the souls known to God alone. *May they rejoice in your kingdom, all our tears are washed away.*

LOOKING FOR THE LOST

If there's a lonelier place on earth, I've never seen it. Phelipeaux Inlet is accessible only by water and boasts a population of twenty thousand: all of them dead. This is where New Orleans dumps her forgotten souls. The misfits are buried here. The drug addicts and prostitutes and runaways. Unclaimed. Abandoned. Misplaced. Don't know what it means to sign papers for a "city burial" when you're standing in the morgue, broke and desperate and trembling from the shock of identifying your loved one? This is it. Where they send the remains. You'll never be able to lay flowers on the grave, however. Phelipeaux Inlet is not open to the public. As a matter of fact, admittance is forbidden without written permission from the Louisiana Department of Corrections.

Trespassing.

Add that to my list of crimes.

Forty years ago, a body was found by divers beneath the pier at Orleans Marina. It was chained to a fifty-pound cinder block. Poor bastard sunk like a stone. And he might have stayed there forever—little more than bones and rotted clothing—if city planners hadn't decided that the marina needed some beautification. The skeleton was intact. Male. Middle-aged. And completely unidentifiable. The only thing they could determine for sure was cause of death: blunt-force trauma to the head. The body was sent here in a burlap sack marked *John Doe*. And I will not leave this cemetery until I learn exactly where they buried him.

I believe Phelipeaux Inlet to be the final resting place of the missing and long-assumed-dead gangster Bertrand

Guidry. He's the one stuffed in that burlap sack. I'm certain of it. I know the date of his death: June 14, 1977. I know the murder weapon: a cast iron skillet. And I know why my wife killed him.

Shit.

"Don't do that!" I holler at Vinny. He's kicking a short, white burial marker. There are no headstones in this cemetery, only steel posts stuck in the dirt like Burma Shave signs for the dead. This one reads *173* and it's listing heavily to the side after Vinny's repeated attacks.

"Why do you care?" He stomps it again. In the beam from my flashlight I can see the soil around its base crumbling, showing the gnarled roots of a clump of grass.

"Have a little respect for the dead."

"Fuck." Kick. "The." Kick. "Dead." Kick. With every word Vinny smashes his boot against the post even harder.

Vinny is young and arrogant, and his back is turned to me. When he lifts his foot to deliver another blow, I knock his other leg out from under him. He lands, hard, on his back. I'm quicker than I should be, what with the age and arthritis and a general case of I-don't-give-a-shit-anymore. I've got one foot pressed against his head, shoving it to the ground, before he can even roll onto his side.

The toe of my polished loafer digs into his temple. "You like that?" I ask.

Vinny thrashes on the ground, and Piss just looks at me, stunned. "You like messing with the dead? Go ahead. There's one about twelve inches beneath your mangy skull."

"Get the fuck off me, you fucking old man!"

"Stop using that word. It's rude."

"Fuck you."

I press harder.

He screams, flailing his arms and legs. "Okay, I'll stop. Shit. I'll stop."

"Say, 'Please.'"

"Please."

"Say, 'Please, *Detective* Baker.'"

Both boys freeze. Piss takes a step backward and throws a look over my shoulder to where he dragged the boat onto the shore not long ago.

"You're a cop?" Vinny whines. "You didn't say you were a cop!"

"You didn't ask. But since you're curious, New Orleans PD. Retired. Does that bother you?"

His head shakes beneath my foot. "No. Not at all."

"You want up?"

"Yes, please." He pauses and then adds, "Detective."

"You still want the rest of your money?"

"Yes."

"You won't get it until we're back at the marina."

"Right," Vinny says.

"So no more problems?"

"None."

I lift my foot and step away.

Vinny scrambles to his feet, shoulders squared, and turns back to the boat. He gives me the one-fingered salute and shouts over his shoulder, "Fuck you, old man! I did my part. I got you here. Find me when you're done."

Piss found the boat and brought the flashlights, but Vinny is the genius with maps. He's the one who navigated the river and the estuaries and brought us to the inlet without a single wrong turn. I don't need him for the next part. Let him sit and pout, for all I care.

"This way," I say to Piss and turn my flashlight toward the overgrown road that leads into the cypress forest. The trees look humanoid in the dark, with their bulbous trunks and fingerlike roots, as if they might stand up and start moving toward us at any moment. The air smells of moss and river and damp soil. It smells like the sweat of a teenage boy.

Piss looks back toward the boat. Vinny sits in the prow, scowling at us. "What if he leaves without us?"

"He won't."

"But—"

"He won't."

"Whatever you say, old man. Now where are we going?"

"To commit a felony."

Piss grins for the first time since we pulled ashore. There's a gap between his front teeth wide enough to spit through, and I think this makes him look younger somehow. "Why didn't you say so in the first place? I specialize in felonies."

I'd be lying if I said this surprised me. He's the sort of kid I'd have enlisted as an informant if I was still on the force.

It takes us less than ten minutes to hike across the quiet, overgrown inlet. We can see only as far as the beam of our flashlights will reach, but the road is clear enough. After a while we pass a redbrick chapel drowning in vines. It's an empty nest of a building, front door boarded with plywood, stained-glass windows pitted by the straight aim of vandals. No one prays there anymore.

And yet June would have loved it, would have insisted on stopping. *Isn't it sad? Isn't it lovely?* she would whisper, and grab my hand. She'd climb through one of the low windows to inhale the scent of decaying wood and damp stone, kneel before the altar, and breathe prayers—for me, perhaps. God knows I need them.

My body aches, desperate for her phantom touch, the way she'd tug my earlobe between thumb and forefinger. Her cool hand at the base of my neck. Feet tucked between my calves as she slept. Anything. Everything. I miss the entirety of her. Forty years has not diminished this longing.

We move on, and the chapel is soon hidden behind a bend in the road. It's a bit lighter now, getting closer to dawn, and the vision of my wife evaporates. Her departure is like pulling the scab from an aging wound, one I pick constantly to keep the pain fresh.

Another building comes into view—a workhouse where the female inmates of Bergeron Asylum were put to work re-soling shoes. I am told that the floor is piled with hundreds of rotting shoes, that it looks like a cobbler's nightmare inside. But I don't care about the workhouse tonight. I'm looking for the asylum itself, the former Bergeron Chateau. A century-old, three-story brick manor built to look like a sprawling home in the

French countryside. It became an asylum when its owner, Sabine Bergeron, began seeing snakes on the walls. Until her death, she was the only patient. Afterward, her family realized they could make a fortune housing New Orleans' psychotic upper crust. Then, decades later, the city bought the entire three-hundred-acre estate and turned it into a taxpayer-funded cemetery.

Another bend in the road and the Chateau looms before us, dark and imposing. At one point the house was blocked by heavy, wrought-iron gates, but these have come loose from their posts and hang lopsided at either side of the driveway. Weeds have choked out the lawn, and vines cover much of the building.

Once burials became the primary function of Phelipeaux Inlet, the Chateau fell into disrepair. It is, apparently, bad form to house the mentally ill in the same location they will most likely be buried after one too many shock treatments. I have elected not to tell Piss most of what has happened here over the years. Adolescent boys are famous for their lack of courage. So it is with complete ignorance that he struts down the driveway, up the crumbling steps, and picks the single padlock barring us from the Chateau.

The doors swing open with a groan and reveal a cavernous entry hall filled with cobwebs, scattered leaves, and the smell of mildew. Beneath the clutter I can see patches of a large tile mosaic on the floor. Swirling bits of green and yellow tile are illuminated in the beam of my flashlight. I think they might be vines or a wreath, and I understand why Sabine Bergeron lost her ever-loving mind. I'd start seeing snakes on the walls, too, if I spent the better part of my life trapped in this house staring at something like that.

"There," I say, pointing to a set of closed doors on the right. "The records room."

The heavy French doors are swollen shut, and it takes both of us yanking on them with all our strength before they wheeze outward. Inside are tables and file cabinets and crates piled high with leather-bound books. There is no apparent order, no rhyme or reason to where things are placed. Unlike most archives, you will not find a card catalog or sections of any kind. There are only piles and piles of log books.

"You're kidding me?" Piss says.

"Surely you weren't expecting the Library of Congress?"

He gives me a blank, clueless glance, then reaches toward the crate nearest him. He lifts a logbook from the stack and waves it in front of me. "We came here for *this*? I thought we'd find something valuable."

"It's valuable to me. You're welcome to wait at the boat until it's time to go."

Piss hooks a thumb behind him. "Out there? With the bodies?"

"I won't be long."

He grips his flashlight a little tighter and slides out the door. I wait until I can't hear the soft thump of his footsteps or his muttered curses. I wait until the crashing in my chest slows and I've caught my breath. I wait until I can almost feel June's phantom breath on the back of my neck, urging me on. She would want me to do this, I think. Her choice wasn't so dissimilar in the end. But God, I wish she could see me finish it on her behalf. She was the reason for it then, and she's the reason for it now. At least that's what I tell myself. Because if I don't finish this, Guidry will eventually be found. John Doe will be identified. And I can't let that happen. Not after all this time.

Trouble is, it would be hard to find the burial manifest even if I knew what I was looking for. But this... this is a rat's nest. Yet there has to be some sort of order. So I step back, slowly illuminating the room with the beam of my flashlight. Dozens of file cabinets are shoved up against the wall. Each cabinet has the year stamped on a metal plaque at the top. But they aren't in numerical order after 1960, and they stop altogether after 1981.

I can tell from the occasional open drawer that each cabinet is stuffed with book after book of burial manifests. A quick glance at the nearest one shows that each logbook has one hundred pages and there are five names per page, listing occupant, age, relatives, plot number, and any other pertinent information. So, math. That's what this will take. Math and a reason and patience. All things I possess in abundance. It's clear that the boxes and crates stacked on the tables are the newest arrivals to Phelipeaux Inlet, which means the file cabinets hold the earlier residents. 1977 is shoved into a far corner.

I find Bertrand Guidry as the sun comes up. He's in the third drawer down, fifth book in. *John Doe. Remains found beneath the pier at Orleans Marina. Brought to Phelipeaux on*

June 14, 1987. Buried under plot marker 185. No other infor-mation available.

The irony of this notation makes me snort. Guidry was brought here ten years to the day after he died. No wonder I don't remember. I observed that particular anniversary by listening to Louis Armstrong on vinyl and marinating my liver in cheap bourbon.

I tap his name—handwritten in a blockish script—and then rip the page from the book. It's impulse, really. I could fold the paper and take it with me, a memento. But instead I wad it in my hand, overcome by sudden, raging emotion. If not for this bastard, I might still have June. She might have lived long enough to bear us a child or get lines around her eyes or complain of fat thighs and gray hair. She might not have died so young and so hor-ribly, and I wouldn't have spent the last forty years of my life alone.

So I crush the paper in my fist, and I clutch it like I'm squeezing the life out of Guidry's very heart. And damn if it doesn't feel good.

I draw a lighter from my pocket and strike it with my thumb. Yes. There. Just a spark. A tiny curve of flame. But it's all I need. I hover Guidry's burial record over the lighter with my trembling hand. And it catches, like the most glorious kindling. A bright, lazy flame licks its way up the edge of the paper, and I'm so mesmerized by this moment of triumph that I don't turn my hand in time to shift the fire away from my wrist. It only takes one sear-ing bite before I drop the paper. I watch it fall as though in slow motion. Turning, tumbling toward the nearest table and its pile of teetering logbooks. It collapses in a shower of sparks.

At first I think the flame has gone out. But a dozen tiny embers have burrowed deep within the dry and brittle pages on the table. A dozen little fires erupt. It only takes a few seconds of beating at them frantically with my coat before I realize I'm standing in a tinderbox.

I'll have to repent for a dozen things when I leave this place. My parish priest will accommodate me. He always does. But it's the sin of arson, and how I'll phrase those words in the confessional, that I'm pondering as I watch the fire spread.

I am struck by a brief remorse for what I've done as I see the names of strangers—men, women, and children—blacken before my eyes. I have ruined any chance of them ever being found. But as I stumble backward toward the door, I realize what an idiot I am. No one is fool enough to come here, looking for the lost. No one but me.

I turn and run from the Chateau.

The entire records room is an inferno by the time I stumble, breathless, to the gates. The fire is beautiful and horrible at once, giving the dilapidated Chateau its first semblance of warmth in decades. It almost looks as if the lights are on in that room, as if a merry fire is burning in the fireplace. And then the windows explode and the flames rush outward with a greedy scream, sucking up the air, licking the exterior walls, engulfing all the tangled, climbing vines. It is mesmerizing, and I want to watch it burn to the ground.

But the Potter's Navy will arrive soon with their daily delivery of the dead. We only have a short time to get away. So I turn off my flashlight and leave the Chateau, her secrets, and this all-consuming fire behind me.

I find Piss and Vinny at the boat. They don't see me at first. Their eyes are on the billowing smoke and climbing flames that now stretch well above the tree line.

"He burned it down," Piss says. "I didn't know he was going to burn it down."

Vinny's eyes are huge and his hands shake. "Like I said. Batshit crazy."

"We gotta get out of here."

"Can't," Vinny says. "That old fucker has the boat keys."

"Well, I'm not stupid," I say as I draw the keys from my pocket and jingle them for effect. They startle so badly, I'm worried Piss might live up to his moniker. I climb into the boat and hand him the keys. "Stop staring. Let's go. We don't have all day."

Vinny wastes no time pushing the boat into the water, and then the outboard motor roars to life and we're off, back the way we came.

I watch the malevolent, hellish glow of the fire until the river bends and the current drags us out of sight. But even then the acrid scent lingers. It is the smell of charred memory. Names, dates, lives all turning to ash.

"Another hundred bucks when we reach the marina," Vinny shouts over the roar of the motor. "Don't forget!"

I am many things, but forgetful is not one of them. It is the curse I live with. A clear and perfect memory. For decades, I've prayed that I will lose this gift, that the edges of my mind will blur and crumble. They don't. My punishment is to remember. June, mostly. The high, soft curve of her breasts. The deep black of her hair. The sweet lilt to her laugh. The elegant arch of her hands as they work the beads on her rosary. I remember it all.

And I remember the night I came home from a double shift to find my wife, frying pan in hand, standing over a dead body. I remember the blood on the linoleum and the splintered bone of his skull. I remember the look of horror on June's face, how she dropped the pan and backed away.

"He propositioned me at the restaurant. I didn't see him follow me home." I remember the lump in her elegant throat as she swallowed, hard. "He tried to—"

I pulled June into my arms and pressed her face to my chest. "Don't worry," I said. "I'll take care of it."

Things might have ended differently if I'd called the precinct before I checked his wallet. Neither of us recognized him. We had no idea he was Bertrand Guidry. Corrupt. Legendary gangster. Connected. Lecherous. Vengeful. But it probably wouldn't have mattered that she was defending herself. It wouldn't matter that I was a detective. Hell, that might have made it worse. There was no getting out of it.

So I took care of everything. The chains. The cinder block. The early morning trip to the marina. I just couldn't take care of June.

Guidry's men did that three weeks later.

The next body I find will be June's.

CONTRIBUTORS

Jeff Abbott is the *New York Times* bestselling, award-winning author of eighteen mystery and suspense novels. *The Washington Post* called him "one of the best thriller writers in the business." His novels have been Summer Reading Picks by the *TODAY Show*, *Good Morning America*, *O the Oprah Magazine*, and *USA TODAY*. His latest novel, BLAME, centers on a young amnesiac trying to solve her own attempted murder. He is currently adapting his novel PANIC for television with The Weinstein Company. Jeff is a winner of the Thriller Award (for THE LAST MINUTE). He is a three-time nominee for the Mystery Writers of America's Edgar Award. His first novel, DO UNTO OTHERS, won the Agatha Award for Best First Mystery. Jeff lives in Austin with his family.

Helen Ellis is the author of the national bestselling short story collection AMERICAN HOUSEWIFE. She is a poker player who competes on the national tournament circuit and, in her spare time, watches *The Walking Dead* with her husband in New York.

Patti Callahan Henry is a *New York Times* bestselling author of twelve novels, including THE BOOKSHOP AT WATER'S END (July 2017). A finalist in the Townsend Prize for Fiction, an Indie Next Pick, an OKRA pick, and a multiple nominee for the Southern Independent Booksellers Alliance (SIBA) Novel of the

Year, Patti is a frequent speaker at luncheons, book clubs, and women's groups. The mother of three children, she now lives in both Mountain Brook, Alabama, and Bluffton, South Carolina, with her husband.

Amanda Stevens is the award-winning author of over sixty novels in multiple genres, including thriller, paranormal, and romantic suspense. Her Graveyard Queen series, optioned by both ABC and NBC, has been described as eerie and atmospheric, "a new take on the classic ghost story." She is a three-time RITA finalist and a 2016 nominee in the Goodreads Choice Awards for Best Horror. Born and raised in the rural south, Amanda now resides in Houston, Texas, where she enjoys binge watching, bike riding, and the occasional Horror and Heineken Night with old friends.

Paige Crutcher is a writer, reader, yogi, and journalist. She's written for a variety of literary publications, including *Publishers Weekly*—where she worked as the Southern Correspondent and contributing editor. She's currently co-owner of the online marketing company cSocially Media. More often than not, Paige has her nose in a book (occasionally while inside her book fort), because inside story is where the magic waits. She lives in her hometown of Franklin, Tennessee, with her family, overactive imagination, and a houseful of books.

Dana Chamblee Carpenter is the author of THE DEVIL'S BIBLE, the sequel to BOHEMIAN GOSPEL, a supernatural historical thriller which won the 2014

Killer Nashville Claymore Award and which *Publishers Weekly* called "a deliciously creepy debut." Edgar Award nominee and author of THE ABANDONED HEART Laura Benedict says, "Look out, Dan Brown. Dana Chamblee Carpenter is the angels' new champion in the timeless battle between darkness and light. THE DEVIL'S BIBLE is not just a book, but a shining, vibrant tale for the ages—told with history and heart—that will have readers both weeping and cheering not only for brave Mouse, but for all of humanity." Carpenter's award-winning short fiction has appeared in *The Arkansas Review, Jersey Devil Press, Maypop,* and in the anthology *Killer Nashville Noir: Cold Blooded.* She teaches at a private university in Nashville, Tennessee, where she lives with her husband and two children.

Laura Benedict is the Edgar- and ITW Thriller Award-nominated author of six novels of dark suspense, including the Bliss House gothic trilogy: THE ABANDONED HEART, CHARLOTTE'S STORY (*Booklist* starred review), and BLISS HOUSE. Her mystery/suspense novel, ONE LAST SECRET, will be published by Mulholland Books in 2018/2019. Laura's short fiction has appeared in *Ellery Queen's Mystery Magazine, PANK,* on NPR, and in numerous anthologies like *Thrillers: 100 Must-Reads, The Lineup: 20 Provocative Women Writers,* and *St. Louis Noir.* A native of Cincinnati, Ohio, she grew up in Louisville, Kentucky, and claims both as hometowns. Read her daily blog and sign up for her newsletter at laurabenedict.com.

Bryon Quertermous is a writer and editor. He was shortlisted for the Debut Dagger Award from the Crime Writers Association, and his short stories have appeared in a number of print and online journals of varying repute. His latest novel, RIOT LOAD, is available now from Polis Books. Bryon lives somewhere between Ann Arbor and Detroit (metaphorically as well as physically), where he can be found screaming at the TV with his wife during football and baseball season and playing Ninja Turtles and My Little Pony with his kids the rest of the time. Visit him at bryonquertermous.com and follow him on Twitter @BryonQ.

Dave White is the Derringer Award–winning author of six novels: WHEN ONE MAN DIES, THE EVIL THAT MEN DO, NOT EVEN PAST, AN EMPTY HELL, and BLIND TO SIN in his Jackson Donne series, and the acclaimed thriller WITNESS TO DEATH. His short story "Closure" won the Derringer Award for Best Short Mystery Story. *Publishers Weekly* gave the first two novels in his Jackson Donne series starred reviews, calling WHEN ONE MAN DIES an "engrossing, evocative debut novel" and writing that THE EVIL THAT MEN DO "fulfills the promise of his debut." He received praise from crime fiction luminaries such as bestselling, Edgar Award–winning Laura Lippman and the legendary James Crumley. His standalone thriller, WITNESS TO DEATH, was an e-book bestseller upon release and named one of the Best Books of the Year by the *Milwaukee Journal-Sentinel*. He lives in Nutley, New Jersey. Follow him at @dave_white.

Lisa Morton is a screenwriter, author of nonfiction books, Bram Stoker Award-winning prose writer, and Halloween expert whose work was described by the American Library Association's Readers' Advisory Guide to Horror as "consistently dark, unsettling, and frightening." She has published four novels, over a hundred short stories, and three books on the history of Halloween. Her most recent releases include GHOSTS: A HAUNTED HISTORY and CEMETERY DANCE SELECT: LISA MORTON; and the forthcoming anthology HAUNTED NIGHTS, co-edited with Ellen Datlow. She lives in the San Fernando Valley, and can be found online at www.lisamorton.com.

David Bell is a bestselling and award-winning author whose work has been translated into multiple foreign languages. He's currently an associate professor of English at Western Kentucky University in Bowling Green, Kentucky, where he directs the MFA program. He received an MA in creative writing from Miami University in Oxford, Ohio, and a PhD in American literature and creative writing from the University of Cincinnati. His novels are BRING HER HOME, SINCE SHE WENT AWAY, SOMEBODY I USED TO KNOW, THE FORGOTTEN GIRL, NEVER COME BACK, THE HIDING PLACE, and CEMETERY GIRL.

New York Times and USA Today bestselling author J.T. Ellison writes standalone domestic noir and psychological thriller series, the latter starring Nashville Homicide

Lt. Taylor Jackson and medical examiner Dr. Samantha Owens, and pens the international thriller series "A Brit in the FBI" with #1 *New York Times* bestselling author Catherine Coulter. Cohost of the EMMY Award-winning literary television series *A Word on Words*, Ellison lives in Nashville with her husband and twin kittens. Follow J.T. online at Facebook, Twitter @thrillerchick, or Instagram @jt_thrillerchick for more insight into her wicked imagination.

Ariel Lawhon is a critically acclaimed author of historical fiction. Her books have been translated into numerous languages and have been Library Reads, One Book One County, and Book of the Month Club selections. She is the author of I WAS ANASTASIA, FLIGHT OF DREAMS, and THE WIFE, THE MAID, AND THE MISTRESS, all published by Doubleday. Ariel is also co-founder of the popular reading website SheReads.org. She lives in the rolling hills outside Nashville, Tennessee, with her husband, four sons and a black lab—who is, thankfully, a girl.

ENJOY THESE STORIES?

PICK UP MORE THRILLERS FROM
TWO TALES PRESS!

Short Stories & Novellas by J.T. Ellison

Blood Sugar Baby (a Taylor Jackson novella)
Chimera
The Endarkening
Gray Lady, Lady Gray
Killing Carol Ann
The Number of Man
The Omen Days
Prodigal Me
Where'd You Get That Red Dress?
Whiteout (a Taylor Jackson novella)
X

Short Story Collections by J.T. Ellison

The First Decade
2 Novellas from the Taylor Jackson Series
Three Tales from the Dark Side
Mad Love

CPSIA information can be obtained
at www.ICGtesting.com
Printed in the USA
LVOW11*1810140917
548741LV00008B/109/P